THE HAUNTING OF
WOUNDED BIRDS

OTHER BOOKS
BY BEVERLEY LEE

The Making of Gabriel Davenport
A Shining in the Shadows
The Purity of Crimson
(The Gabriel Davenport series)

The Ruin of Delicate Things
The House of Little Bones
The Sum of Your Flesh

Jointly with Nicole Eigener
Crimson is the Night
A Conclave of Crimson: A Queer Vampire Romance Trilogy

Jointly with Keith Anthony Baird
A Light of Little Radiance

Find out more about Beverley's work at
beverleylee.com

THE HAUNTING OF WOUNDED BIRDS

BEVERLEY LEE

Published by Ink Raven Press

ISBN-13: 978-0-9935490-7-6

This book is wholly created
by human intelligence.

Cover design by
Elderlemon Design
Interior formatting/design by
Nicole Eigener

READER ADVISORY

Death of a parent, suicide, use of hallucinogenic substances,
death by hanging, bird death.

For Nicole, my ride or die, who nurtured this
story from nest to flight, and for loving Jackdaw
from the very first moment you met him.

PRAISE FOR
THE HAUNTING OF WOUNDED BIRDS

Lee's ability to offer small rural town claustrophobia, ghosts that command every beat of your heart, and sinister folklore, would make Shirley Jackson envious. *The Haunting of Wounded Birds* is alchemy on the page.

CRAIG WALLWORK
Author of *The Skin We Feel Most Comfortable In* and *Human Tenderloin*

The Haunting of Wounded Birds is a coming-of-age folkloric feast for fans of Andrew Michael Hurley and Michelle Paver. With a perfect blend of heart and horror, I defy anyone not to be moved by the plight of our protagonist (Jackdaw).

CATHERINE MCCARTHY
Author of *Mosaic* and *Death of a Clown*

There are moments of genuine terror in this tome, others of heartbreaking sorrow and loss, all built into an intricate world whose village centre the reader is so sucked into, it could well be sitting there, waiting to be visited in the English countryside.

A masterfully written tale of friendship, loss, and a past that simply refuses to be forgotten.

KEV HARRISON
Author of *Pyres* and *Shadow of the Hidden*

Beverley Lee's writing has always pulled me in, but *The Haunting of Wounded Birds* truly cemented why she is one of my favourite authors. She's got this incredible knack for balancing warmth with pure dread. It's like a lullaby wrapped around a sharp blade. Her prose doesn't just tell a story, it unsettles you, comforts you, then just claws at your spine.

MATT COXALL
Goodreads

Martinmas heralds the wintering of ghosts…

CHAPTER ONE

At the exact moment Jack Dawtrey's mother died, a bird flew into the lunchroom window.

Every face turned to him, as though he was single-handedly responsible for this unexpected incident. He kept his head down, his gaze focussed on the charred edge of a slice of cold pizza.

Mocking laughter and taunts filled the stuffy air as they tried to ruffle his metaphorical feathers.

His heart ached. Not for himself, but for the bird. He could go out and look for it, but the sound it had made when it hit the glass was enough to shatter a small skull. It had thought the window was a way out, a way through. But really, there was no way out for anything, not here, and the way through was a minefield of wrong choices and dead ends.

Only the lucky ones found a window in their glass.

Everybody leaves. That wasn't a cry for pity, it was just a cold, hard fact.

The boy sat on the bus, a battered holdall on the seat next to him, watching the landscape crawl past in the dark. He traced his name on the grimy film on the window to prove he'd been here.

Jack Dawtrey. He didn't particularly like his name, but wasn't that what he was supposed to do? Rail against authority until he became who he was meant to be?

And no one called him Jack, anyway. He was always Jackdaw, because kids always found a way to twist a name, to make someone who's slightly different the odd one out. It didn't help that he had a mop of unruly black hair – not just dark, but ebony black. It was futile to point out that jackdaws have a distinctive silvery sheen to the back of their heads. There were other things that made him different, too. But he didn't like to think about those.

Everybody leaves. The phrase smudged against his mind's eye, and for a moment he saw it in indelible ink, a mark he'd never be able to erase. He'd never known his father. When he asked about him, his mother retreated inside of herself, hunching her shoulders, as if the thought of that man was a weight she didn't want to carry. All Jackdaw knew was his father had left before he was born.

Everybody leaves.

A fact cemented at a tender age. He'd been almost four when this truth shattered his innocent world. His mother let go of his hand to put something on the back seat of the car and he ran off to stand by the front door, triumphant in his new found freedom.

'Get in the car, Jack.' He could still hear the impatience in her voice eleven years on, see the tightness of her lips as he defied her. 'Get in the car or I'll leave you here.'

Of course he didn't believe her. His mind wasn't mature enough to know a threat when he heard it; his universe barely stretched farther than the street they lived on. A bird landed on the patch of grass—the symbolism wasn't lost on him now—that served as a lawn and he held out his arms, a naïve invitation to come closer. He wasn't aware of the car engine starting, of the sound of tyres on tarmac, his attention fixed on the bird as it cocked its head to one side then snatched a wriggling earthworm from the grass.

When he looked up, the car and his mother had gone.

A cold prickle of fear ran across his scalp at the memory.

This was it, wasn't it?

The first time he knew people could be cruel, even though he had no language for it at the time. The stomach-churning dread. The acute loneliness as he was separated from the one person who was the light in his little world.

His mother had only driven around the corner and was watching him the whole time. But he didn't know that. She was trying to teach him to obey but the only thing it delivered was the splintering of innocent trust, an event traumatic enough for him to remember, traumatic enough to leave that indelible stain.

The memory was like a starting gun in his life, and, as the years went by and other people avoided him, he stopped being surprised and retreated into the armour of his own shell. Words such as *unfocussed* and *withdrawn* began to appear on his school reports. His grades suffered and his mother did what she always did—she took away what gave him comfort. First his phone and his TV, then his laptop, and finally, as she became more and more distant, her company.

When the other boys talked about what they were streaming or trending video games, he couldn't join in. That set him more and more apart. Some of them stopped talking to him. As if he didn't even exist, as if he didn't breathe the same air as them, seven hours a day.

In the end, he stopped caring at all. He got up, he went to school, he went to the library because it was warm, where he sat and read until it closed. Then he walked home and found scraps in the fridge for supper. It wasn't that they had no money. It was because his mother spent all her time locked away upstairs on a project: and preparing meals would have torn her away from it. He did chores, homework, took a shower, and went to bed.

The same old routine.

Until it wasn't.

He was sitting at a workbench in chemistry, scribbling notes for revision, when the door opened and Alice Hobb, the school secretary, called out his name.

All eyes wheeled to him, and he was caught like a specimen under a microscope. For one moment he was *somebody*.

Expectation followed him out of the room. They all needed to know what was happening, this exciting interruption to the tedium of their day.

'Come with me, Jack.' Alice's voice washed over him, a little too soft and tender. He tried to think of anything he'd done wrong but came up empty. When they got to the school office, he saw Mr. Balkin, the headmaster, through the open door. Under the fluorescent lighting his pallid complexion looked like a death mask.

The next few minutes passed in a milky haze. Mr. Balkin told him to sit so he did. Alice brought him a glass of water.

His heart hammered a staccato rhythm in his throat and his palms began to sweat. There was ink on the back of his hand, dirt under his nails.

When the two police officers entered the room, their caps in their hands, his reality skewed sideways and he wanted to melt away into the harsh, nylon carpet under his feet.

He didn't really process what they were telling him, not whilst it was happening. He had to replay it all later, when he was alone, to make any sense out of their words.

His mother was dead. Struck down in an instant by a fallen roof tile which had somehow targeted her of all the people rushing around on their lunch hours on the pavement below.

A freak accident.

A huge tragedy.

The words hummed around his brain.

The bottom fell out of his world. He felt like he was a gush of liquid circling down a drain into an infinite black void. A high-pitched buzzing sounded in his ears and he grabbed a hold of the desk in front of him, barely able to keep the flood of nausea from erupting from his throat.

Then the double blow.

The hushed voices. The concerned glances in his direction. The knowledge delivered calmly, becoming increasingly foreign like ancient Egyptian. No one had ever told him he had a sister.

Even though he didn't remember her at all, she was someone else who had left him.

CHAPTER TWO

The woman waited in her car, the engine running to keep the early November chill at bay. The sodium streetlight above her cast a sickly yellow glow onto the road, the light barely breaching the dark pressed beyond the name sign for the village.

The bus was late. Maybe even that form of transport didn't want to pass through here.

She edged forward in her seat and focussed her gaze on the winding road, blanketed in night, that disappeared between the hills, willing headlights to appear.

Movement in her peripheral vision and she turned, but it was only a lonely crisp packet skittering along the pavement.

A gust of wind rocked the car and her hands tightened on the steering wheel.

Callie Dawtrey didn't want to be here, at this moment, just as she knew who she was waiting for didn't want to be here either.

In truth, the only people who came to the village by choice were summer tourists.

But two years ago, she hadn't known that. It was just a place where she could afford to settle down, a place which had room for her workshop, somewhere she could disappear.

The cottage was old, late 1700s, a stone-built dwelling with a slate roof and a dilapidated barn. It had three rooms and a tiny bathroom on the ground floor and two rooms above, but the only way of reaching these was by way of the original wooden staircase, a rough-hewn and steep affair that definitely wouldn't have passed today's building regulations. It didn't bother her, as she slept in one of the downstairs rooms and only used the ones above for storage.

Until now.

She drummed her fingers on the dashboard, then turned on the radio in her battered Ford. Static screamed from the speakers, the faint murmur of music tantalising but unobtainable.

Not that she was surprised. The signal here was awful, the village nestling between two rolling hillsides—both of which did their level best to keep anything modern at bay.

She should be at home, examining the pots from her kiln, selecting the ones she would set aside for overglazing.

'Come on, come on,' she muttered, staring out into the dark. Her stomach growled because she hadn't eaten supper. It was waiting in the crockpot for her—and her guest.

Although, *guest* really wasn't the right word. But then what is the right word for a fifteen-year-old boy you've never met who happens to be your half-brother?

Up until the phone call from the police, she hadn't known Jack existed. Callie had left home at sixteen, travelled to London, and had somehow managed to scrape an existence together sleeping on a friend's couch, working three jobs at a time, and putting herself through a college course which led to her first proper position in a design studio.

She had her life in order now, and taking care of a sibling was definitely not in her five-year plan.

But what could she do? She was Jack's only family, named as such in her late mother's will.

That particular document was a surprise. Her mother had always dreamed her way through life.

A will seemed too adult. Too responsible.

Oncoming headlights split the darkness apart, and Callie took a deep breath. She watched as the lights meandered towards her along the winding road, becoming ever brighter, watched as the life she didn't want forced its way forward.

Her lips tightened.

The bus stopped, its windows so steamed up she couldn't see inside. A blast of pneumatic air as the doors opened and closed. It moved away, slowly.

Callie got out of the car and took her first look at what was left of her family.

CHAPTER THREE

They stood staring at each other in the wake of the exhaust fumes from the bus. Jack was shorter than Callie had imagined, and the dark padded jacket he wore looked as if it had been inflated to give him the appearance of someone older. A beanie hat was pulled down over his ears, so all she could see was a pale face and large, dark eyes.

She managed to suppress a groan as she felt her life turning in on itself.

Somehow she forced her feet to move and crossed the road.

'Hi.' The greeting slipped out, every bit as awkward as she felt. She pulled him into a hug he didn't respond to, his body stiffening.

This was the first time they'd met, although they'd had a few stilted conversations on the phone. It had taken the authorities a while to track her down, and by that time, her mother was dust in an urn. Some part of her was glad that she hadn't had to endure the funeral.

His gaze tracked over her shoulder, and something flickered across his face, a slight frown creasing his brow.

'Is this all you've got?' she said, indicating the holdall. Inwardly, she grimaced. Of course this was all he had.

'It's all I want,' he said, with a small shrug.

'Possessions are just things you drag along with you. Most of them you don't need.' Her attempt at smoothing the waters earned her a measured glance from those dark eyes. She picked up the holdall, but he took it from her, clutching it to his chest like a shield.

'Come on, let's get you back to my place.' Callie almost said *home*, but Jack didn't have a home, not anymore. There was no way this was going to be a permanent thing. She preferred her own company, she always had. She'd sorted her life out from the trainwreck of her childhood. A little voice told her she was being unreasonable, none of this was his fault—but she pushed it away as Jack stowed his bag in the boot of the car and climbed into the passenger seat.

A fine white mist had fallen, as it often did in the valley, and she dipped her headlights as they pulled onto the road.

'So, Jack...'

'Jackdaw,' he interrupted. 'Everyone calls me Jackdaw.'

He swiped off his beanie, revealing a tussle of black hair.

It wasn't much, but it was the first thing he'd volunteered.

'Callie,' she said, 'short for Calliope.' She screwed up her nose. 'But I can't sing a note that doesn't sound like a rusty wheel in pain.'

He ran his fingers through his flattened hair then hung his head, but not before she saw the shadow of a grin on his face.

'I ditched the name when I left home,' she said, wondering how much was too much to tell him at this point.

They were in the heart of the village now, on the main street that ran right through the middle, tiny ribbons of light peeking out from behind the closed curtains of the cottages lining the road. Summer brought coach loads of tourists, all of them squealing with delight at how quaint and lovely the village looked, snapping photos, recording videos on selfie sticks.

But Callie knew how un-lovely it could be.

She indicated to turn right even though she was the only car on the road. In fact, she couldn't recall seeing another vehicle on the drive down to meet Jack—Jack*daw*, she corrected herself.

'Like possessions, then,' Jackdaw said softly.

His face was turned to the passenger window, his fingers playing with a loose thread on his beanie.

It took Callie a moment to catch on that he was replying to her comment about discarding her name.

'Yep, just like possessions. We choose what to take with us.'

'Cool.' A one-word answer but it smoothed out the taut wall of awkwardness between them. Maybe his visit wouldn't be so bad after all?

She turned on the CD player nestled in the dash. A soft piano melody filled the car. Something classical she couldn't name. She half expected Jackdaw to scoff but he was intent on staring into the swirling mist.

They were out of the village now, travelling on the narrow, undulating lane towards her cottage. Overgrown hedges spilled out, the occasional whip of a wayward branch scraping over the car.

The road surface was pockmarked and uneven. Ruts lined the edges of the rough tarmac, caused by years of overflow water from the fields.

She relaxed a little, settling back in her seat, her gaze firmly on the road. Even though she knew the way well, the mist had a way of skewing the landscape, of making you believe things were there that didn't exist.

It was only when they were two minutes from the cottage— and food—that she allowed her concentration to shift. Her stomach grumbled, right on cue, and she laughed, turning to Jackdaw. 'I hope you like chilli. I didn't make it too hot just in case you don't like…'

'Watch out!' Jackdaw yelled, his hand grabbing the steering wheel, the expression on his face one of wild-eyed terror. The car veered to the left. A loose bramble whipped across the windscreen, and they both ducked on instinct.

She tried to fight the wheel, but an acute bend threw them sideways, and the back end swung out. The car skittered on loose gravel, sending it into a spin.

An instant where she was aware of Jackdaw's terrified face, one hand clutching the grab handle, one braced against the seat.

A bone-jarring wrench as the car lurched over a hillock of scrappy grass at the entrance to a field. It tottered, and she knew with a bolt of panic that she had no control over what happened next. She covered her face with her hands. Her seat belt locked, pinning her to the seat. A scream tore from her throat.

But it was a sunken tractor rut leading from the field that came to their rescue. The rear off-side tyre slid into it with a jolt that shook the whole car—they shuddered to a halt, the engine pinging in distress.

Adrenaline surged through her veins, together with the unwelcome sting of tears behind her eyelids. She clutched the steering wheel as anger swamped the relief, her emotions a tangled mess where common sense had no place.

'What the hell, Jackdaw?' She turned to him, her jaw set tight. 'What the fuck were you playing at?'

He shrank back against his seat, and for a moment, a shadow of fear played across his sharp features.

'I…' he began, and the rest of his words hovered on his lips before he swallowed them back down.

'You could have got us both killed.' She spat the words out knowing it was an accusation, but it was uttered as a knee-jerk response to a situation that could have been a whole lot worse.

'I thought I saw something… someone,' he said quietly, his chin on his chest, his fingers squeezing the beanie.

'We're in the middle of nowhere,' she replied, this time managing to keep her tone level. 'Look at the weather. Who'd be out in this? *I* wouldn't be out in this if I hadn't needed to pick you up.'

That was uncalled for.

They'd had a near miss, but they were both okay.

She opened the door, grabbing a torch she had stowed under her seat. Freezing fog coated her skin, the moisture creeping under the collar of her jacket. Crouching, she angled the torch beam behind the wheel, half expecting to see broken metal work, but apart from the tyre sitting in the tractor rut, everything looked normal.

Normal.

The word irritated her like sand against bare skin.

No part of this was normal.

The only saving grace was that this had happened so close to the cottage. Callie opened the driver's door and leaned in.

'Grab your things. We'll need to walk the rest of the way.'

The chilled air had cooled her anger, and regret for her accusation poked her in a tender place.

'Look, I'm sorry I snapped.' She held up her hands, hoping he'd yell or shrug or *something*.

But there was no reaction other than a certain guardedness in his stance, as though he had expected something like this to happen.

They set off along the road, her torch beam lowered to the tarmac. The ghostly forms of hedges shadowed their steps, and an eerie disorientating silence settled.

'What do you like to do, Jackdaw?' She tried for conversation.

'The usual stuff,' he finally said, and this time, she did get a shrug. Okay, he was going to make her work for this.

She deserved that.

'I'm not clued into the language of teenage boys,' she said with a grin, pausing at a five-bar gate. A wooden stile stood beside it, and she clambered over. 'Come on, let's take a short cut, the cottage is just over this field.'

They tramped through the wet grass, the field sloping uphill, until a dim light broke through the mist. Callie thanked her past self, who'd had the common sense to leave an outside light on. At least she'd done something right tonight.

Jackdaw had paused about ten feet away, his gaze fixed on… *what?* There was nothing there, at least nothing visible.

A shiver tripped down her spine.

But she knew that across the valley, on the slope of the opposite hill, stood a tall, wooden structure with an ominous history.

And the only reason she had been able to afford the cottage was because of its history with that structure.

Because no one in the village would touch it.

Jackdaw didn't need to know that where she lived now had a brutal and macabre past.

CHAPTER FOUR

Jackdaw set his bag on the red, quarry-tiled kitchen floor.

A welcome blast of heat had greeted them, and his gaze found the source: an ancient Aga stove set into the far wall. A pitted wood table, oblong in shape, took up most of the space, three mismatched chairs around it. Two shirts and a jumper on hangers swung from nails in the timber beams that crossed the ceiling.

Callie slung her coat on the back of one of the chairs. 'It's the warmest place in the cottage, so it doubles as a laundry room.'

She went over to the Belfast sink and washed her hands, then took the lid from a crockpot on the worktop next to the range. Jackdaw's mouth watered as something that smelled really good wafted out.

'Come on, I'll show you your room before we eat.'

She disappeared through a doorway, and he snatched up his bag and followed her. The room beyond was dimly lit by a tired lamp in one corner. There was a squishy sofa occupying the far wall with a coffee table in front of it, but the atmosphere didn't feel very lived in, and he quickly crossed to a rickety-looking staircase where he could see her through the open slats.

'Careful,' she yelled down. 'It's sound but steep. Use the hand-holds on the wall.'

Metal rings had been cemented into the stone at some point, a rough rope threaded through them. Taking his bag in one hand he climbed up after her, his fingers glancing over the cold metal. A burst of saliva in a copper-edged rush as he bit the edge of his tongue.

'My bedroom is next to the living room, so this whole floor is private for you, although I'm afraid there's only one bathroom downstairs.'

Her voice drifted across from a room on the left.

The landing was a small, square space with two doors leading from it.

'Watch your head.' She motioned with one hand, and he ducked instinctively as he went into the room, even though he didn't need to. 'People were much smaller when this place was built.' She hugged her arms around herself as she surveyed the room. 'I know this isn't much, but I never thought I'd have guests.'

He dropped his bag on the floor, pondering her words.

So she was a loner, too.

'It's great,' he said, although there was nothing great about a single bed with a faded green duvet, a wooden chest against a wall, a battered bedside table, and an ugly wardrobe tucked under one of the eaves.

He reached out to touch the wall as he crossed to the window, a strange disorientation pulling him off balance.

'Yeah,' she said, grimacing. 'I forgot to say, the floor slopes a bit up here. It's one reason I didn't make it mine. You'd have thought that when they renovated this room that they could have levelled it, but no…I guess it all adds to the charm.' She climbed onto the bed and pulled a single lace curtain back. 'Although it does have the best view, and in summer the sun comes right through…' Her voice trailed off. He knew she didn't think he'd be here in the summer.

'It's great,' he repeated. 'Can we eat soon?'

He *was* hungry, but more than that, he needed some space to think. When his peers were about to decide the course of their lives, his had been thrust into mayhem. His old life hadn't been anything special but at least it was familiar, and he could get by at school by flying under the radar. They had long ago decided he wasn't worth bullying or beating up because he made a pretty good job of that himself.

He was a nobody, a kid who would drift through school and never be remembered.

But now he was still a nobody in a fresh place, and the prospect of a new school loomed—although he'd been given a month off for compassionate reasons.

There was nothing he could do about his situation, and that just added to his sense of helplessness.

'Five minutes,' she said as she crossed to the door, hovering on the landing for a few moments before going downstairs.

He unzipped his bag and carried an armful of clothes over to the wardrobe. It had a small key balanced in the lock, and as he turned it, the door swung open sharply, the edge of it catching his brow. *Of course, the floor…*

A scent wafted from the interior and his nose wrinkled. It was something herby, but he couldn't identify it. A scattering of tiny dried white flowers lay clustered in one corner.

A few crooked wire hangers hung from a rail. He bundled his

clothes into the bottom of the wardrobe because he didn't really have anything worth hanging anyway.

His hand flew to his chest as his heart began to race, a galloping, forceful rhythm that pounded in his ears and made his fingertips tingle. *It's just stress,* he told himself, repeating what the school therapist had told him. He was almost sixteen years old and already labelled as frayed around the edges with self-confidence issues, and more than likely he was on some social services watch list. If it wasn't true, he would have laughed… but there was nothing humorous about his current situation.

He scrambled over the bed to the window. It was iron framed, a single casement on the right with an ornate iron latch. Jackdaw could feel the chill of the night through the glass. The front wall was thick, the angled sides leading to the window, roughly plastered. If he'd been six years old, he could have taken a pillow and a blanket and curled up here to read.

He banged his fist against the stubborn latch, the window swinging open into the inky darkness.

Callie had said the room had the best view, and he studied the new landscape through the bare branches of an oak tree right outside his window. The mist had cleared slightly but still hung in the valley, obliterating most of the village—apart from the church he'd seen from the car. Its tower stood proud under the cloud-scudded sky, a haze of moon illuminating its neo-gothic spire. It was closer than he had thought… the road must have zigzagged a lot on their journey.

He chewed the edge of his thumbnail, grateful for the cold wash of night to clear his thoughts. Just what *had* he seen on the road? As Callie had said, who would have been out on a night like this?

It must have been the mist playing tricks with his eyes like drifting shadows do. Plus, his contacts were screaming to be removed, so anything was possible.

'Supper's on the table!'

Callie's voice echoed through the floor.

He pushed his hair back from his face, his hand reaching to close the window. But as he did so something else caught his eye on the opposite hill, something beyond the church, etched against the gauzy clouds.

A tall, wooden pole with a cross rail.

He flinched back, horror crawling over his skin.

It was a gibbet.

CHAPTER FIVE

Jackdaw excused himself right after supper, saying he was tired. It wasn't strictly untrue, but he didn't need company right now. Callie had made small talk all through the meal, nudging him with questions, telling him what she did—she was a potter; his eyebrows had shot up at that—avoiding any specifics about The Thing hanging between them: that he didn't want to be here anymore than she wanted him here.

She did this weird thing with her nose when she was thinking, a little nostril flare most people wouldn't have noticed. His mother had done that, too.

Now he stood in front of the mirror in his bedroom, moving his head from side to side as parts of the glass were clouded with age. The mirror was old and ugly with a domed top and a battered, moulded frame. His exhaled breath of frustration fogged the surface even more.

But he didn't need a mirror to know his eyes were burning. He didn't want to go downstairs to wash his hands, so he pulled a pack of emergency wipes out of the pocket of his bag and scrubbed one over his fingers before pulling down his lower eyelid and pinching the lens off with his thumb and index finger.

It was second nature now, but he remembered when he'd first started to wear them and how difficult it had been to take them out. All through primary school he'd worn glasses, but before he started secondary he'd begged his mother for contacts—coloured contacts—telling her glasses would get broken easily in the chaos of a much larger school.

Again, not a lie. Jackdaw was very adept at bending the truth.

Music filtered up through the floorboards, and he heard Callie rinsing the dishes in the sink. It was an old song with a melodic guitar intro, one he couldn't name but yet somehow knew because he'd heard it at various times throughout his life. People call those a classic, but he liked to think of it as something grounding to remind you that you were real.

He removed the other contact lens, then tipped his head back and dripped a couple of eye drops into each eye. This was the point where he had to fight an impulse to rub the hell out of them because in the short term, that would feel *so* good. But he'd learned that gratification wasn't worth the after-effects.

He squinted at the mirror, saw his true self staring back, pale and sharp-featured, ebony hair that refused any style but the one it was now, falling over his face. Thick, dark brows, but the eyes that looked back at him weren't dark at all.

Little Crow, his mother had called him as a term of endearment when he was younger because she didn't know much about birds. He remembered the day he'd thrust out his bottom lip and stomped his foot. *I'm not a crow, I'm a jackdaw!*

He slid his glasses on and pulled off his jeans, replacing them with a pair of worn tracksuit bottoms before padding across the floor and opening the heavy, wooden door. Light spilled up the staircase, light that only reached about halfway, leaving any steps he would tread first in complete darkness. A dryness lined his throat and he desperately needed a glass of water, so he'd just have to suck it up and go get one. He hoped Callie would be too busy to notice his eyes—he kept his head down as he descended the staircase, testing each step with his weight because he didn't want to use the metal rings.

The song was still playing as he went into the kitchen, but Callie wasn't there. Relief escaped as a breath through his lips. He opened a few cupboards until he found one containing glassware, then stuck a squat tumbler under the tap. While it was running, he stared out of the window. His reflection stared back, ghosted in the glass, but something else caught his attention. A sound outside he instantly recognised.

He turned off the tap and crossed to the door. The old iron drop latch chilled his fingertips as he opened it. Freezing air rushed in, numbing his bare feet, but his focus was elsewhere. Grimacing, he edged over the gravel in front of the cottage to a rough grassy area. An old horse trough filled with wilted summer flowers stood to the left of the oak tree. Through the gap between he had a clear view of the darkened meadow beyond and the gibbet he'd seen on the hill. The sound came again and he shivered as an eerie drawn-out screech filled the night.

An owl. A barn owl. He'd never heard one in the wild before. A smile curled onto his lips as he craned back his head and answered the cry with one of his own. Not a perfect imitation but enough for the owl to reply. He turned towards the echo of its call, aware that he wouldn't hear it approach on silent predator wings.

A moment where he felt a rush of air, then claws brushing through his hair.

The momentum dragged him a few feet forwards. He reached up, his fingers digging into soft plumage. Wings beat against his face, muffling his cries, and then he tipped forwards again as the owl released him, tumbling down a steep embankment behind the trough.

He lay on his back, winded, as the owl circled him once and then glided away. Raising himself up on one elbow, he rubbed his shoulder which had taken the brunt of his fall, and watched it disappear gracefully as though it had never been here at all.

Another sound echoed over the dark-drenched meadow.

But this wasn't an owl.

It was a crow. And the call wasn't a normal social caw—it was the harsh defensive shriek of a bird whose territory had been breached.

CHAPTER SIX

Callie set the tray of pots from the kiln onto the wooden work-bench. She cast a critical eye over their forms, instantly discounting two with hairline cracks. She sighed. The kiln really needed replacing as the heat distribution wasn't up to par, but that was out of the question right now—unless her upcoming show in London was wildly successful. She was lucky her name was well-known and she'd had good sales in the past, but art, like any creative process, isn't a guaranteed cash cow. Maybe she should have stayed in design, working 9-5 then going out for cocktails and food at some trendy restaurant.

Money was easy back then, but it came with a price—because there's always someone wanting to take advantage of those with disposable cash. Some low-life had slipped molly into her drink one night at a club, and the resulting energetic high had been a chaotic fever dream filled with loud music and a complete loss of inhibition. When she'd woken up with her tongue stuck to the roof of her mouth, she was in an unfamiliar penthouse apartment with a view of the Shard and a strange man sprawled out on his stomach beside her.

This was her wakeup-call moment. Actually, it was her second wakeup-call moment.

The first was when she decided to leave home at sixteen to go and live in London. She slept on a friend's couch in a grimy upper-floor flat overlooking Highgate Cemetery, working in a coffee shop near the Archway tube and taking evening classes in art and design. Her mother had made no attempt to bring her back... which wasn't a huge surprise.

A freezing gust of wind snaked under the ill-fitting door of her workshop, pulling her from pondering about her not-so-fabulous past. *Hey, at least I got away.* The thought unfurled in her mind, casting its net between the past and the present. Jackdaw hadn't had the option to leave, but fate obviously had other ideas. She'd watched him during supper, his eyes downcast, hair falling over his face. Had noticed his slim-boned wrists and the way he chewed every mouthful carefully as though he wasn't sure where the next one was coming from.

Meals had taken a backseat in the Dawtrey family, Francine Dawtrey too caught up in her never-ending research into some element of history, forgetting that her own present was right in front of her. Callie wasn't even sure what she was working on long into the night, only that the back bedroom walls were covered in tacked-on paper with datelines and names and places, the thin light from a north facing window never quite reaching the corners of the room.

Just before she'd left, Callie got up in the middle of the night to find her mother in a white lace nightgown, plaited hair trailing down her back, standing in the dark, muttering like some Victorian madwoman.

Jackdaw had probably gone through the same neglect and she saw herself as a young teen in him, even though she hadn't known he'd existed until the phone call. What makes a parent get so caught up in their own world that the bond between them and their children untethers one strand at a time?

Callie had discarded that rope long ago, but Jackdaw?

Maybe he was just hanging on by a thread.

CHAPTER SEVEN

Jackdaw was yanked from sleep by a knock on his door.

His muddled brain fought for clarity because he'd been lost in the snares of a dream. He sat up abruptly, his heartbeat drumming against his rib cage.

'Jackdaw? Are you awake?'

Callie's voice.

Jackdaw shot out of bed and stumbled across to the wooden blanket chest where he'd left his bag.

'Just a minute!' he yelled, desperately searching through the inside pocket for his contact lenses. He didn't want her seeing his eyes.

Not yet.

His fingers closed on the packet and he drew out the slim foil, his mind still rooted in the dregs of sleep. He rubbed the hem of his sleeve over the fog on the mirror, then remembered it was part of the glass. What was the point of a mirror you couldn't look into? He punched out a lens, aggravation tightening the muscles in his jaw.

Squinting, he balanced the lens on his forefinger and peered into the usable section of the mirror. There was something on his cheek. He lifted his other hand and brushed away a droplet of moisture, wiping it on his T-shirt before popping both lenses in.

He didn't want to think about why it was there.

Another knock.

'Look, I only need a minute.'

Jackdaw cringed, because this time Callie's voice had an edge of frustration hanging on the syllables.

'Coming.'

He stepped away from the mirror, blinking to settle the new lenses. His knee caught the edge of his bag, and the foil, which was balanced on top, skittered across the floor.

He fought a sudden urge to crawl back under the covers. Padding over to the door he opened it, leaning against the frame.

'How did you sleep?' Callie tracked her gaze over his face.

'Not bad,' he said, which was a lie because everything was too strange and too tense, and they were both skirting around each other like they'd wanted their lives to be thrown together. 'The mattress is a bit lumpy.' As soon as the words fell, his gut clenched. What did he think this was, a five-star hotel?

He wasn't spoiled, far from it, and now this simple phrase made him sound selfish and ungrateful.

'We can see about getting a new one,' she said, her voice softening. 'Look, I have to go see someone, and I wanted to make sure you'd be okay on your own.'

'Why wouldn't I be?' The reply plummeted from his lips like a diver from a high board. He pressed them together. There were multiple reasons why he might not be okay.

'Go.' He dredged up what he hoped was a confident smile.

She hesitated, rocking back on her heels. 'There's bread for toast and juice in the fridge. I shouldn't be too long.'

He waited for a few moments, watched as her fingers trailed lightly across the metal rings, listened to her footsteps on the quarry-tiled floor of the kitchen, the slam of the front door.

Now he allowed himself to relax.

He didn't need babysitting.

Crossing to the bed, he drew back the lace curtain and watched as Callie wheeled an old bike from the side of the cottage.

She disappeared down the track.

The sky was leaden grey, a weak sun pressing against the heavy cloud, a stiff breeze bending the tops of the trees.

The weight lodged in his chest lightened a little.

Now he could explore without feeling like Callie was plugged in to his every move.

He changed into jeans and a jumper, shoved his feet into socks and trainers, and went downstairs to the bathroom, washing his hands and face and cleaning his teeth in the avocado-coloured wash basin. A shower could wait.

There was no background chatter of a radio, no hum of traffic—only birdsong.

He identified a harsh, scolding outburst—an irate blackbird— then made himself breakfast, acutely aware of how the silence in the cottage wrapped itself around him like a glove.

As much as he didn't want to be here, this was home now.

Pulling on his jacket and beanie he shut the door behind him, stepping out into a sullen November morning.

Callie hadn't left him a key. Maybe people didn't lock their doors here?

There was an outbuilding set to the right of the cottage, and he peered behind the rickety door. Rows of pots sat on a long, wooden bench. A potter's wheel stood in the corner with the lurking shape of a kiln behind it.

A stable sat between the outbuilding and an old, wooden barn. Jackdaw opened the top half of the stable door and peered in.

A rope halter hung on a peg, dusted with cobwebs. The air was musty, and it made his nose itch. It didn't look like a horse had been here for a very long time.

He stood outside the tall double doors of the barn for a few minutes, his lips pursed. A padlock hung open from an iron clasp. The building was rectangular in shape, the long side facing him. The slats were weathered and peeling. Moss-draped slate tiles covered the gable roof but some were missing, showing glimpses of wooden struts.

He wrenched one of the doors open. The bottom edge stuck slightly on the concrete yard, jarring into his wrists. The gloom reached out to greet him, thick and dark and mouldering.

Gingerly, he eased himself through the gap, staying in the wan strip of light from outside. He waited until his eyes became accustomed to the blackwash. Gradually, dim shapes appeared— an old cart at the back, under a hayloft with steps off to one side.

He left the comfort of the light and walked deeper into the shadows. Some kind of farm tools were hung on the wall opposite the door and other things he couldn't quite make out. A rustle from above. He jerked his head towards it, but it was only a bird resting in the rafters.

The cart loomed from the darkness. It had one large wheel at each side and a wooden body. The remains of a bale of hay dusted its interior. Cobwebs shivered in the slight draught from the door, and as Jackdaw drew closer a fat spider scurried along a web. He raised one hand towards the nearest wheel.

'Leave it be!'

The sharp voice drilled into his thoughts, and he stepped back as though the wheel had grown fangs.

'You should not touch what you do not understand.'

A small figure appeared from the hayloft. She settled herself on the top step, her hands clasped between her knees. She had dark hair, plaited over one shoulder, and a long floaty dress at odds with stocky black boots.

'Who the hell are you?' he asked, maybe a little too angrily as she couldn't have been more than ten.

'Ophelia,' she replied, without missing a beat. 'Who are you?'

'What are you doing here?' he said, wandering across to the steps, feeling like *he* was the intruder. He didn't offer his name.

'I play here,' she said. 'I do not like other people.'

Jackdaw understood that sentiment bone-deep. 'What did you mean when you said I shouldn't touch what I don't understand?'

She fixed him with a green-eyed gaze, too piercing for a kid of her age. A strand of hay clung to the tail of her plait.

'It is not time yet,' she said, solemnly. 'But you will see.'

Now Jackdaw felt like he'd entered some fifth dimension. 'You're not making any sense.' He was too weary to bother about some irritating girl and her made-up stories.

She raised her chin, knocking the toes of her boots together. Jackdaw turned on his heel.

'Whatever,' he sighed. 'Just go play. Forget you ever saw me.'

He was two steps away when her next words rooted him to the spot.

'He will find you.'

He glanced over his shoulder, heated words fizzing on his tongue, but she'd gone back up to the hayloft.

As he went outside, blinking at the sudden light, her words needled under his skin. He kicked at a stone, sent it clattering against the side of the barn.

Forget it. She's just a kid trying to spook you. What he didn't want to admit to himself was that she already had.

CHAPTER EIGHT

Maggie O'Reilly lived in a tiny, stone-built cottage at the other side of the lane. She was a no-nonsense woman whose dress sense was best described as broad-ranging, but she was never seen without a hat of some description.

As Callie propped her bike up against the gate, Maggie opened the door, shaking out a tablecloth.

Callie remembered the first time they'd met. Callie's car battery had given out on a freezing winter's day and Maggie found her with the bonnet up in the yard, swearing as she poked the crusted terminals.

Maggie had lived in the village for decades. If there was ever a crisis, she knew exactly who to call. Callie had watched, transfixed, as Maggie phoned the local garage, ignoring their insistence that they were booked up.

Within two hours, a battered truck appeared and an overall-clad mechanic had her car up and running in minutes.

Callie arrived at Maggie's door the day after with a bunch of flowers, and their friendship had blossomed from there. Although Maggie's parting comment had made Callie's brows hike.

'Now you can see that I don't bite.'

It was ironic that if Callie asked anyone else in the village they would have assured her that Maggie O'Reilly probably did bite—and if she liked the taste, she'd take another.

'Kettle's on,' Maggie said, as she ushered Callie inside. A black range took up most of the back wall. Rows of copper pans hung above it. The morning sunlight streaming through the window glinted from the burnished metal.

Callie pulled out a chair and sat at the table.

People in the village whispered about Maggie, said she was tainted with her past. But Callie didn't believe them. Maggie was one of life's rare souls with a heightened perception for simply knowing what the other person needed. She read body language as easily as if it were painted on the other person's face.

'How about you tell me what's bothering you,' Maggie said, pouring boiling water into a brown earthenware teapot, 'and then I'll tell you if you left anything out.'

Callie laughed, the sound easing the tension across her shoulders.

She'd been right to come here.

Maggie would set her straight.

And Jackdaw would be fine. If living with a parent who didn't actually parent had taught Callie anything, it was that Jackdaw would have learned to fend for himself at an early age.

Maggie lifted the lid on the teapot and began to stir the loose leaves. A haze of steam blanketed her face.

She splashed some milk in a couple of mugs and tilted her head, her elbow resting on the table, her hand cradling her chin. A knitted hat hid most of her hair, this one a riot of pinks and yellows and greens.

'You can do this,' Maggie said, fixing Callie in her gaze as her friend unloaded her trepidation over how the hell she was even supposed to be qualified to nurture a half-brother she never knew existed. 'But no one said it would be easy. You just need to let him know that he's safe and give him boundaries. Then let him figure the rest out for himself.'

It all sounded so simple, and Callie wished that it was.

'I don't know how to speak to him, Maggie.' She sighed and played with an unravelling thread on the hem of her jumper. 'I think he knows I don't want him here.' She glanced up and chewed the edge of her lip. 'Does that make me a rotten person?'

Maggie laughed, and the lines around her eyes crinkled.

'No, it makes you a very honest person.' She poured the tea into the mugs—ones Callie had made. 'Jack will come around eventually.'

'Jackdaw,' Callie said, cupping her hands around the mug. 'He was very insistent on that.'

'Jackdaw?' Maggie's voice wavered in surprise, and something flashed across her face, an expression Callie couldn't decipher. As though a corner of the night had unpeeled itself for an instant.

'Yeah. It's a play on his full name. Jackdaw. Jack Dawtrey. I guess he feels comfortable with it. It's not like I use the name I was given.'

As she stared into the tea, Callie found herself pondering that the names we're given don't actually define us. It's what a parent thought we were, not what we decide is right. Not what life makes us into.

'Maybe he's here to discover who he is?' Maggie said softly, sipping her tea.

Not for the first time, Callie wondered if the other woman

could read her thoughts, but she pushed the idea away.

It was irrational, and God knows she didn't need that particular emotion right now.

They sat in companionable silence for a few minutes, and the conversation changed to Callie's forthcoming show and how far she was behind. As she finished her tea—carefully, as Maggie didn't believe in tea strainers—Callie felt lighter than she had since the news of Jackdaw's existence had interrupted her routine.

Everyone deserved a Maggie in their lives. Someone who would listen and advise. Someone who would give you a swift kicking if you needed it.

'Could I borrow your car?' she asked. 'Just for a few hours. I hit a rut in the dark last night. Joe Hobb picked it up this morning to check it over.'

Part of her wanted to tell Maggie about why she had hit the rut, but maybe it didn't even matter.

She owed Jackdaw some loyalty.

As they said their goodbyes and Callie drove off down the lane, the sun had forced itself through the dark bank of cloud, turning the hovering mist on the low-lying fields to molten gold.

Maggie waited for a few moments before gathering the mugs from the table. She had hidden her unease from Callie because the last thing her friend needed was any reason to be more apprehensive.

Jackdaw.

The name tumbled around her mind, wild and youthful—and totally unknowing.

But she couldn't ignore the fact a boy with that name was living in the cottage on the hill. She chewed the edge of her thumbnail.

Maggie didn't like it one bit.

She rinsed the mugs and climbed the narrow staircase.

Her bedroom door was slightly ajar. Ribbons of sunlight wavered on the washed floorboards, streaming in through the detailed lace of the curtains Maggie's mother had made.

The door to the room opposite was closed. She always kept it closed, for it faced the forest. Any sunlight that bled through this window barely breached the glass.

As Maggie pressed the iron latch to enter the room, she paused. Goosebumps crawled over her scalp, a harrowing remembrance uncoiling from the depths of her mind.

Something she tried to keep buried.

She rested her brow against the old, slatted door.

The hinge creaked as she slowly pushed the door open, her gaze on the dusty floorboards. At first glance, this room looked unused. There was no furniture. No curtains at the window. The painted walls cast a pallor that could best be described as funereal.

Any observer would be filled with unease at the rows upon rows of rustic shelving attached to these walls.

Because on every surface rested an array of different animal or avian skulls.

Maggie took a small bowl from one shelf and scattered its

contents in a circle in the middle of the room. Then she took a skull from an adjacent shelf and placed it in the centre of the circle.

A salt circle.

It's all she could do right now to protect Jackdaw.

She was powerless until future events shifted into place.

As she closed the door she hesitated for a moment, looking back over her shoulder.

'Little bird,' she whispered to a boy she had never met. Her gaze rested on the crow skull in the centre of the circle. 'I hope you're strong enough to meet him.'

CHAPTER NINE

Jackdaw couldn't settle.

He'd gone back into the cottage after meeting Ophelia, angry at himself for letting a little kid's words get to him. She shouldn't even be in the barn.

He pulled out his phone, hoping that he'd find… *nothing*. Again. No one had messaged him to ask how he was doing. He'd been forgotten, conveniently deleted from the memory banks of the few classmates he thought might care a little.

Is that a surprise? he asked himself. And even though the answer was a loud and unanimous *No,* it still stung. He knew it was because he didn't conform to what they considered necessary for acceptance, and that fact labelled him as *persona non grata,* not that he'd ever been truly welcome. And he'd only made it worse by acting like he didn't care. At least the other kids who were taunted, and who responded emotionally, had friends who were there for them.

A memory surfaced, something bitter and shameful.

Heat crept over his face. He'd been eleven years old, his first term in secondary school, and he wanted to fit in back then. He was with four other boys sitting on the grass behind the tennis courts.

Across were two girls taking turns to do handstands.

One of the boys—Jackdaw didn't even remember his name, only that he had a cruel mouth always curved into a sneer—bet him that Jackdaw couldn't do a handstand. And because Jackdaw so desperately wanted to be part of a group, he stood and performed one, his legs spindly and ungraceful. The other boys laughed and nudged each other. Jackdaw was so incensed that he kept on trying, telling them that he was doing this for *fun*.

It wasn't fun. It was humiliating.

Okay, stop!

Bringing up this demeaning fragment wasn't helping at all.

He poked around in a few kitchen drawers because he was bored, slamming them shut just to hear something. Here, there wasn't *anything*, like the world had folded in on itself.

He went up to his room and threw himself on the bed, studying the grooved surface of the dark beam above. It made him feel a little bit dizzy. And then he remembered the contact lens foil that he'd dropped earlier. It wasn't on the floor or behind the chest. Scrabbling on his hands and knees, he peered underneath the bed. His brow furrowed.

A fierce determination flooded through his veins, probably on the heels of his embarrassing recollection. He sighed and heaved the heavy, wooden bed to one side, inch by inch. The floorboards beneath were covered in light dust, the knots in the wood more pronounced. The boards were crudely laid and when he inspected them closer, a draught whispered over his face.

He grabbed his phone again and flicked on the torch, angling it so it illuminated the gaps. There, nestled and just out of reach of his fingers, was a slight glittering.

How the hell?

It was impossible that the packet had fallen into the gap, but there it was, sitting smugly, sending his already intense irritation into overdrive.

He didn't have the luxury of leaving it there. He only had a few days' supply left, and he couldn't let Callie see how he really looked. He knew it was stupid, that she wouldn't care, yet allowing people to see his eyes felt like he was stripped naked in front of them.

He ran downstairs and grabbed a knife from the kitchen. Positioning it between the boards he wiggled it about, trying to scrape the packet closer to where a knot in the wood was missing.

His whole focus was on this task, and it felt really satisfying to be in control of *something*. His hair hung into his eyes and he swept it back constantly, dragging the packet slowly towards the hole. He could see the edge of it, but now it wouldn't budge any further. Laying his cheek against the floor, he squinted into the gap. The packet seemed to be caught on something else.

He stuck his finger into the hole. The edge of his nail grazed the foil. *So fucking close!* Jackdaw sat back on his heels for a moment, wiping the back of his hand over his nose to clear the dust. A muscle in his jaw twitched. He was getting that foil if he had to tear the floorboard up.

Oh.

The realisation hit him like Arctic water.

How did that other object get there? It looked too big to slip through the gap.

He poked his thumb through the hole, jamming it beneath the board and pulling to test its solidity. It shifted, only a smidge, but it was enough to cement his resolve, and with the aid of the knife and brute force, he jemmied the board up enough for him to get his whole hand underneath.

A splintering of wood and the board gave, sending him hurtling backwards, the wood clasped in his hands. His spine hit the wall, and pain ricocheted along his vertebrae.

The wood in his hands was maybe thirty centimetres long, both short edges planed. It had been cut. Cut to hide something.

He just hadn't seen it because of the dust.

He scrambled back across, and as his fingers closed over the foil he brought it to his lips and kissed it, a ridiculous grin of triumph lighting up his face. Placing it to one side, he removed what it had caught against.

A book—covered in chalky dust, tied together with old string.

He sat cross-legged and blew away the powdery dirt, easing the cracked leather cover open. The edges of the spine and one corner were scuffed. The pages were thin and yellowed and most of the ink had faded away on the first few, leaving only fragmented letters. Jackdaw's breathing started to race, prickles of sweat forming under his arms. He was looking at something *really* old. Something that had been hidden away.

He skimmed gingerly through the pages. There were ancient dates now, written in a column.

Names sat opposite the dates, the letters carefully penned.

1799 James Elliot.

1802 Tobias Granger.

1804 Thomas Brown.

He turned another page, and this time his breath caught in his throat. The date was bold and heavy, written in anger, the paper slightly torn by the pressure.

IZA.

Thick, black strokes underlined the name.

The final entry came at the bottom of the page.

And as Jackdaw read the words he dropped the book in his lap, gooseflesh creeping over his arms.

Never rest. Never forget. Never forgive.

Say his name.

Find his…

The last word was illegible, marred by a spot of water into an inky smudge.

CHAPTER TEN

Callie only went down to the village when she was forced to.

When she'd first arrived, she tried to insert herself into local life, offering her wares as prizes in village shows and school fundraisers, but it soon became very apparent that no one truly wanted to make friends. She was the Outsider and would remain as such even if she ended up living here for decades.

She could already feel the scrutiny as she walked down the narrow street and entered the shop which served as a post office, too. Two women browsing greetings cards turned to stare at her, but Callie refused to be rattled. She pushed her shoulders back and went about the task of filling her basket with groceries.

Maybe she should have driven the extra fifteen miles to Meadowford Bridge, but she didn't want to leave Jackdaw by himself for longer than necessary.

As she rounded the end of the aisle, a snippet of conversation drifted across from the two women. '…and there's a boy living in *that* cottage.'

Callie gritted her teeth, indignation bristling through her veins. *Ignore them,* she told herself. *They're not worth it.*

Her temper didn't listen. She wheeled, fixing them both with a glare that was close to incineration. 'Excuse me? What business is this of yours?'

The older of the two, a thin woman with greying hair and a gaunt face, eyed her with something Callie recognised.

Disdainful pity.

'It's our business when strangers meddle with things they don't understand,' the woman said. 'There's a reason that cottage has stood empty for years. No one around here would have touched it.'

The other woman found her voice. 'And now you bring a boy to live there. It's just wrong, that's what it is.'

Callie's tolerance level for strangers notched rapidly towards meltdown. 'Wrong?'

It was bad enough that they were disparaging her, but to bring Jackdaw into it?

'I'm just stating a fact. Take it or leave it.'

Callie wasn't a violent person by nature, but right now she was dangerously close to marching over and demanding answers— by force, if necessary.

She dropped the wire basket on the floor.

The noise reverberated around the shop, a satisfying sound that said everything she couldn't.

'Keep your small-minded opinions to yourself.' The words fell from her tongue quietly, but nonetheless potent. She raised a hand and resisted clenching it into a fist, instead concentrating all of her rage into a pointed finger. 'My brother is living with me now, and if anyone hurts a hair on his head I *will* come after you.'

With that, she turned on her heel and marched out of the

shop, not stopping until she reached a side street with no prying eyes. Her heart felt like it was somersaulting against her rib cage, and she was both proud of herself for standing up to their prejudice and concerned that she'd really alienated them now. No doubt the events of the last ten minutes would spread around the village like wildfire, twisting with each gossip until Callie was the one who had started it.

By the time she reached Maggie's car sweat pricked the back of her neck, and she both wanted to curl up into a ball and set something alight.

Fuck them!

She slammed the car door closed and started the engine, swinging out from her parking slot. As she turned the corner and drove along the high street, the two women were standing by the post box, deep in conversation with a tall, raggedy man she recognised. Sometimes she saw him in the field opposite her cottage, just watching.

A full-body shiver ran through her as she passed him. A glance in her rear-view mirror—his gaze followed her, and there was something about the lack of emotion in it that imprinted the image against her mind's eye, long after Combe Hurst was a blur in the distance.

As she joined the road that led to Meadowford Bridge, her fingers were white-knuckled on the steering wheel.

What was so wrong about a boy living in her cottage, and why did she feel that every word the women had said had been a threat?

CHAPTER ELEVEN

The journal sat on Jackdaw's bedside table. He'd covered it with a sweatshirt in case Callie came in, but the edge of it poked out beneath a cuff, reminding him that he hadn't dreamt it.

Now, lying on his bed with the afternoon sun dappling the walls, he tried to make sense of the words and what the missing one could be.

Find his... what? There were a thousand things that were possible. But the wording above and its angry rebelliousness wouldn't stop circling around in his mind.

He sighed, propping himself up on one elbow to look at his phone. Two fifteen.

Callie wasn't back. She might not be back for hours.

He flopped down on the bed with his hands behind his head and stared up at the dark wood beam. There was something about it he didn't like. Something he couldn't pinpoint. A gut feeling he couldn't shake.

He turned to look out of the window. From here, he could see the top of the oak tree. A crow sat on the uppermost branch preening a wing feather.

Get out, a small voice said. He wasn't a prisoner here but he felt untethered, as though if he went too far away from the cottage, he'd float away like a balloon with a snipped string.

With a growl of irritation, he stuffed his feet into his trainers and grabbed his jacket. He needed to walk to clear his head.

As he closed the front door behind him, pulling his collar up, he realised that at some point he'd need to ask Callie about getting more contact lenses.

A spike of anxiety worried at his nerve endings. He didn't want her to see the true colour of his eyes. He didn't want to see pity etched across her face, like he was the runt of a litter—the kind that was always the last to be homed.

The afternoon sun skulked behind a bank of dark cloud, and a stiff breeze knifed across from the field. Dried leaves skittered around his feet.

A surly anger churned alongside the anxiety, a potent mix of emotions that drew all his common sense into a ball and left it shivering in his gut.

He picked up a stone and hurled it against the oak. A satisfying *thunk* echoed across the yard and the crow took flight, cawing indignantly. It was a stupid act, but for a few moments it made him feel better.

His situation could definitely be worse. Callie could be fussing over him, invading his space and asking constant questions.

A thought took hold, and he chewed it over as he set off up the hill. His mother had left him to his own devices, too, holed up in her room with the radio and the bits of paper taped to the wall. Callie was doing the same thing, but in a different way.

He came to the conclusion that it was again up to him to decide how he wanted to spend his time. The prospect of a new school loomed and his anxiety laughed, swamping his mind with taunting and the hollow ache of being different.

He'd do what he always did. He'd keep his head down, grit his teeth, and refuse to let them see how much it hurt.

Survival wasn't always about the fittest.

He found a trail at the other side of a crumbling stone wall, which he guessed was the cottage boundary. He trudged on, the uphill climb leading to a stile.

In the field beyond, black-and-white cows raised their heads to watch him, their jaws masticating clumps of foamy grass.

He watched them for a moment, then plucked up the courage to walk past. They were bigger than he'd imagined and smelled rank. His nose wrinkled as one lifted its tail and deposited a steaming liquid cowpat on the ground.

Further on, an orchard beckoned beyond another wall.

He could see drooping branches covered in fruit. Hunger growled in his stomach, the slice of solitary toast he'd eaten for lunch already digested. His steps quickened and he scrambled over the wall, his feet sinking into long, damp grass. Rows of heavily laden apple trees stood as far as he could see, the ground beneath them littered with fallen fruit. For a boy who had only seen apples in a bag from a supermarket, it was a magical sight.

But he was hesitant. Why hadn't someone picked the harvest?

The orchard must have an owner.

He checked no one was near, then plucked a rosy-red apple from the nearest tree. It came away in his fingers easily, as though it had simply been waiting for him. Rubbing it on his jeans first, he took a bite and the flavour burst onto his tongue, crisp and sweetly tart with an aromatic scent.

A grin quivered on his lips. This was wild and surreal.

He was in the middle of the countryside, eating an apple that he hadn't paid for straight from the tree. And he liked this feeling, this throwing caution to the winds and jumping into something that felt a little bit wrong—but in a good way. He took another bite and spun in a circle with his arms outstretched, awestruck as golden sunbeams glittered through the clouds.

A lone crow circled above him. Jackdaw wondered if it was the same one from the tree at the cottage and he called to it, the sound vibrating easily in his throat. It answered and he laughed, racing through the orchard, jumping over trailing boughs, the heady scent of ripe fruit filling his senses.

The sky darkened as though the clouds had swallowed the sun in one bite. He stopped, slowly looking around, joy fading as quickly as it had begun. Something was different about this part of the orchard. The trees were gnarled, the apples on them either wizened or rotting.

Branches creaked in a cruel north wind. He was small here. An insignificant speck on the landscape. All around him were piles of rotted apples, and the scent now wasn't sweet at all. It smelled like meat left out of the fridge for too long on a hot summer day.

The apple was still in his hand, its juice sticky against his palm. He looked down, saw the core clearly visible with its dark pips. His eyes widened in horror as one of the pips trembled, slipping from its pith. Behind it the mucous-covered body of a plump maggot slithered out, twisting and turning until it squirmed onto his palm.

The apple tumbled from his fingers as his stomach heaved.

He skittered backwards, his spine hitting the rough bark of a tree as thunder rumbled overhead.

Fat drops of rain began to fall, and in a matter of moments his hair was plastered to his scalp.

Beyond the orchard, stretching high up on the hill, was the beginning of the woodland he had noticed when he set out.

Back then it had seemed so far away.

Now it was his only form of shelter, so he sprinted through the long grass, vaulted the low wall, and ran towards the darkened arms of the forest.

CHAPTER TWELVE

The sky had turned from a gloomy grey to a churning mass of storm clouds by the time Jackdaw reached the tree line.

Why had he come here?

Maybe it was because of the Punch Bowl woods at home.

Home.

It was such a messed-up concept, especially now. He slicked his wet hair back from his face, buried the observation—but it wouldn't stay dead.

The Punch Bowl woods had been his safe place, a small rural oasis on the outskirts of a sprawling town with its hordes of people and ugly concrete lives. It stood at the top of a hill, just beyond a scattering of mostly abandoned allotments, banked at one side by a supermarket home delivery factory and a DIY store at the other.

He'd discovered it in his first year at secondary school, slipping away at lunch time to avoid the jeering and the bullying from his peers. He'd found a hole in the fence at the back of the playing fields, and if he ran both ways he had just enough time to sit on a fallen log and eat whatever lunch he'd prepared.

It was calm there, with just the trees and the wind whispering through them. Sometimes he saw grey squirrels, their twitching tails a blur as they leapt from branch to branch. Here he could practice calling to the birds, and sometimes they answered him. Back then, in his naivety, he'd imagined living in the woods, away from school, away from being in a house where, despite his mother's presence, it had always felt like walking into a forgotten room. He was a ghost in his own life, and he'd hardly begun to live.

Thunder rumbled overhead, a noise so loud Jackdaw felt it vibrating in his chest. The rain was cold and harsh and unforgiving as it pelted the tree canopies above him. Here, at the edge of the woods, they gave him little cover. He turned away from the orchard, his gaze skimming over a carpet of copper ferns and ropes of brambles so thick he couldn't see the other side.

A flash of movement in the corner of his eye as a squirrel scampered up a tree. His eyes tracked it, then stopped.

On a branch jutting out above sat an adult jackdaw. It watched him, its head cocked to one side, its pale eye studying him dispassionately.

'Hey,' he said. The sound was swallowed by another rumble of thunder, and he shivered. 'I could do with a little help here.'

I am losing my mind. The thought sliced through him. Yet he couldn't help but think of his namesake as some kind of sign.

Raindrops showered him as the jackdaw took flight, landing on another tree. A hard *tchack-tchack* call—the one that gave it its name—and a ruffle of its feathers. It hopped to the end of the branch and called again.

Jackdaw tried to replicate the sound in his throat, but this time the retort sounded like a laugh, an avian, 'You seriously need to work on that!'

He wound his way through a clump of thin trees, their spindly branches snagging strands of his hair. Another boom of thunder and his heart rate rocketed. Rain pelted down, carving dying leaves from the trees. The rich scent of petrichor filled the air.

Up ahead was a fallen tree, lying right across the path. Its roots reached out, entangling around the trunk of a larger oak—as if, even in death, it was clinging desperately to some form of life.

Jackdaw stopped as the thought took hold. Tears filled his eyes and he swiped them away with the back of his hand. He didn't know why it had affected him at such a visceral level.

He clambered onto the fallen tree. Most of its bark had been stripped away, leaving the pale skin of the sapwood. It rested here like a beached whale in the forest. From this vantage point, he could see over the thick tangle of woodland cover. A narrow track snaked into the distance. Winding deeper into the woods.

A shiver ran through him again, but this time it wasn't because of the rain or the cold. It was the same feeling he'd had when he discovered the journal. It was something that was inherently his, something he could control.

He could explore a little bit. What harm could it do?

Maybe he could pretend he was back at the Punch Bowl. He jumped down and his feet sank into a bed of decaying leaf mulch. He looked back the way he had come, and part of him wanted to retrace his steps. The fallen tree seemed like a demarcation line, a boundary that once crossed could never be forgotten.

It's just a tree, for God's sake.

Gloom deepened as he trekked farther, the trees older and broader, their late autumn branches intertwining until very little of the sky was visible. Still the thunder rumbled, but now it wasn't as loud. Unless the forest was masking it.

His wet clothes clung to his body and his feet squelched in his trainers. It was colder here amongst these ancient trees, and he couldn't imagine any sunlight penetrating the oppressive darkness. The excitement he'd felt drained away, leaving him edgy and unsettled.

He made a pact with himself. He'd walk for a count of one hundred, then turn around and backtrack. It's what he'd done when the taunts resounded in his ears—walked for a hundred steps—but at school he never looked back.

The track narrowed and he pushed through a throng of waist-high copper bracken, emerging at the other side into a clearing. Silver birch trees circled it, the ground beneath them strewn with fallen leaves.

Silence throbbed against his ears. There were no bird calls. The rain had stopped. Even the thunder had disappeared. His mouth twisted into a grimace, sweat beading in the small of his back. He felt rooted to the spot as though there was a beast hidden, drool dripping from its jaws, and if he ran it would know and leap, and—

His fingers curled into his palms and he dug his nails into flesh, using the pain to focus. He forced himself to breathe in, then exhale. There were no beasts hidden, unless he counted his own freaky imagination. Still, it was a strange place.

Why am I here?

An unbidden thought, brought to life by the ache of dread

lining his gut.

A whisper of wind in the trees, a susurrus that caused the occasional stubborn leaf clinging to a branch to shiver.

His gaze tracked to other movements.

Adrenaline spiked through him. Hot and sharp and feral.

A cry of alarm stalled in his throat.

On every tree encircling the clearing, a small object twirled. He'd not noticed them before, but now he wondered just how he'd missed them.

Dangling, as though they had a noose around their necks, were small bundles of woven sticks.

Sticks that formed human figures.

CHAPTER THIRTEEN

Maggie O'Reilly rode Callie's ancient bicycle down to the village. She avoided the road, keeping to the bridleway that skirted the fields, one eye on the rapidly darkening sky.

A cold breeze had blown in from the north, making the hedgerows whisper.

She didn't go into the village very often.

The tongues there wagged enough without her presence, but Terry Gillam, the postman, had told her there was a letter waiting at the post office with excess postage to pay. Maggie couldn't remember the last time she had received something that wasn't a bill reminder. And this one had piqued her curiosity because Terry had emphasised the word *letter*. It twinged against her intuition—the one that shadowed her constantly. The one the villagers loathed.

She dismounted, pulling her knitted hat firmly down over her ears, and snuck through a bridleway gate, making sure it closed behind her. It was to keep the beasts safe in the fields, but the villagers would say the real beast lurked in the forest.

Maybe she should have been more open with Callie, but Maggie had no real proof that the wild was biting back. That the past didn't want to stay there.

Yet a certain date *was* looming. It was pointless to worry the young woman who had befriended her, both outcasts in their own way—Callie because she was a newcomer, and Maggie because, well… she was part of the fabric of this place, and they all knew her history.

Thunder rumbled to the west, and Maggie's gaze flicked towards the gibbet on the hill. The gibbet that still held such a sway in this small-minded community. Once, someone had suggested cutting it down, saying it was archaic and unnecessary. But no one here would have allowed that.

Not even Maggie.

Over one more field and the village came into view, nestled in the palm of the valley. Rows of picturesque cottages with rambling roses tumbling over their porches, all adding to the charm. Old-fashioned shops lining the street—butchers and bakers, greengrocers with their rainbow wares arranged outside. Cobbled back streets that hadn't changed for hundreds of years. A setting that would give a film location scout a wet dream. But beauty can be rotten, and this place knew that all too well.

The post office sat smack bang in the middle of the high street and, as it doubled as a convenience store, it was rarely empty.

As Maggie leant her bicycle against the bright-red post box, she straightened her shoulders. A moment of relief as she saw there was no queue at the counter. It quickly sank without a trace as a voice assaulted her senses.

'Maggie. How lovely to see you!'

Despite the greeting, the words carried a snide undertone. Elspeth Hargreaves was the self-appointed chairwoman of just about everything in Combe Hurst.

They used to be friends—Maggie's fingers found the edge of her hat— before the night that had shocked this tiny community to its core. When the reminder that the past was always watching came back with tooth and claw.

'Elspeth,' Maggie said, keeping her voice as civil as she could. 'You know how it is. Busy, busy.'

Maggie made for the post office counter, but Elspeth appeared around the end of the aisle clutching a loaf of sliced white bread. She gathered it to her chest like a shield, and Maggie inwardly cackled.

'Are you here for the letter?' Elspeth said. She had a grey, chin-length bob, small eyes, and a mouth that always looked disapproving even if she was smiling.

Of course Elspeth knew about the letter.

Nothing was a secret here.

Or at least, nothing to do with everyday business.

'I am.' Maggie took her purse from her pocket. 'Don't let me keep you, Elspeth. I'm sure you've so much to do.'

The girl behind the counter looked up from a stamp book she'd been checking. Her name tag declared that she was Ruby Allen.

'I've come about a letter,' Maggie said.

'*The* letter,' Elspeth interrupted, her emphasis heavily on the first word.

A pink flush spread across Ruby's cheeks. Elspeth was never subtle. Maggie had once told her that her genetics must be part steamroller.

Ruby pulled a wrinkled envelope from a pigeon hole on the side wall, smoothing it over before she passed it under the glass partition. 'I'm sorry it's such a mess,' she said, as though she'd been single-handedly responsible for its long-winded journey and its tattered state. 'But the address isn't complete, and there's no stamp. It's a wonder it actually got here.'

Ruby's voice faded as a cacophony of noise exploded in Maggie's head. Her gaze was fixed to the scrawl of handwriting across the envelope. Handwriting she thought that she'd never see again.

She didn't notice the amount Ruby asked for. She simply tapped her card against the terminal, her fingers closing around the envelope.

'Oh, I do hope it's not bad news,' Elspeth said, appearing at her shoulder.

Maggie slipped the envelope into her pocket.

'I've no idea. I haven't opened it yet.'

It was a lie. Both women knew it. But this was a battle line they weren't prepared to cross.

Elspeth's gaze raked over Maggie, her small eyes glittering, laser beams looking for a chink in armour. 'Do let me know if I can help.'

Elspeth moved away, the loaf she held flattened out of shape.

She discarded it in a basket filled with brightly coloured après Halloween sweets. 'And Maggie.' A pause as she pulled on knitted gloves. 'You haven't forgotten about Friday, have you? We'd love to see you again.'

With that carefully orchestrated shrapnel, she disappeared through the doors.

'Are you okay, Ms O'Reilly?' Ruby asked. 'You look like you've seen a ghost.'

Maggie turned, plastering a smile on her face. 'No ghosts, only a woman who doesn't know how to keep her nose out of everyone's business.'

Ruby's cheeks flushed again, and Maggie softened towards her. She didn't recognise the young girl. Perhaps she was new here. To be completely oblivious to the history of this place was a blessing.

'Thank you for keeping the letter, Ruby,' she said as she made her way to the door. The envelope crinkled in her pocket.

Dried leaves skittered along the street, the wind tugging at the few strands of hair loose under her hat. She retrieved the bicycle and walked it along the pavement, deep in thought.

By now, Elspeth's infamous gossip trail would have gathered its wings.

Was it coincidence that the letter had arrived now?

With Gala Day so close? With the arrival of Jackdaw?

Cogs were slipping into place, the past and the present lining up as Martinmas loomed, blood sacrifice and remembrance and a bygone coming-of-age steeped in tragedy.

Something wanted her to help. Something wanted her to go out into the dark night following the day.

A memory scoured through her with wire fingers, pain as raw and as sharp as it had been on that awful night.

They had called to him and he had come, merciless in his wrath. Some said he had traded his heart to a traveller woman so he could roam.

What Maggie would find in the letter would fuse the past and the present.

Words for her eyes only, after all these years.

Words from a dead woman.

CHAPTER FOURTEEN

Callie parked the car in Meadowford Bridge, finding a spot close to the river. Despite being farther away, it was her favourite place to shop. The village still had a fraction of old-world charm about it, and sometimes, she wished she'd chosen this area instead of Combe Hurst. But that was a pipe dream. She'd seen the house prices in the estate agent's window. Her cottage might not be in the best location, but she'd got it for far less than it was worth.

She was lost in these musings and didn't see the woman with the baby on her hip exit the chemist shop. A paper bag tumbled to the ground and a plastic bottle of yellow medication rolled out. The standard children's banana-flavoured medicine.

'I'm so sorry.' Callie threw her hands up in apology, crouching to retrieve the bag and the bottle. Her eyes skimmed over the name label. *Theodora Gabriella Taverner-Isaacs.* She handed it back to the woman, the dark-haired tot on her hip studying Callie solemnly. Phantom fingers dusted Callie's spine.

An old soul. That little girl is an old soul.

Callie pulled herself back into focus, grimaced and apologised again, but even as she walked away she knew the woman was still watching her. *Okay, just another dose of weird.* She shook her head, her lips twisting into a wry smile. People thought country folk were odd, but really, they had no idea *how* odd they could be.

Her phone began to ring, and she extracted it as she ran across the road to the small grocery store. It was her agent, Adele Hopkins, who also owned the London gallery where her show was scheduled in just four short days.

'Hi, Callie, I've got fabulous news!' Adele launched into the reason for her call, which might last two minutes or twenty. Callie had learned by now just to listen and make encouraging noises. 'Remember Diego Acala, from San Francisco? He bought the main pieces from your Winter Haunts range last year. Well, he's flying over especially for the show, and I know for a fact that he'll have an open wallet.'

Callie remembered Diego well, and she also remembered how healthy her bank balance had looked after the show.

'We need more creations, Callie, darling. Something that will blow him away. Is this going to be a problem? I know it's very last minute.'

It was ridiculously last minute, but Callie had Jackdaw to think about now. He was fifteen, nearly sixteen. He'd maybe stay on for sixth form, but what if he wanted to go to uni? She'd need extra funds. Even basic living costs would be more with another mouth to feed. Last night, she had been sure that Jackdaw's presence in her life was temporary, but now…

'I can do it,' Callie said in a rush. 'I know exactly what I can use as a theme.'

Truth be told, she didn't have a clue on that front.

'Marvellous, darling. Must dash. Keep me in the loop. See you in four days!'

Four days. *My God, that was* so *close.* Callie would have to pull a few midnight sessions.

It was a huge relief to fill her basket without worrying about prying eyes or judgemental comments. By the time she got to the till, the basket was overflowing, but at least she had enough for meals for the next few days and some treats for Jackdaw.

She pushed away the thought it was guilt demanding these extras, knew that she should be spending time with him.

The show had come at the worst possible time. Or maybe it was Jackdaw who had arrived at the worst possible time?

Callie hated herself for even considering the latter.

Thunder rumbled in the distance as she unlocked Maggie's car. The skies overhead were clear with cotton wool clouds, but over to the east, where Combe Hurst lay, they were a sullen shade of steel grey. By now, she was used to the sudden unpredictable weather changes in this region, but still a flutter of apprehension raised the hair in the nape of her neck.

A few miles out of Combe Hurst, fat drops of rain began to fall, and by the time she reached the village boundary, she had to set the windscreen wipers to double speed. Water gushed along the roadside as the drains became flooded with the downpour. Lamps shone in cottages as the dimming light turned day to dusk, time rushing forward towards night.

'Fuck!' She braked heavily as the bright yellow Belisha beacons at a zebra crossing loomed out of the murk. A line of school children filed across it, flanked by two teachers. They were all dressed in dark cagoules that covered them from head to knee, hoods obscuring their faces, rain glistening on their shoulders.

One of the children lifted their arms, and the cagoule fanned out like wings.

A murder of crows, Callie thought. *They look like a murder of crows.*

Her blood ran cold, as though ice crystals had formed in her veins. If she'd been standing, her knees would have given way.

All she could do was watch as the group finally crossed the road and entered the schoolyard.

A flash of headlights in her rear-view mirror refocussed her thoughts, and she held up her hand in apology to the car behind.

Now that the initial shock had worn off, heat flushed her skin, adrenaline making her fingertips tingle. They were just kids, kitted out for English weather. But there was something about how they'd looked—*what* they'd looked like.

She needed Maggie's guidance, a strong cup of tea, and a stiff drink. As she set off again, negotiating the narrow road as it wound up to Maggie's cottage, her unease deepened. She couldn't help feeling something was changing...

And that she was powerless to stop it.

CHAPTER FIFTEEN

The tall man took the sack from his back, placing it on the ground by his makeshift hut. He was a wanderer of no fixed abode, but this month, he lived in the woods above Combe Hurst. Come rain or shine, he needed to be here.

The land needed him to be here.

There was no sign of the boy who had discovered the clearing —but the man knew he had been here because the wind whispering through the stick figures told him so.

They were agitated. He brushed past each one, quietening them with a touch, for they were his children, and he had created them from the bounty of the forest. The trees remembered everything. Each sin and each curse and each promise to stay together.

He hummed to himself as he sat on a fallen log, extracting a bundle of willow rods from his sack. The days were rapidly turning, and he would need to work quickly to have all of his sticklings ready. The young ones were relying on him.

Sometimes he wondered what would happen if a year went by without this ancient ritual, but he had no desire to find out. Not when his memory was as clear as crystal concerning the night he had almost touched the past.

No, this had to be done, to lead the next generation into the future whilst ensuring that they never forgot. Because forgetting could only spell catastrophe for the village. It was blessed, and it would always be blessed as long as they remembered.

As long as the boy who had once lived here was remembered.

It was a pact between them.

He was an old man now, seven decades under his belt, but he'd always been tied to the land, a slave to her whims.

All land is scarred with ghost soil where blood soaked into the earth. Where wrongs were committed by those with privilege and power, where tortured souls can never rest.

If anyone dared to come here in the dead calm of night, they would meet the very worst version of themselves. He was only immune because he had already suffered this.

As a boy, he had a given name, but it was lost to time—and now he only went by the name of Twig.

He took a length of willow and wound it deftly between his calloused fingers, adding extra smaller lengths for limbs. When half a dozen sticklings lay on the ground before him, he paused.

The rain had stopped but still cold, fat drops spilled down from the skeletal branches above, soaking through the tattered padded jacket he wore—which once had been a deep red but now had faded to a colour like old blood. His clothes were all hand-me-downs from the villagers. They left them outside their houses in plastic bags, a hurriedly snapped twig placed on top so everyone would know that these were for him.

He looked down at his feet, at a pair of garish trainers with graffiti scrawled across them, the laces now lengths of string.

These were not the garments of his heart, they merely acted as a covering so he could move freely around people. What really mattered was the clothing he would wear on Gala night.

The night where they came to ask the blessing of a boy who had died two hundred years before.

Twig stood and stretched his back, his spine cracking.

He swept a covering of woven stems and trailing bracken aside. There, behind, was his home, a hut assembled from materials he had scavenged through the year. A sheet of corrugated metal, a faded tarpaulin, a fence panel bowed in the centre. It did little to keep the cold at bay if November grew teeth. But he was not here for comfort.

Each night he would take the mushrooms he'd collected at dawn and press them into a paste. This he placed on his tongue, even though the taste was bitter and repulsive and made him gag.

He laid upon the earth, where echoes of the past thrummed in time with his heartbeat. He waited for the dreams, waited for the portal to quiver like a mirage in his mind's eye. Because he needed to see for himself what had really happened on this land. It was an itch that had burned through him year after year, stifling logic, a driving force hellbent on devouring what was left of his sanity.

Yet despite all of his preparations and his serfdom to this cause, he had only caught tantalising glimpses.

You are not worthy, a small voice mocked. But still he persevered.

He sighed, an exhalation that was not unlike the whispering of the wind through the trees. It was still a few hours before nightfall. Time still to gather berries and apples to stave off his hunger.

A crow cawed harshly in the trees, and his gaze tracked it immediately. He bowed his head in respect then hurried through the clearing, stopping when he found the spot where the new boy had stood. Stooping, he took hold of a handful of wet leaves and brought them to his nose. A rush of wind tugged at his hair, and the trees creaked around him.

Twig fell to his knees on the earth as the sound vibrated through his core, and it seemed to him then that the creaking was less about the trees whispering their discontent...

And more about a rope swinging with a heavy weight kicking at its length.

CHAPTER SIXTEEN

Jackdaw ran like the hounds of hell were on his heels. On more than one occasion his feet slipped from beneath him in the wet sludge of leaves, sending him scrambling for balance, his breath rasping in his throat.

He didn't look back.

Brambles tore at his wet clothes, and his cheek stung where a particularly vicious stem had landed a barbed swipe.

Birds called through the trees—the high-pitched alarm chit from a blackbird, the harsh caw-caw of a crow. He was aware of them in the branches above him, and in his panicked state he wasn't sure if they were warning him about a danger or trying to lead him away.

His foot caught on a half-buried root and he fell, his arms flailing, hitting the ground shoulder first. He lay there, winded, the ache throbbing through him, staring up at a huge, towering oak. From this perspective, its bare branches looked like they touched the sky. Other trees surrounded it in a circle, their limbs intertwining.

As though they're protecting it.

The thought cut deep, and his lips parted.

As his heart rate settled, he gingerly raised himself into a sitting position, picking dead leaves from his jacket.

A watery sun spiked through thinning cloud and suddenly the woodland was filled with the glisten of moisture. Beads of water dripped from the tips of bracken fronds, cobwebs strung between them. Raindrops shivered on the ivy leaves clinging to tree trunks. Jackdaw rested his brow on his raised knees, his hair falling forward.

The sun on the back of his neck felt like a hug from someone he loved… he grimaced and lifted his chin. How did he even know what that felt like? His mother had never really demonstrated this kind of affection, at least none that he could remember. He'd had no friendships where this was ever a thing. Callie had hugged him, but he knew he'd stiffened and given nothing back.

Maybe he'd convinced himself he was strong enough without it, but sitting here, in the still and feral beauty of the woodland, he would have given anything for arms around him.

'Just get a grip,' he said under his breath, rising to his feet. It was pointless wishing for make-believe.

The bark of the oak was thick and weathered, moss staining its deep fissures and ridges like wrinkles on an old face. Jackdaw placed his palm against it, his fingertips pressing against the rough surface. His gaze tracked upwards to the sky and then back to the base, and he felt his own insignificance against this titan that had seen so much and would still be here when he was dust.

A small clump of fungi sprouted from the tangle of grass at the bottom of the trunk. The vivid red–orange caps with white flecks were fly agaric, poisonous and hallucinogenic.

It was a weird fact for a modern boy to know, but he'd spent a summer identifying different fungi in the Punch Bowl, just for something to do.

It had become an addictive game trying to find each one.

Fly agaric didn't normally grow close to oak trees, though.

His mouth twisted to one side.

Jackdaw knelt in the wet leaves and brushed away a tangle of ivy winding its way through the brightly coloured caps.

There, carved deep into the bark, was a name.

A name he had seen in the journal.

Iza.

He traced it with his forefinger, then let the ivy fall back into place. Who was this boy, and why did everything seem to point towards him? Maybe Iza had been a loner, too, or maybe something had happened to him out of his control? That last reflection he understood soul deep.

Whatever the reason, Jackdaw made a pact with himself, a fierce determination settling deep in his chest.

'I'm listening, Iza,' he whispered as he set off again along the track, sunlight dappling his path.

It led him a different way out of the forest, emerging at the far end of a field beyond the orchard. He followed a trail of molehills running the length of the drystone wall sloping down towards the cottage. His damp clothes clung to his body and he desperately needed a shower. He could smell his own fear oozing from the collar of his jacket.

Luck was on his side as he drew closer to the cottage. It didn't look like Callie was back yet, so there'd be no searching questions about the state he was in.

He glanced back over his shoulder at the forest as his hand reached out to push open the door.

A sticky softness brushed against his fingers and he turned, his brow furrowing.

His hand flew to his mouth, shock rasping in his throat.

There, pinned to the door, were two black wings edged in gore—torn from a crow or a raven or a jackdaw.

The feathers lifted in the stiff breeze as though they still remembered how to fly.

CHAPTER SEVENTEEN

Deep in the earth something stirred, an awareness soaking through the heavy mantle of soil and grass and age. A name tore through it, vibrating inside its empty skull. Despair uncurled itself, fingers of rage tearing the binds of its restless sleep.

It felt the weight of the moon biding her time, and the glare of the sun keeping the orb prisoner in these daylight hours, and if a sound could have come from its incorporeal lungs it would have been a howl to make the very ground tremble.

Hush, said the moon. *It will be your night soon.*

CHAPTER EIGHTEEN

Jackdaw was standing under the porch with a rag in his hand as Callie parked her car. It had been given a clean bill of health, and the guy from the garage had offered to drive it over to Maggie's. Callie took the call as she peered through Maggie's kitchen window, but the older woman wasn't in.

She grabbed the shopping bags from the boot, balancing them on her knee as she slammed it shut.

Her car didn't understand subtlety.

'Don't tell me you're cleaning the paintwork,' she said. A roll of kitchen towel tumbled from an overfilled bag and bounced onto the ground. She swore under her breath.

'I've got it,' he said, bending to pick it up.

Her brow creased as she saw that his hair was wet, curling around his collar, and that the shoulders of his jacket were darker, soaked with rain. It shouldn't really have bothered her, but as the realisation dawned that this was a fraction of maternal instinct, she shrank back into herself. She'd never wanted kids, especially after her own upbringing.

'Where did these come from?' she asked, refocussing her thoughts as a few downy black feathers danced around her feet. 'Did a bird fly into...'

Her voice trailed off as she looked at Jackdaw.

His face was ashen.

'Okay.' She pushed the bags of shopping into his arms and opened the door. 'We need to talk. Take that wet jacket off and hang it by the Aga.' She shrugged out of her own coat and hat, relishing the warmth from the quarry tiles as she pulled off her boots. 'I had to go into Meadowford Bridge for supplies, but at least they had more choice. Check the orange bag.' She dived for the other one, which was in danger of toppling from Jackdaw's arms. 'I know this is way too late for lunch, but I got cheese pasties from the bakery. They should still be warm.'

She busied herself grabbing plates and filling the kettle, intensely aware that he hadn't said a word.

'Has someone said something to you?'

She wanted to put a hand on his shoulder, but his stance said *don't touch me.*

For a few moments, he didn't move. Then, with a sigh, he pulled out a chair and flopped bonelessly into it.

'The vibes of this place are seriously off.' He glanced up at her through a fall of damp hair. 'Did something happen here, like, in the past?'

Callie could have gone into great detail about exactly how *off* this place was, but she was an adult, and so she had to behave like one.

'Not that I'm aware of.' The lie stuck in her throat as she rifled in the bag, pulling out two foil packets. She shook a pasty onto a plate, shreds of light pastry flicking onto the table, and pushed it across to him. 'But you have to remember, this is a rural community, and they have lots of traditions that might seem weird to outsiders, but it doesn't mean that they're wrong.'

He poked at the pasty with one finger, drawing his lips around his teeth. 'Is it a tradition to nail bird wings to a door?'

Now it was her turn to pale. She could almost feel the blood draining from her skin.

'Is that what you were doing when I arrived? Cleaning it off?'

He shrugged. 'I dug a hole and buried them. It didn't feel right to put them in the bin.'

Her heart clenched at Jackdaw's empathy whilst annoyance simmered in the pit of her stomach. She thought about the indignant women in the post office, and yet this act seemed like a step too far. What was so wrong about him being here? Maybe Maggie would know, but then wouldn't she have said something when Callie was there earlier?

Questions rolled around her mind, but any answers she came up with only spawned more questions. 'Damn it.' She slapped her hands on the table. Jackdaw flinched and she was immediately filled with remorse.

'I'll ask around,' she said, reaching to tentatively rest her hand on his arm. 'But I don't want you to be scared. Whatever this is, it isn't your fault.'

But there was something else she needed to talk to him about. 'I got a phone call when I was out, from my agent.' She paused as his mouth twisted in confusion. 'God, you don't even know. I'm so bad.' A sigh escaped her lips. There hadn't been time. There never seemed to be enough time. 'Once a year I have a show in London, and lots of people come and pay ridiculous amounts for my work.' It wasn't that she wasn't proud of what she did, but in the long run, they were just heaps of formed clay. 'She asked if I'd make more—special ones—as she has an American buyer coming in. That means I'll have to work when I should be spending time with you. But it's only for a few days. And then the show will be here, and when I get back, we can both relax.'

'It's okay,' he said, finally taking a bite of the pasty. 'I'll be fine here. I'm used to fending for myself, remember?' He brushed away a few crumbs from his lips with the back of his hand.

Callie inwardly grimaced. Of course he was used to looking after himself. Some of the agitation fluttering in her gut settled. They could get through this one day at a time.

A sudden thought ended as a question. 'Do you want to come to London with me?'

He stopped chewing, one brow hiking. 'And spend my time making small talk with people I don't know about things I know nothing about? No, thanks.'

She couldn't blame him.

Putting it like that, it sounded tedious.

'I can ask my friend Maggie if you can stay with her, if you want.' Callie wasn't used to the logistics of caring for other people.

'Come on, I'm nearly sixteen. I've been looking after myself all my life. I'm not going to stay with someone I don't know. That would give me a menty b.' His jawline suggested this wasn't up for negotiation.

'Menty b?' Callie said. A vertical wrinkle appeared between her brows.

'Mental breakdown,' he said, without missing a beat. 'Gen Z in the house.' For an instant, she saw his sharp sense of humour, a flash of the boy she had yet to get to know.

'Okay, that's my cue to work.' She laughed as she pushed back her chair and grabbed her tea. 'If you need me, I'll be knee-deep in wet clay.'

As she went out into the cold late afternoon light and entered the gloom of her work space, she pondered Jackdaw's words. He was right. It was unfeeling of her to expect him to go stay with Maggie.

Yes, he wasn't yet an adult, but he wasn't a kid anymore.

She had to trust him.

Or this wouldn't work for either of them.

CHAPTER NINETEEN

Jackdaw slept as if he'd been awake for days. He'd only meant to close his eyes for a few moments after his shower, his conversation with Callie ping-ponging around his skull. He'd missed supper, and his grumbling stomach reminded him of that fact.

'Ow.' He grimaced as he tried to rub the sleep out of his eyes, cursing at his own stupidity. His lenses were still in, and his eyes weren't happy about it at all. Blinking, he stared up at the dark wood of the roof beam.

A bitter taste flooded his tongue and he shivered.

His phone told him it was 9.28am. A few short weeks ago he would have been sitting in tutor with the day's lessons looming. A few short weeks ago he would have been trying to make himself as invisible as possible.

He swung his legs out of bed and padded to the mirror, tilting his head to the only spot where his reflection wasn't blurred. Going to bed with wet hair was never a good thing, and now he looked like a bird that had been run over—tufts like feathers sticking out at odd angles.

Like the wings nailed to the door. He pushed the thought away.

Red-rimmed eyes looked back at him, the corners crusted. Just great. A perfect start to his day.

He pulled his bag out from under the bed and rifled in the front pocket for his eye drops. The bottle felt too light, and when he stuck his hand back into the pocket, he knew why. The material was damp. He can't have put the lid back on properly the last time he used it.

All that came out when he tipped his head back was tiny puffs of air.

Panic fizzed through his fingertips and he had to pause and take several deep breaths. *Okay, I can do this.* In the scheme of all the messed-up things that had happened, this was a small blip. At some point, he'd have to talk to Callie about the one thing he desperately tried to hide.

Footsteps sounded on the stairs and he spun, his heart rate rocketing.

'Jackdaw? Are you awake?' Callie's soft knock.

'Yeah,' he said. 'You can come in.'

The door opened, and he was greeted by a smile. Then it fell as though someone had turned off a switch, rapidly followed by a look Jackdaw knew well. Pity.

It took a few moments for him to realise why. She'd seen his red eyes and thought he'd been crying. As soon as this thought hit, tears welled up, causing them to sting even more.

'I'm okay,' he said, holding his hand up, keeping her at bay. 'I just left my contacts in overnight, and my eye drops are finished. I don't suppose you have any so I can get these out?'

Her gaze scrutinised him for too long, and he knew she was trying to work out if he was telling the truth.

'Sure.' Her hand touched his shoulder lightly, and then she retraced her steps, the sound of her feet on the wooden stairs echoing through the still air. When she returned, clutching a small bottle, Jackdaw nearly snatched it out of her hand.

She motioned to the bed. 'Sit. Turn your head to the light.'

'I can do it,' he said, a little too quickly, because it was too soon for her to see him as he truly was. But she was already pushing him gently down onto the bed. His eyes watered as shafts of morning sunlight spiked through the window.

'I did call you for supper.' He could see the backs of her hands, speckled with red clay. An old, white scar across her wrist bone. 'But you were fast asleep, so I left you to rest.'

She squeezed the bottle, filling his right eye with liquid, and he shrank back instinctively. 'I know it stings,' she said calmly. 'Just blink. Here.' She pulled a small mirror and a pack of wipes from her back pocket. 'Oh, can you see okay?'

Tears ran down his cheeks, but at least these were from the drops. 'I'm near-sighted.'

He cleaned his fingers on a wipe and took the mirror, angling it so that he could see. After a few fumbled attempts, he managed to remove the offending lens. Balanced on his fingertip, it looked like snail slime, the gunk from his eye glistening on its surface. The memory of the maggot sliced through him, and his nose wrinkled.

The other lens came out a lot easier, and he managed to resist the urge to rub the hell out of his eyes. He looked down at his hands folded in his lap. There were moss stains from yesterday embedded under his nails.

Please go.

But she didn't.

'Jackdaw, if there's something bothering you, you know

you can talk to me, okay?'

She crouched, and through a fall of hair, he could see the worry etched on her face.

Slowly, he raised his head until their eyes met.

'Wow,' she said, her lips parting in wonder. 'This is your natural colour? That's so unusual.'

Now she could see what he'd kept hidden. That his eyes were a bright summer-sky blue—exactly the same as a young jackdaw.

He hung his head as soon as her words hit, unsure if they carried other connotations. He'd spent so long hiding his truth and automatically assumed everyone would think he was a freak.

'Can you order me some more lenses? The optician where I live…used to live, has the prescription.' It felt like a big ask to a boy who flew under the radar.

'Of course I can,' she said, screwing the cap back on the bottle and setting it on the nightstand. 'Keep this. I'll buy another one.'

A few moments of silence ticked between them.

'Do you wear them, too?' he asked, studying her face. Her eyes were blue-grey, the colour of light on the ocean.

'No, this is something I have in. You wouldn't believe how often I flick clay into my eyes. Occupational hazard.' Her mouth twisted into a rueful grimace.

She patted his leg and stood. 'I came up to tell you that I'll be working all day, but just knock if you need me for anything.'

Gentle sunlight dappled the walls, soft shadows dancing

across the painted surface. He could hear the rapid hammering of a woodpecker somewhere close, and the orchard and the strange stick figures in the woods seemed like a world away.

Maybe being here wasn't so bad after all.

'You can borrow my bike if you want to explore,' Callie said, as she paused in the doorway. 'It's in the barn.'

Jackdaw opened his mouth to tell her about Ophelia, then shut it again. The little girl was obviously happy playing there. It was her little secret. Jackdaw knew how important those were.

And in the wardrobe, wrapped in a dark hoodie, was his own.

Sure, he could tell Callie about it, but she had enough to do with the show. This was his mystery, his ghost from the past, and he was determined to solve it.

A memory of his mother tacking scribbled notes to faded wallpaper flitted across his mind. He'd always thought it was crazy, the amount of time she spent in her own insular world.

The sudden realisation hit him like a derailed train: she'd done it because it was important and there'd been something inside her that wouldn't let her stop.

He wondered what was going to happen to all of those scraps of paper, all of her notebooks. Would someone just take them and fling them into a bin? A pang tore through him at the thought of all her hours of work being discarded like they meant nothing.

For the first time, he truly understood her passion.

And now his own was waiting for him tucked away in the dark.

After all, what harm could it do?

CHAPTER TWENTY

By the time Jackdaw took a quick shower and wolfed down a fried egg sandwich, his eyes had settled enough for him to pop his last set of contacts in. He took the journal from the wardrobe, still wrapped in his hoodie, and placed it carefully in his backpack.

Today, he was on the hunt for clues—and having the old words close made him feel like he wasn't alone.

He grabbed his jacket from the peg in the kitchen and jammed the beanie over his hair. Pushing the door open on the barn, he found Callie's bike leaning against a hay bale. A long time ago it had been red, but now only patches of the paint remained on the rust-flecked frame. He closed his hands over the handlebars. Intense burning cold bit into his fingers.

A sudden rustling came from the deep shadows at the back of the barn and his head snapped up. No light reached that far. It was like a slice of night had curled up there to sleep. He chewed the inside of his cheek.

A creak of wood and his gaze flicked across to the old cart. Musty straw hung over its edges, trembling in the draught from the door.

As an object it was tired and unloved. A relic from the past.

But he didn't like it, and he didn't know why.

Gooseflesh tingled across his arms, and his tongue felt glued to the roof of his mouth.

'Are you going out?'

Callie's voice from behind made him spin, his eyes wide, as though she'd pulled him from some lost world.

'Yeah.' He tried to sound unflustered, but to his own ears, the unease still hung in his voice.

'I saw you through the window,' she said. Her hands were covered in dried clay, a few speckles on her cheeks.

'What's with the old cart?' He jerked his head towards it.

She followed his movement.

'Oh, that. It's part of what I inherited when I bought this place. Nothing of any value.'

He tore his gaze away and wheeled the bike through the door.

The wan daylight on his face felt soft and comforting.

'What's the quickest way to the village?' he asked.

A flicker of apprehension in her eyes. He wanted to ask why, but how could he ever put that into words without sounding like some spooked-up kid?

'Go out onto the lane for about fifty yards, and there's a sign in the hedge on the right for a bridleway. Follow it, and it will take you to the church. The road from that leads to the village.'

She pressed a ten-pound note into his hand, her fingers grazing his for a few seconds. 'For lunch,' she added. 'Most things here are cash.'

The note of brightness in her voice felt too false.

'Thanks,' he said, shoving the note into the back pocket of his jeans. He wheeled the bike over the tufts of grass growing through the gravel. The back wheel creaked in protest.

As he reached the point where the driveway kinked towards the lane, he glanced over his shoulder, but she'd already gone back into her work shed.

Something about her behaviour needled against his senses as he went out onto the lane. A harsh cry from the skies and he tipped his head back to see a lone red kite circling against the clouds. He mimicked it without thinking and it circled lower, its great wingtips shivering in an air current.

The bridle path skirted around the edge of the field he'd trudged through with Callie the night he'd arrived. As he reached the dip, he dismounted and pushed the bike along. The waterlogged ground squelched under his feet.

Sweat coated his skin by the time the gate to the churchyard loomed. He took off his beanie and shoved it into his backpack.

Autumn sunlight dappled through the trees onto the old, moss-covered gravestones. Dead flowers toppled from urns. A tap dripped on the church wall. Dried leaves skittered across the path. It was all so ordinary.

He paused at the entrance to the church. One of the double doors stood open, leading to an interior porch. The scent of old stone curled into his nostrils. Tucked under a narrow wooden bench was a rectangular wicker basket with a lid, a stack of hymn books with scuffed spines resting on the top.

'Can I help you?' A voice drifted out from the main body of the church and Jackdaw shrank back. A figure appeared from the shadows, a slim woman with a blond ponytail. A small girl dressed in pink leggings and a fluffy white jacket held her hand.

But it was what the child carried under her other arm that made Jackdaw's head spin.

A white chicken with a red comb and bright amber eyes tilted its head to look at him.

The thought he'd had only moments before—about everything being ordinary—dissolved.

He shook his head at the woman's question and hurried away, feeling her scrutiny like a knife in his back.

'Chickens in church are perfectly normal,' he muttered, huffing out a breath.

He continued on the pathway as it wound past a stone war memorial with a Celtic cross, then onwards towards the main road. The lychgate drowned him in shadow as he passed beneath its roof. A clock tower on the high street chimed the hour.

And then he was sailing down the road the bus had driven on only a few short nights ago. Wind tousled his hair and he laughed, enjoying the speed and the high adrenaline buzz of freedom. Cars passed him and he had the sudden urge to pedal faster, to leave all this uncertainty behind.

So he wasn't really paying attention as an electric scooter shot out of a side street on his left. A flash of sunlight on metal. He braked hard, but the old bike wasn't listening. A moment where he knew he was going to collide with the scooter and that it would *really* hurt.

A face turned towards him, shock painted across its features.

And then a bone-crushing impact sent him sailing over the handlebars, defying gravity. Pain coursed through his side as he hit another solid body, a cry he wasn't sure came from his throat or not, and the unmerciful ground hurtling towards him.

CHAPTER
TWENTY-ONE

The letter still sat in the drawer. Maggie had stuffed it there yesterday when she'd returned from the village, telling herself that she'd read it later. But that was a lie.

Part of her knew she was only putting off the inevitable, that the words she would read there would only confirm her worst fears. She just needed a little more time.

Yet time was one thing she didn't have.

The moon cycles would not wait.

Whatever was out there stirring would not wait.

And nature knew. This morning, the trees had been coated with frost, her breath escaping in spectral clouds as she set out seeds for the birds. There were more of them now, perched in the trees, waiting on the old telephone wires that still crossed by her cottage. Their calls echoed into the freezing dawn and she shivered, but not because of the cold.

The smaller birds huddled together—safety in numbers—because they knew that the crows held court here. They knew that the corvids sensed the wheel turning.

Soon, he would roam—and the gods help anyone who was out after dark. That was how it had always been since that awful day so many years ago. When something pure and good had been ripped away. When desperation and grief had driven a boy to commit a horrific act.

Today, there was someone she had to see.

After breakfast, she stood in front of the hall mirror, adjusting the woollen hat she always wore in the winter. She tucked a few strands of hair back into her thin plaits. There was a time when her hair was her crowning glory. It hung long and thick halfway down her back, shining like golden wheat in the sun. But one night had changed all of that, had sent her scurrying away like a beaten dog until she finally found the strength to return. And when she did her greatest friend had disappeared, too.

How vain they had been. How desperate to cling onto the beauty that was fading with each passing year. How stupid to believe that they could reach into the past.

With a heavy sigh, she sat on the bottom step of the staircase and pulled on her waterproof boots, making sure that she had a packet of seed in her pocket.

November sunlight had melted the frost on the meadow, leaving a glistening coating on every blade of grass. But there was no birdsong. She didn't look up, just kept her gaze firmly on the leaf-strewn bridlepath as she walked. Her heart would know the way blindfolded.

She paused at the bottom of the hill, glanced across to Callie's cottage. Her gaze flicked towards the old barn. A sharp pang tore through her at the knowledge that her friend would be caught up in this dark chaos, and there was nothing Maggie could do about it.

She'd known the instant Callie had arrived that afternoon a few weeks ago, her face drained of colour, worry etched across her brow. The sudden death of her mother. The stunned awareness that she was going to be responsible for a half-brother she had never met.

Maggie leaned against a gate post and shook a stone from one of her boots. A crushing weight settled across her shoulders.

Boys did not do well in this place.

It was useless to wonder at fate. To wonder at an unravelling that had been carved upon this land all those years ago.

The village would do what it always had to survive. It laughed in the face of contemporary thinking, of those who spurned the heartbeat of the past.

She set off up the incline, her gaze firmly fixed on the treeline at the top of the hill.

He would know she was coming. He always did.

An eerie silence greeted her as she stepped into the forest, as though the trees had closed in, suffocating any sound. *As though they want to silence me.* The thought tore through her, but she fought free. She hadn't come this far to be intimidated.

Gorse thorns tugged at her clothes as she pushed her way along the track, her boots sinking in patches of rich, damp soil.

As she stepped into the clearing the years fell away, and she was back on that fateful night—filled with life, filled with determination. But by dawn, she was bloodied and shivering and almost hysterical.

How she made it home was still a blurred mystery shrouded with pain and terror.

Maggie ripped her thoughts back to the present. The past was over and done, and all she could hope to do was mitigate the damage the future held in its jaws.

The stick figures hanging on the trees quivered as though that concept was insanely comical.

Part of her agreed with them.

Twig sat on a fallen log at the end of the clearing, his calloused fingers deftly weaving willow rods.

A hard lump formed in her throat.

'Have you ever stopped to think what might happen if you didn't do that?' She gestured to his hands, now stilled as he watched her approach.

'I don't have a choice,' he said. 'You should know that.'

It wasn't a criticism. It was a cold, hard fact.

She continued until she was standing over him—this man who had taken it upon himself to live so meagrely, who still hungered for the truths from the past, even though every time he tried to push through the veil he was slowly poisoning himself.

He was a slave to this lore, just as she was. As Naomi was, wherever she was now.

'Have you met the boy?' he asked, starting to weave again. 'He was here. My sticklings told me.'

That was the term he used for the stick figures. As though they had come from his loins.

'They said his blood is ripe.'

Maggie tightened her lips before her words could escape.

Emotion had no place here. She stuffed her trembling fingers into her pockets.

She'd wanted to mention Jackdaw almost as a postscript to why she was actually here, to gauge Twig's reaction.

'I came to tell you that I'll be at the Gala Day.' She refused to acknowledge his last comment, hitting him with one she knew would startle him.

He blew a fragment of loose willow from the figure he was fashioning.

Blood streaked his fingers where the bark had bitten back.

'Why this time, Maggie?' he said, his pale eyes rising to meet hers. 'You've not walked the path since that night.'

'Times change,' she said, her tone a little sharper than she'd meant. She turned on her heel and was halfway across the clearing when his voice came behind her, certainty in every syllable.

'But you know as well as I do that they don't, Maggie Moon. That's why we're still here.'

His words might as well have been a punch to her gut, but she squared her shoulders and carried on walking until her steps led her out of the forest to the top of the hill.

Maggie Moon. A name he hadn't called her since that night.

Her gaze flicked across to find Callie's cottage perched on the shoulder of the hillside, where a boy called Jackdaw now lived.

A harsh caw sounded from above, and she instinctively ducked as two large crows swept in and landed on an abandoned hay bale partly shrouded in a black plastic covering. They watched her with foreseeing eyes, assessing what she knew.

She dug into her pocket and retrieved the packet of seed, scattering a handful as she passed.

A humble offering as a phantom pain seared across her skull.

CHAPTER TWENTY-TWO

Images blurred against Jackdaw's half-closed eyelids. Everything had happened so quickly, and now he was leaning against the reason he was here with blood dripping into his eyes. The reason was talking to him and the voice was soothing, so Jackdaw gave in and let himself be led into the stuffy heat of a building.

Something shimmered close by, a nightmarish skeleton.

A large bird. Only it wasn't just a skeleton. He could see the bones through a gauzy covering of pale skin.

I am losing it…

The reason pushed him gently down onto a hard, plastic chair. 'Wait here.'

Jackdaw gingerly raised his hand to his brow and found an inch-long cut across his temple. A paper towel was placed into his other hand, and as he dabbed the blood away his vision finally settled. He was in what looked like a village hall. A stage loomed at one end, stacks of chairs and fold-up tables against an adjacent wall.

A door to the right of the stage creaked open, and a figure emerged carrying a small bowl.

'I'm glad you didn't make a run for it.'

The voice belonged to the reason Jackdaw was here.

He sauntered across and crouched down.

His hands were covered in blue surgical gloves, and he held a wad of cotton padding in his fingers.

'First of all, I'm so sorry about the accident. It was all my fault for not stopping.'

A face looked up at Jackdaw. A boy, slightly taller and older with wild, sandy-blond curls and a smattering of freckles over his nose.

'To be fair, you were trying to break the speed limit careering down the hill.' A grin followed, one that lit up the boy's whole face. 'Now hold still whilst I clean you up.'

Jackdaw opened his mouth to say something, but everything felt like he'd just turned around and around in circles for a minute, his thoughts a dizzying spiral of jumbled nonsense.

The water in the bowl turned pink as the boy rinsed the wadding. Nausea rose in Jackdaw's throat but he managed to swallow it down.

'It's not as bad as the blood looks,' the boy said. 'Heads bleed a lot because of all the blood vessels. I don't think it will scar.'

Jackdaw gazed into two solemn, light-green eyes as the boy dabbed his brow again.

'Look,' the boy said, drawing his lips around his teeth. 'The whole thing *was* my fault. If you want to report it, I'll take the blame.' He cocked his head to one side, and this time the grin was partly a sheepish grimace. 'I'm Oscar, by the way.'

'Jackdaw,' Jackdaw said without thinking, inwardly wincing that he'd now have to explain the whole name thing.

'Yeah,' Oscar said. 'Jack Dawtrey. Jackdaw. I get it.' He pulled a paper packet from his pocket and tore it open. Nestled inside was a strip of butterfly plasters. He tore two off and pressed them against Jackdaw's temple. 'There you go.' Oscar sat back onto his heels with a satisfied smile. 'Don't look so surprised. News travels fast. You're new here and a boy.'

'What's wrong with being a boy?' Jackdaw asked, sure that somewhere in this conversation he'd missed something critical.

A dismissive sound fell from Oscar's lips. 'Some folklore thing. You know what it's like in the country. They like to build fires and sacrifice people for good harvests.'

Jackdaw's jaw slackened. 'You're kidding, right?' He didn't like the pensive expression on Oscar's face.

'Of course I'm kidding, you idiot,' Oscar said as he stood. 'Just, everyone here likes to live in the past and they have weird customs. It's why my parents relocated when I was eleven. I'm only back as they're away on some fancy holiday, and they don't trust me not to burn down the family home in their absence. A whole glorious week in the company of Aunt Elspeth. Although, there was the small matter of the last time they left me alone, and when they got back the fire brigade were in the driveway.' He cleared his throat and bit the edge of his lip. 'Do you know that, if you leave a pizza in the oven for an hour, it starts to char and smoke? And that my parents have the most sensitive smoke alarm known to man connected to the fire station? So, yeah…'

Jackdaw had never had someone be so open with him.

So non-judgemental.

'I am incredibly trust-worthy though,' Oscar said, 'in case you're getting the wrong idea.' Again that serious expression, before the sunshine smile. 'Come on, I'm starving. And I'm not letting you wander off by yourself in case you have a concussion. But then I *could* try out my doctorly skills.' Oscar reached out a hand and helped Jackdaw to his feet. 'Well, not quite doctorly. Yet. But that's what I want to be, a doctor. Or rather a surgeon. An orthopaedic surgeon.'

Jackdaw's mind skittered to a halt. He had absolutely no idea what he wanted to do with his life, but here was this boy who was so confident and had everything mapped out. *What the hell just happened?* But a grin found its way to his own lips.

The grin was still there as he followed Oscar out of the door.

They went back to a little terraced cottage at the end of the high street with yellow roses scrambling over the stone walls. As Oscar opened the door, he ducked under the lintel, something Jackdaw didn't have to do.

Gloom greeted them, courtesy of the tiny windows. Beams crossed the ceiling, and Jackdaw raised his head to look at them. Something queasy cramped in the pit of his stomach. He curled his hands around the back of a flower-patterned sofa.

'Hey, are you okay? You've gone really pale. Here, sit down.'

Oscar guided him to a high-backed armchair, and Jackdaw flopped down into it. 'It's probably just adrenaline leaving your body.'

Oscar went around flicking on the lamps. 'Ssh, don't tell.' A rendition of his aunt followed. 'Electricity doesn't come cheap.'

Jackdaw couldn't help but laugh. He pulled the cushion out

that was behind him and clutched it just for something to do with his hands.

Would Oscar be a friend?

Even as the thought settled, a flutter of fretfulness sprang across his hope—Oscar was only here for a week.

He lived somewhere else.

Take the week, you idiot, he told himself. *It's better than nothing.*

'You're not vegan, are you?'

Oscar's shout came from the kitchen. The clattering of knives and opening of cupboards filled the air.

'Because I've put a shitload of ham in your sandwich.'

They ate sitting at the kitchen island, Oscar regaling Jackdaw with tales of his school and his twin sisters and his hopes for the future.

'You've got everything figured out,' Jackdaw said, his voice laced with awe.

'Listen,' Oscar said, stuffing the final piece of his sandwich into his mouth. 'You've got to make your own decisions. You've got to own them.'

Jackdaw chewed a crust as he let this remark settle. And then a bolt of dismay shot through him. 'My backpack. Did you pick it up?'

Oscar's face was hidden behind the fridge door.

A muffled reply.

'Damn, it's at the hall. Your bike is there, too. Someone saw what happened and helped me. What have you got in there, state secrets?'

Jackdaw paused. He really wanted to tell Oscar about the journal, about the names and the dates, but he didn't want to risk Oscar looking at him like he was a loser.

'No, just some stuff,' he said, trying to make his voice sound casual.

'We can grab it when we go back over,' Oscar said, planting a slab of chocolate brownie on the worktop and breaking off two pieces. 'I'll look at your bike after I walk you back. It's the least I can do.'

Jackdaw took a bite of the brownie. It was soft in the centre, just as it should be. Saliva exploded onto his tongue.

'Here, you have a crumb.' Oscar reached across and swiped a fragment of brownie from Jackdaw's chin.

Jackdaw flinched, instinctively pulling away.

Oscar held up his hand, chocolate smears on his fingers.

'Hey, I'm sorry. I shouldn't have done that. I'm just naturally full-on.'

Jackdaw didn't know what to say. How would he even begin to explain that he'd been touch-starved, that random shows of affection made his gut clench, that he was always looking for an ulterior motive for when the other person walked away?

'Well, shit,' Oscar muttered, pushing back his stool.

The legs squeaked against the tile floor, a noise like chalk on a blackboard. He grabbed their plates and began to stack them in the dishwasher.

Jackdaw picked at the skin around his thumb.

He cleared his throat. 'It's fine,' he said, taking a breath. 'I'm just not very good at this.' He gestured towards them both with his hands.

The front door creaked open and an older woman bustled in, setting two bags of shopping down onto the floor.

'This is Jackdaw.' Oscar nudged the dishwasher door shut with his hip. 'I knocked him off his bike, so lunch was the least I could offer him.'

'I've told you before about that infernal scooter, Oscar,' she scolded. 'You're a disaster waiting to happen.'

She looked Jackdaw up and down slowly, an expression he couldn't decipher, before disappearing into a scullery behind the kitchen with her coat.

'Can I borrow the car to take Jackdaw back, Aunt Elspeth?' Oscar shouted. He counted down with his fingers, and a reply came swiftly.

'No, you certainly cannot. You haven't passed your test.' Elspeth reappeared, fixing Oscar with a glare that made Jackdaw wince.

'In that case, can you run him home? I don't want him passing out on the way.'

Oscar had neatly corralled her into a corner without missing a beat.

Jackdaw sat in the back of the old Mini. It had furry, tartan seat covers and a dashboard that looked like it belonged on a Lego car. Oscar sat in the front, occasionally turning to point out something of interest on the way.

As they turned onto the lane, Jackdaw swivelled to look out at the gibbet on the hill. His scalp tightened. He wanted to ask about it but felt like that was a subject no one talked about.

Elspeth stopped at the end of the driveway, and Oscar climbed out. He tipped the seat forward for Jackdaw, then fell into step beside him as they walked towards the cottage. Gravel crunched under their feet, and Jackdaw glanced up as a crow shadowed them from above.

'This might sound weird, but don't go out tonight, Jackdaw.'

The solemn expression was back on Oscar's face and Jackdaw waited for the grin, for the boy to say he was teasing.

The expression stayed, along with something else in his eyes. A pleading.

Oscar squeezed his arm, then smiled. 'Be careful, okay? Watch out for any signs of concussion.'

Unease unfurled inside Jackdaw's veins, a nagging inkling that stayed with him as Oscar waved and disappeared behind the hedge. He didn't think that Oscar was talking about the cut on his head.

Jackdaw waited until he heard the car chugging down the lane, one hand on the door. He wanted to trust Oscar, yet the misgivings from all the other kids who'd ridiculed him over the years refused to quieten down.

But beneath these chaotic feelings a fear fermented, thick and oozing. He thought about the forest and the stick figures. The cart in the barn and the rotten orchard.

What if there *was* something here to be afraid of?

CHAPTER TWENTY-THREE

Callie sat on an old milking stool she'd found in the house when she moved in, a thin paintbrush in her hand. In front of her stood a wooden crate on its end, the perfect height to place whatever she was working on.

A cold wind knifed over the meadow making her nose run, but she needed daylight to paint the image on the jug. That was the nearest description she could come up with for what she'd produced after Adele's phone call.

It stood about eight inches high, wider than it was tall, crafted in local red clay. The spout curved slightly into a beakish shape that resembled a crow. Maybe it was fate. She'd noticed the birds more in the last few days.

Now it was time to apply the underglaze, which gave her work a unique feel. The images were always nature-inspired, a leaf or a flower or a sheaf of corn. But they always carried a shade of the uncanny, be it a dying petal or a rotting stalk.

This one was going to be different.

She'd known from the moment she'd helped Jackdaw with his eye drops, when somehow she'd managed to keep her true emotions under control. Even as she started the first tentative lines, her tongue protruding slightly over her bottom lip, an easy calm settled. Her surroundings faded away, and all that remained was her artistry.

This would be the piece to turn Diego Acala's head—something slightly off-kilter with a stunning depiction as its focal point. She'd already worked on a set of four ceramic tiles, moulding one corner of each into feathers so, that when placed together, the centre formed the torn wings Jackdaw had found on the door. The piece had a solitude to it along with a forlorn grace, an acceptance of the inevitable.

And that's what she had named it.

Inevitable.

It wouldn't go on public display, and neither would the jug. They would be set inside a private viewing room for Diego, their singularity and their lack of a price making them instantly sought after.

Adele would orchestrate the sales from other buyers for the rest of the pieces, and inform Callie after the show had closed and the shutters came down on the little gallery. Callie already knew that Diego would offer more than last year—he was just that kind of collector. That knowledge burned behind her rib cage as she worked, head bowed, as the light began to fade

Gods willing, after the weekend, she'd have enough in her bank account to last the year and to be able to put some aside for Jackdaw's education.

As she added the final flourish, she angled the design to the sky. The colour was just about perfect, and the transparent overglaze shouldn't disturb that. The summer-sky blue staring back at her was wholly her brother's natural colour, framed by thick, black lashes, one corner fanning out into a feather.

A satisfied hum vibrated in her throat, and she grinned. Who would have thought that Jackdaw would become her muse?

With the glaze safely applied and the jug in the kiln, she gathered all her work tools and set them to soak in the clay-spattered sink, hanging her apron on a nail on the wall.

Dusk had fallen quickly, and gloom drenched the yard as she closed the door to her workspace. Loose strands of straw danced around her feet, carried by the wind.

A sudden creak made her wheel sharply, her eyes finding the culprit—the barn door was slightly ajar. She was sure she'd shut it earlier after Jackdaw had left. Her conversation with him replayed in her mind as she walked across to close it.

She'd never really bothered much with the barn. It had come along with the cottage and she didn't need the space, so had simply left it alone.

Now as she edged inside, she looked at it with new eyes.

The cart stood at the back, dark shadows lurking behind the cobweb-strewn wheel facing her.

At its rear was the hayloft, a narrow wooden staircase climbing to pitch-darkness at the right.

Farm implements hung on the walls—scythes and pitchforks—along with an old horse collar, the kind used to pull a cart. Coils of rope hung on rusty nails. Her eyes flicked to the shadows.

She walked slowly towards the display she'd never taken any notice of, her feet disturbing dust that hadn't been trodden in centuries. The scent of age and mould assaulted her senses, and she wiped her nose with the back of one hand. Mildew encrusted the leather on the horse collar, its once-shiny brass fixtures dulled. A bridle hung next to it, a nameplate attached to the brow band. She rubbed it with the corner of her sleeve but couldn't make out the name etched on it.

A rustling in the rafters and her heart shot into her throat. *A bird,* she told herself. *Or a very agile mouse.* She clung onto her attempt at humour.

It was too dark here and the gloom felt heavy and oppressive, like the air before a thunderstorm. Sweat formed on her upper lip. *Go get a torch,* her logic told her, but she didn't listen.

There was something here that held her, that pulled her close like a whisper from a long-dead lover.

She ran her tongue over her lips, tasted the dust and the years.

Her feet led her forward past the implements and the harness, on towards the space at the other side of the hayloft. The deep, dark space where no light gathered.

She stopped about five feet from the opening, stared into a cavernous maw of nothing—knew the stout wooden pillar that supported the back of the hayloft stood hidden in that darkness.

But yet, that's not what she felt.

'Maybe there's something in front of it,' she murmured, her own voice raising the hair in the nape of her neck.

She edged forwards until the ink-drenched dark was an embrace away, reached out for something she could only sense. Her fingers grazed something rough. Something awful.

A cold terror raced through her—unlike anything she'd experienced before. She stumbled back, her hand clamped over her mouth, unable to tear her gaze away from the impenetrable shadows. Her hair blew back from her face as though something had breathed against her. Something close.

The barn door creaked open, and she spun to find Jackdaw

silhouetted in the frame.

'Hi.' His voice filtered across the space between them, and she clung onto its grounding force. 'Don't freak out. I was in a bit of an accident, but I'm okay.'

He had no idea what had just happened to her, and she had to keep it that way.

Somehow she forced her feet to move, even though the act felt like tearing skin away from bone.

She reached the door, wanting to hug him and protect him, but all she could do was lay her hand on his shoulder.

'Don't ground me. I had to leave your bike at the village hall, but I'll get it tomorrow.'

She saw the patched laceration on his temple, tension lining his jaw, a muscle standing out against his pale skin. But he was okay. Tears welled in the corners of her eyes.

'Dust,' she said with a small laugh. 'Let's get inside, and you can tell me what happened.'

She could feel his gaze upon her as they trudged over the yard, towards the welcoming glow of the cottage.

He was expecting her to freak out, to demand an explanation, but right at this moment all she could do was hang onto the tattered shreds of her sanity.

CHAPTER TWENTY-FOUR

Jackdaw had expected Callie to hit the roof when he appeared with plasters holding a bloody cut together. Or fuss over him to the point where he'd have to excuse himself and escape into his room. He'd seen the way she looked at him, like she wanted to hold him close, and he really wasn't sure how to process that.

But she'd done neither of these, just ushered him into the cottage, her eyes flicking over his shoulder as she closed the door.

He decided to be proactive before his reality slipped even more than it had already.

'I was going too fast down the hill to the village,' he said, watching as she filled the kettle. 'This kid came out of nowhere on an electric scooter. He didn't see me.' Jackdaw paused as the images flashed through his mind. 'He took me into the village hall and cleaned me up, then insisted I go back with him for lunch.'

Stringing the words out like that, the events of the day seemed even more insane.

She set the kettle on the stove and came across, leaning on the edge of the table. Dried clay stuck to the bottom of her jumper. He wondered if she'd even heard him until her focus shifted, and she was suddenly the Callie he knew.

'God, you might have a concussion.' She peered closely at him, her gaze fixing on the cut, and he shrank back.

'Are you sleepy?' Her hands rose to her hair, raking it through her fingers. 'We should get you checked out.'

'No need,' Jackdaw said. 'Oscar said I was fine.'

'Oscar?' Her head tilted to one side.

'The boy who crashed into me. He said he's staying with his aunt this week.'

'And this boy has medical training?'

An arched brow accompanied this question.

'Well, kind of. He said he wants to be a doctor, and he did seem to know what he was doing.' Jackdaw took a breath. 'Honestly, I feel fine. I'm sorry about your bike, though. I'll get it tomorrow.'

The shrill whistle of the kettle interrupted their conversation. Jackdaw watched as Callie poured water into an ancient teapot. He traced a deep groove on the kitchen table with one finger.

'Did something happen in the barn?' he asked, his voice edged with caution. He had his own experience there running through his mind on repeat, and some part of him wanted Callie to say she'd felt something, too, so he'd know he wasn't going crazy.

She paused and pushed her hair back from her face, glancing towards the door. Her tongue swept over her lower lip.

'No, nothing happened. I'm just a bit preoccupied with the show and thought I saw something. But it was only a rat.' She shrugged and smiled.

But Jackdaw saw through the mask.

She was hiding something.

And he wasn't sure how he felt about it.

She crossed to the pantry and returned with two large potatoes, rinsing them under the tap.

'Baked potato okay for supper?' She wiped a splash of water from her cheek with her sleeve. 'Maybe you should go stay with Maggie when I'm gone? Just to be on the safe side?'

Jackdaw didn't want to be on the safe side with someone he didn't know. In fact, it filled him with abject horror.

'Maybe I'll just stay here and make sure the door is locked at night.' It wasn't a question, and the firmness in his tone made her glance over her shoulder.

'I don't know…'

He flung his hand up in a gesture of exasperation. 'Look, I'll ask Oscar to come and stay with me. Will that make you feel better?' He had no idea if he'd even see Oscar again, but he was desperate enough to use him as a bargaining tool.

A few moments where she seemed to be mulling his words over, and when she finally agreed he couldn't stop a wide grin from lighting up his face.

Jackdaw made sure to keep the conversation on Callie's show as they ate, and she seemed genuinely touched that he was interested enough to ask. It wasn't like he didn't care exactly, it was just that he didn't want the discussion to shift to his accident or Callie's concern for him.

After they'd tidied up the supper things, she went out to check the kiln and pack some of the pots. The kitchen bin was full, so he pulled out the bag and went outside to find the wheelie bin.

Oscar's warning vibrated through him and he stared into

the darkness, pausing for a moment to look up towards where the forest stood. A shiver ran through him. He forced himself to focus, concentrating on the cold nipping at his cheeks and the way his breath fogged the air. His feet crunched on the gravel lining the path as he went around the side of the cottage.

This was obviously the side few people saw, where quaintness gave way to a garden hosepipe curled snakelike by the wall and a rusty wheelbarrow by a crooked door with a broken hinge. A pile of old bricks were stacked Jenga fashion against a low stone water trough.

He edged around them, avoiding a rambling rose that had taken rambling to a new extreme and had interwoven itself through the handles of the wheelbarrow.

The grey bin sat behind all of these, melding into the shadows. He flung the bag in and wiped his hands down his jeans.

It was so still here, as though the November air had frozen everything into place. Constellations glittered overhead and he lifted his face to them, suddenly feeling as if he'd been sent here for a reason.

This time and place and moment were his alone. He didn't want to fade into obscurity. He wanted to live.

A shiny pebble caught his eye, and he stooped to pick it up.

It was almost oval in shape and worn smooth, as if it had come from the sea. He clasped it in his palm and walked back to the front of the cottage, a sense of purpose thrumming through his veins.

If he'd looked down into the calm water of the stone trough, he would have seen the face of a boy looking back at him.

But the face wouldn't have been his own.

CHAPTER TWENTY-FIVE

Sleep didn't come easily for Jackdaw that night. He couldn't get comfortable, and the gash on his temple throbbed every time he turned over onto that side.

At three minutes past midnight his eyes finally fluttered closed, and his breathing became even.

The cottage settled, old wood creaking into the still night air. Tiny claws scuttled across the attic floor—a small field mouse intent on bringing a scrap of food back to its nest. It stopped suddenly, rising onto its haunches, whiskers twitching, long tail curled around its body. Small mammals understand fear as well as they understand the need to feed, but the former always wins any battle. It's called survival.

The mouse dropped the morsel of food and raced across a rafter, burrowing into its nest of gathered straw and shredded paper. Only its bright, black eyes were visible, and these were dilated in terror.

A barn owl hooted in the large oak by the cottage, its pale plumage a sharp contrast against the ink of nightfall.

It cocked its head to one side, its sight firmly on the window of Jackdaw's bedroom.

A stirring in the dark, the sound of wings slicing through the night. The owl took flight, a ghostly form, as eight crows alighted in the oak, all dark, glossy feathers and fevered eyes.

Roused from their roosting they had come, the reason burning in their ancestral blood.

Because they never forget.

Jackdaw stirred, his closed eyelids twitching.

The bedroom door opened, its hinges creaking, the sound filtering through his sleeping senses. He turned over onto his side, his face towards the window.

The temperature in the room dropped like a stone into a well. He pulled the covers closer, swatting at a strand of hair as it tickled his cheek. His nose wrinkled in disgust as a smell assaulted him. Something high and rotten. Something spoiled.

Instinct told him to wake up, but the dream he was floating in was soft and warm and safe.

A shiver ran through him as an intense cold seeped into his bones. The smell grew stronger and this time, his eyes flickered open. The dark, wooden beam on the ceiling was a palpable mass against his chest.

Moisture coated his face.

A weight settled at the bottom of the bed, but the springs in the old mattress didn't creak.

Fuck, fuck, FUCK.

Something was in the room with him.

The realisation sent firework sparks of panic shooting through his veins. Jackdaw sat bolt upright, then scrabbled back against the headboard. The knowledge undid him to his core, his heartbeat thundering in his ears, his eyes wide as he stared into the thick dark at the bottom of the bed, completely frozen into place.

The weight shifted.

The awful smell faded a little.

Logical thinking grappled against his fear—*a nightmare, a nightmare that seemed real, but how could it be…?*

It was only when his eyes adjusted to the dark that any common sense faded. The door to his room slowly closed. He watched it, his fist stuffed against his mouth to stifle the scream lodged in his throat.

Just a draught, his distraught mind insisted.

But this thought died brutally as the iron latch on the door lifted and dropped into place with a metallic rattle.

The silence that followed was deep and crushing.

Jackdaw understood it soul deep. It was the same feeling that had shrouded him on the day of his mother's funeral. Grief wasn't just an emotion. It was tangible. And he felt it here in this room, that same emotional awareness. A loss like a black hole, the never-ending nothingness sucking every scrap of goodness into its maw.

He launched himself across the bed, flicking on the lamp, and the glow from it was so welcome it brought tears to his eyes.

Wide awake now, he pulled the curtain back cautiously, saw the bright, pearl glow of an almost full moon hanging over the forest on the hill.

A sharp caw sounded, and his eyes narrowed searching for the source. Another followed, and another, and now he saw them on the bare branches of the oak.

Their appearance wasn't anything random—he knew that, even as his mind scrabbled for reasoning. Cold sweat pricked his pores and he reached for his hoodie at the foot of the bed.

He hadn't dreamt it.

He hadn't dreamt the smell, or the icy temperature.

Something *had* been in his room.

CHAPTER TWENTY-SIX

When Jackdaw came down to breakfast, feeling as if he'd been dragged behind a truck for a few miles, the first person he saw as he came through the kitchen door, yawning, was Oscar.

Jackdaw stopped, mid-step, his jaw slackening. For a moment he thought he might be dreaming again. He dropped his chin, desperately trying to hide his eyes.

'Morning,' Oscar said with a grin, raising a mug in the air. 'You took your time. I've been up for hours… wait. Hold on.' His last words held a question.

Jackdaw took a deep breath and slowly raised his head. It wasn't as if he could hide his eye colour, and maybe it was better that Oscar saw it now. But still, his heart hammered behind his rib cage.

Oscar let out a low whistle. 'Jeez, Jackdaw, your eyes. They're beautiful. Is that your natural colour?'

Jackdaw mumbled something about contact lenses, watching Oscar's reaction through a fall of hair.

'Well, I wouldn't be hiding them,' Oscar said, with a smile that lit up his eyes.

The tightness in Jackdaw's chest lightened as though a great stone had been slid away.

'Oscar brought my bike back,' Callie said, by way of an explanation. She was standing at the stove, bacon sizzling in an ancient frying pan.

In spite of everything, Jackdaw's stomach growled. He caught a sidelong glance from her, and one corner of her mouth quirked upwards. She was changing the subject for him.

'I had to bring it back, considering that it was my fault you had to leave it,' Oscar said, as he caught the cue effortlessly.

Jackdaw wondered how it felt to be so socially aware that everything flowed into place, where you didn't have to second-guess if you were doing the right thing or not.

He ran his hand through his hair, gingerly touching his temple. The plasters were still intact. His whole body ached. He wasn't sure if it was from the accident or what had happened during the night. He'd left the lamp burning, curled into a tensed, tight ball, one eye open as he tried to get back to sleep, and when he did it was fitful.

'Here you go.' Callie placed a heap of crispy bacon onto two white rolls and slid the plates across the table. Jackdaw raised his eyebrows to her as he slumped into a chair. This was clearly not how he'd envisaged his morning starting.

He watched as Oscar picked up a roll and bit into it as though he hadn't been fed for days. 'This is so good,' he said, his mouth stuffed with bacon. 'If you don't eat yours now, I'm stealing it.' He gestured to the roll in front of Jackdaw.

Jackdaw's reality unravelled like a ball of wool.

'Okay, boys, I'm heading out to pack some more boxes. Have fun today.' With a coffee mug in one hand, Callie grabbed scissors from a kitchen drawer.

Jackdaw watched her leave, and when he turned around Oscar was studying him, his chin propped against his hand.

'I didn't think I'd see you again,' Jackdaw blurted out. He knew it was rude, and Oscar had done him a favour returning the bike, but he was still rattled about what had happened during the night.

Seriously, how the hell was he supposed to process any of it?

Oscar didn't speak for a moment, just chewed his mouthful thoughtfully.

'I thought we could hang out,' he said. 'God knows there's hardly anything to do in this place, but doing nothing with someone is better than doing it by yourself. Agreed?'

Jackdaw couldn't help it. The smile that curled his lips was part wonder, part appreciation. He couldn't fault Oscar's logic. He took a bite of his roll. Oscar was right. It was really good.

'Ha, I knew I'd break through that serious shell,' Oscar said, a note of triumph in his voice.

'Serious?' Jackdaw repeated. And then he thought about it. His mouth twisted to one side, his lips dusted with flour from the roll. 'I guess I am. I'm different.' He paused and felt Oscar's gaze upon him. 'I'm weird.' He shrugged his shoulders. 'Don't you mind that?'

Oscar snorted. 'You're talking to a kid who was brought up in this place. Weird things happen every day. Especially,' he held up a finger, 'at this time of year. You've heard about the Gala Day, right?'

Jackdaw shook his head.

'It's something that's been going on for years. I mean, literally centuries. It's a festival where everyone in the village gathers and has fun. Then, when it gets dark, they light torches and march after a big-ass paper bird held up in the air on sticks, ending up at the gibbet on the hill.'

Goosebumps prickled across Jackdaw's shoulders. He ran his fingers through his messy hair.

'When does that happen?' he asked.

'In two days. And this year it falls on a full moon, so it's even more special. Apparently, the bird likes to fly towards the light.'

Oscar's expression was so solemn Jackdaw swallowed his next bite of sandwich before he'd chewed it properly.

It lodged painfully in his throat.

A grin burst across Oscar's face, and he shoved Jackdaw's arm playfully.

'You're really gullible, you know that?' Oscar licked his fingers and pushed his plate away. 'I might have made that last bit up. But the old people here, they really believe in it. My aunt says if they don't do it, something awful will happen.'

'And has it?' Jackdaw said.

'I don't know.' Oscar rocked his chair onto its back legs. 'They've never missed a year, even during the wars. So don't tell me again about you being weird. This place invented it.' A shaft of sunlight filtered through the kitchen window, bathing him in a warm glow.

Jackdaw contemplated spending the day alone, chewing over his own thoughts, hyper-focussing on everything that had happened—or going out with someone who really seemed to get him. Who didn't think he was… well, weird.

His gaze fell on his backpack sat behind the front door. He wondered if Oscar had looked inside, could feel his scrutiny in this pause in conversation.

'I'm glad you're okay,' Oscar said softly. 'I mean, after the accident.'

I'm glad you're okay. After last night.

Jackdaw pushed away the subtext gnawing at his brain. Oscar was just being his normal, friendly self. He finished the last bite of his roll, grabbed Oscar's plate, and took both to the kitchen sink. Callie had left it full of soapy water, so he dunked them into it. A chaffinch flew past the window, and Jackdaw followed it as it landed on the bird table, its pink breast puffed out. His gaze tracked over the fields and the church—to the gibbet on the opposite hill.

'What's the story on that?' he asked, as Oscar appeared at his side.

Oscar paused, and Jackdaw turned his head. The other boy was deep in thought.

'It's part of the history here,' Oscar said, meeting Jackdaw's gaze. This time, Jackdaw knew instinctively that Oscar wasn't kidding. A beat of silence. 'Talk about keeping your work visible.'

Jackdaw's fingers curled around the edge of the Belfast sink. 'What do you mean, visible?' He wasn't sure he was ready for the answer. It felt like a guillotine blade about to fall.

'Oh.' Oscar grimaced, his hand coming to rest on Jackdaw's shoulder. 'You don't know? I guess Callie didn't want to spook you. This place used to be the hangman's cottage.'

CHAPTER TWENTY-SEVEN

Callie stood back and admired her work. Fresh from the kiln, the jug she'd painted yesterday was one of her best creations, the eye far too lifelike as it stared back at her. Diego would go out of his mind, and if it loosened his wallet for her other pieces, all the better.

But the timing of this show—and Jackdaw's arrival—couldn't have been worse. Her conscience see-sawed between needing to stay here with him and needing to sell what she'd already produced so they could actually eat for the rest of the year.

He's more than capable, she reasoned. *He's been looking after himself for years.*

Oscar's arrival earlier was a surprise. No one ever visited her apart from Maggie, but as soon as she opened the door and saw him astride her bike, an infectious grin on his face, she'd invited him in.

He was the polar opposite of Jackdaw, very unreserved and chatty, and she found herself really liking his attitude and uninhibited speech.

In truth, he was the perfect friend for Jackdaw, and he'd already proved himself by looking after her newfound brother yesterday. She only just stopped herself from asking if he'd stay overnight when she was away, because it wasn't her question to ask, but deep down she was thrilled at the outcome.

Oscar seemed sensible, and he had an aunt in the village, so along with Maggie, Jackdaw had adults around if anything happened.

Which it won't, she reprimanded herself.

She reached across her workbench for a sheet of bubble wrap, and something fell onto the floor. Swearing under her breath, she stooped to pick it up—and froze before her fingers touched it. A small, doll-like figure, woven from willow, stared up at her. *What the hell?* It had been at the back of the bench with a heap of broken pots and other detritus. Callie knew she wasn't the tidiest person in the world. Maybe it had been there since she moved in, and she'd just never noticed it before.

Her nose wrinkled in disgust as she picked it up by one limb. There was something about it that made her flesh crawl. Her gaze shifted to a heap of unused clay sitting on her wheel. She pulled a section off and flattened it with her fist, then rammed the stick figure down onto it, so the clay oozed through the willow skeleton like flesh. The action raised a warm flurry of triumph in her chest. She nodded, then lifted her chin. *Let's see you get out of that.* She knew it was unhinged but right now, anything that made her feel in control was welcomed.

She busied herself labelling pieces and bundling them in bubble wrap, her thoughts drifting to the barn. Had she really sensed something in there, or was it the product of all the stress of the upcoming show and Jackdaw's sudden arrival?

Maybe it's even grief. She shook her head at that thought.

Her ties had been cut with her mother the day she left home, and she'd never looked back.

As she pushed out into the thin, grey, corpse light of the November morning, her gaze tracked to the telephone wires slung between the wooden poles that crossed the field. Birds sat upon the wires, mainly crows, but other smaller ones, too. There was no jostling for position. No squabbling between them. They were simply perched there, all facing the cottage.

She waved her hands in the air as a resigned sigh left her lips. This is what she got by leaving out food for them. They obviously weren't in the least bit scared of her. Word had got around the avian grapevine, and now they were all queued up, waiting for an easy meal.

A glint of watery sunlight off a windscreen on the lane caught her attention. The sound of a car engine labouring up the hill. Callie pursed her lips. It didn't sound like Maggie's car.

An ancient red Mini came into view, stopping just outside the gate. Callie waited, resisting the temptation to go greet whoever it was, and when she saw her uninvited visitor she suppressed a groan.

It was Elspeth Hargreaves.

'Callie, what a lovely morning,' Elspeth said as she climbed out of the car, a smile plastered on her face.

It *had* been a lovely morning until now, but Callie kept that thought to herself.

'I've come to ask a favour, on behalf of the Gala Day committee.' Elspeth opened the gate and strode towards Callie.

'A favour?' Callie said, the question carrying more than a hint of derision.

Elspeth waved her hands dismissively as though the question

had been a gnat on a particularly hot day.

'I realise the village might have been a little ungracious the other day. News reached me, and I had to come and apologise on behalf of Combe Hurst.' She held out a gloved hand. 'Elspeth Hargreaves.'

Callie clasped it for the briefest of seconds. Of course Elspeth had heard about the altercation in the post office. 'Callie Dawtrey.'

'Oh yes, you're well known.'

Again, the dismissiveness made Callie grit her teeth.

'It was so kind of you to take on this little cottage. We don't like our history to stand empty. The past is very important to us, you see. It helps shape the present, don't you think?'

The cottage door opened and Oscar and Jackdaw tumbled out, Oscar gesticulating wildly about something.

'Oscar, you left very early this morning.' Elspeth's gaze flicked towards the boys, her lips drawing into a tight line.

Oscar shrugged, the action ending in a grimace.

'You were sleeping, and I didn't want to wake you. I brought Callie's bike back.'

Callie caught her jaw before it slackened. Elspeth Hargreaves was Oscar's aunt? Damn it, she never saw *that* one coming.

Callie watched Elspeth's gaze zeroing in on Jackdaw, a strange expression on her face.

She cleared her throat, nudging the older woman's attention back to her.

'Anyway, as I was saying, I think you may be able to help us. I believe you have an old cart in your barn? We'd like to borrow it for the Gala Day, make it part of our procession.'

Callie wanted to say no, just to make a stand, but reasoning overcame her stubbornness.

What harm could it do if they borrowed the cart? It's not as if she used it, and it was just sitting there gathering cobwebs.

'Sure,' she said. 'I don't see why not. When do you need it?'

'I'll send someone to get it tomorrow. It might require a little renovation before we can use it, but we'll pay for that, naturally.'

The wind changed directions and knifed across the field, making the bare branches of the oak sway, and Callie shivered. She lifted her gaze to the birds on the telephone wire. Only the crows remained. They began to caw, the wire bouncing beneath their agitation.

'All sorted then. Good to see you, Callie.'

With that, Elspeth turned on her heel and marched back to her car, leaving Callie more than a little aggravated at the outcome.

She felt as if she'd been backed into a corner, that maybe the cart was more than happy standing in the barn and didn't want to take part in a stupid procession.

Which was absolutely ridiculous.

With her hands stuffed in her pockets against the chill, she looked back over her shoulder to find that Jackdaw and Oscar had disappeared, unaffected by adult bargaining and the politics of politeness.

Part of her envied their freedom.

CHAPTER TWENTY-EIGHT

The boys skirted the cottage and set off up the hill. Jackdaw stuffed his hands further into his pockets. Overnight, autumn seemed to have disappeared and winter was hellbent on making its presence known. He pulled a few strands of hair from his beanie and let them fall over his face.

'You don't need to do that,' Oscar said, taking a stick of chewing gum from his pocket. He offered a piece to Jackdaw.

'Do what?'

'Hide your eyes. You should own how unique they are.'

Jackdaw took the gum and put it in his mouth. Spearmint exploded on his tongue.

'I guess I've always done it. It's just a habit now.' He risked a sideways glance towards Oscar as the sound of his aunt's car chugged down the lane. 'When people ridicule you because you're different, you do what you can to fit in, you know?'

Oscar's mouth twisted to one side. He raised his head and gazed into the distance, towards the forest at the top of the hill.

'You already know this place is weird. And I'm guessing you've had things happen that you can't explain?'

Jackdaw hunched his shoulders. That was the mother of all statements. He took a deep breath.

'Last night.' The words felt like roughly sawed wood in his throat. 'Something came into my room. I felt it sit on my bed.'

He waited for Oscar to laugh, but he didn't.

The silence between them fizzled, charged with static.

Oscar pressed his lips together and Jackdaw saw his throat ripple.

'It's Martinmas.'

They'd reached the first boundary on the hill, a low dry stone wall covered in patches of moss. Beyond it, to the left, was the woodland. Jackdaw eyed it, watched as a small black speck circled above the treetops. 'Corvidae,' he whispered under his breath. *An invocation.* He shook his head and focussed on Oscar's words.

'What's that mean?'

A hare bounded from the safety of the long grass, black-tipped ears twitching, its powerful hind legs propelling it across their path.

Oscar swore under his breath. He tugged at Jackdaw's arm to halt him, watching the hare disappear under a gate.

'It's an old feast time. You'll see people carrying paper lanterns when it gets dark tonight.'

The boyish amusement that normally graced Oscar's face disappeared, making him look older.

Jackdaw hesitated, looked back at the cottage which had almost been eaten by the landscape. Something was off, and he couldn't put a finger on it.

'Where are we going?'

Maybe he should have asked that question before.

Oscar vaulted the dry stone wall and stood waiting, his face a solemn mask. 'I thought you might want to see where all this began,' he said. 'Where all the stories come from? It might help you understand why people are wary of you.'

'But I haven't done anything,' Jackdaw said. He hunched his shoulders, retreated inside himself—his protective default.

The fact that he slept under the same roof where a hangman used to live was like a slab of concrete in his gut. He'd been trying to bury what Oscar said in the kitchen. Trying to file it under things boys told each other. A good-natured scare tactic.

But it didn't feel like that. It felt real and nauseating and terrifying. And now Oscar was acting really erratic. Jackdaw didn't like it, and all his instincts told him to run. His heart ached—he thought he'd found a friend, and now it looked like Oscar was just like all the rest.

Jackdaw backed away, his expression hardening.

'I won't play games,' he said, the edges of his words harsh and clipped. 'And I don't appreciate all of your vague bullshit.' His chin trembled and he turned away, not wanting to let Oscar see how much he was hurting. But if he stayed, he'd capsize and his vulnerability would spill out like an overfilled jug. He marched off in the opposite direction. Tears burned the back of his eyes and he swiped at them angrily.

A sudden rage quicksilvered through his veins, making his fingertips tingle. 'Fuck you!' he shouted over his shoulder, the wind snatching the words from his lips. He suddenly hated this place, hated this life he'd been thrown into, hated being the strange new kid again. He'd let his guard down, and look where it had got him. No more. No fucking more.

When he dared to glance over his shoulder again, Oscar had

disappeared.

Even though it was only late morning, the light was thin and scuds of dark-grey cloud hung over the hills. The gibbet stood silently, an ominous column stamped against the horizon.

He took out his phone, found a faint signal, and loaded a search.

> *Martinmas – old Halloween. A time when autumn is waning and dark winter days are ahead. Lanterns are lit to symbolise the light inside all of us that has to be protected. The time of year where the veil between worlds is at its thinnest, where the lack of sunlight allows spirits to wander...*

Jackdaw's eyes skimmed over the text, pulling meaning from the phrases. Part of him wanted to click away, to stuff his phone back in his pocket. But another part, the part that was the free-spirited boy who mimicked birds and catalogued fungi, was hungry for each sentence.

He ran the back of his hand over his lips.

Old Halloween.

He'd never heard of it before. But it wasn't those words that stuck in his mind like a sharp thorn dragging across tender flesh—it was the last phrase that he'd read.

Martinmas heralds the wintering of ghosts.

He continued to walk, his head bowed, even though he didn't know where he was going, trying to make sense of all the conflicting thoughts in his head.

There was no way he was going back to the cottage, to face a barrage of questions from Callie. She assumed he and Oscar were friends and Jackdaw wanted to keep it that way—because if she found out they weren't, she might rethink him staying at the cottage by himself.

Did he really want to be alone after last night, though?

It was a sobering thought, and one he chewed over again and again. He could stay up all night and sleep through the day. Ghosts didn't come out in daylight, did they?

A fragment of conversation punched through the fog in his brain. His mother a few years ago when she'd discovered him watching a documentary about the afterlife.

'The dead always find a way through if they have unfinished business.'

The comment came out of nowhere, and by the time Jackdaw had time to internalise it, she'd gone back upstairs, her lips moving silently.

What if what had come into his room last night was the ghost of someone who had been hanged? What if it had come seeking revenge?

At that last thought a harsh laugh sounded in his throat.

Now he truly was losing the plot. He puffed out his cheeks and took stock of his surroundings. His steps had led slightly uphill, the thick woodland behind him.

Out here, the land was exposed—the wind knifed across from the west, where the gibbet stood.

Jackdaw shivered, wrapping his arms around his body and clutching his elbows. His nose began to stream and he wiped it on his sleeve. Standing alone here, he was an insignificant speck on the landscape. An outcrop of grey rock stood sullenly at the edge of the field and he made his way towards it. He scrambled onto its top, the added height giving him a better view of the surrounding countryside.

His eyes tracked towards the horizon, where a weak sun was fighting a losing battle with gathering steel-grey clouds. Behind him the valley sat protected between the hills, the village nestling in its palm. And all around the vast expanse of sky.

Movement above and his gaze fixed on a bird, almost too high to make out. He watched it circle in wide loops, slowly descending, until he could clearly see that it was a crow.

He threw his head back and cawed, and the act felt liberating out there with no one to judge him but the bird. When it called back, a surge of euphoria shot through his core.

He raised his arms, letting the wind buffet him from behind.

The crow swooped suddenly, a deliberate nosedive or so it seemed, and Jackdaw ducked, watching with a galloping heart as it sped off towards the forest. He followed it and saw it land in a bare treetop.

Wait.

His lips parted.

I shouldn't be able to see this clearly. It should be blurred…

He was so used to wearing contacts that he hadn't noticed.

He flopped down onto the rock, looking around in wonder.

Every detail in the distance was hyper clear, every tree and every cottage roof. Every cloud. Even the rays of sun spearing through that cloud.

He'd been given the gift of sight, which should have had him buzzing with elation. But the question spinning through his mind was this.

What was he supposed to see?

CHAPTER TWENTY-NINE

Part of Oscar wanted to run after Jackdaw. He hadn't wanted to be vague but hell, how did he even come up with the words to explain the whole fucked-up history of this place?

When you're a kid and live in an isolated community, you do what you're told. Parents, then teachers, become your safety and your authority figures. You don't question what they say. What they do. But there were things here that he'd forgotten, and being back was nudging the folds of his memory, all of the weird things spilling out.

Like boys not being allowed to form close friendships. He could be friends with another boy, but as soon as a teacher or another adult zeroed in on a certain camaraderie, it was snipped off at the root. *You need to socialise,* was the answer they were given if they kicked back. Friendships were split up, put into different classes, not allowed to mingle out of school—so, of course, whatever had been forming dissolved. It was just normal.

And now, looking back at it, with the wisdom of being on the cusp of adulthood, Oscar could see how wrong it had been. He pulled his collar up against the cold wind, his head bowed as he walked. Now he had friends, boys who had his back at school, who came round and played video games—Tyler and

Ravi and Leo. As soon as he left Combe Hurst all the rules changed, and he didn't know why.

He'd never given it a second thought for five years.

He'd been eleven when his family had moved away. They'd told him it was because his father needed to be closer to work, but where they'd relocated hadn't really been closer at all. Back then he'd been more focussed on being the new kid in a much larger school than the reasonings behind the move. And it wasn't as if Combe Hurst had much going for it in the way of entertainment for teenagers. It was a dead end, a place where the past meant more than the present and you could forget about having a future.

All the kids here knew the stories of the hangman and his son, of what happened, and the consequences that followed. It was their very own version of a Halloween scare, made all the more potent by the fact that it happened right here.

His mother had told him that he shouldn't believe all the stories, that tales like this probably had their base in fact, but then it all got added to and tangled with each generation, so any truth had been diluted.

That was the explanation he held onto as he grew, as the time for each Gala Day drew near. All the kids loved it. Or rather, they loved Gala Night. Following the procession in the dark to the gibbet, lit torches held high, watching with wide, bright eyes as the avifauna was set free.

Then there was music and dancing and sweet, hot chestnuts held in gloved hands, and the beacon painting the sky with flame.

It was a time for celebration.

But now he knew better.

Because every celebration has a flip side. And people will do what they need to, whether from tradition—or out of fear.

And now there was a new kid here who knew nothing.

Who lived in the hangman's cottage. Who was scared and lonely and confused.

Oscar tramped off down the hill, occasionally glancing behind to see if Jackdaw had decided to forgive him.

He gritted his teeth against the chill knifing through the valley. He'd forgotten how cold it was here. Living in a city had its benefits. But beneath that thought another throbbed, an insistent heartbeat.

Living in a city makes you soft.

It robs you of certain instincts.

By the time he reached the outskirts of the village, ragged, dark clouds hung in the sky like dirty candy floss. He turned towards them, felt the lack of light against his retinas. Tried not to focus on the wormlike niggle in the pit of his stomach.

As he pushed open the door to his aunt's cottage, he regretted coming here this week of all weeks. But then he hadn't really had a choice.

'Where have you been?'

Elspeth fixed him with a pointed look.

She was peeling beetroot on the kitchen island, her hands stained purple.

'Out with Jackdaw. But he had to go home and do chores.'

The lie tripped off his tongue, and he waited, taking his trainers off by standing on the backs. The sound she made didn't convince Oscar that she believed him.

'What do you make of that boy?' She began to carve the beetroot into chunks, the juice dripping into a cast-iron pan.

Oscar picked an apple from the fruit bowl and bit into the firm flesh just to give himself some time to answer.

'He's cool,' he finally said, through a half-chewed mouthful. 'A little odd, but cool. It can't be easy for him, you know, moving here, considering what happened to his mother.'

Elspeth stopped what she was doing.

She studied him impassively.

Oscar pulled out a bar stool and sat, trying to work out what she was thinking.

'Well, bad things happen,' she said with a shrug of her shoulders. 'Don't you get too close to him, mind. I don't want his misfortune rubbing off on you.' She sprinkled a liberal dose of salt into the pan. 'And anyway, you'll be back home next week, and then what's he going to do?'

This cold, hard truth lodged in Oscar's gut. He could leave this place, but Jackdaw was trapped.

'Misfortune? What do you mean?' he asked, taking another bite.

The apple didn't seem as sweet now.

'No good can come of a boy living in that cottage, mark my words. Places hold on to trauma, and those walls are steeped in it.' She cleared her throat. 'Now take these peelings and put them out on the compost for me.'

He threw the apple into the trimmings as she gathered them onto a wooden board.

'My mother says it's all superstition.' The comment was out of his mouth before he had a chance to think. It was a kickback, a volley of words because he didn't want her to see how much she'd rattled him.

Elspeth thrust the board towards him. Her thin lips curled in disapproval.

'Your mother never did know what was good for her. She was always a naysayer about this place. But she was the one who decided to move away, did you know that?'

Oscar didn't know that, and the expression on his face showed it. He looked at the floor, crestfallen, then made for the back door leading to the garden.

'Oscar,' she said, and he turned. The peelings on the board he carried stained the wood like blood. 'Don't forget that it's Martinmas. Look for signs. Don't be misled.'

What the hell was he supposed to say to that?

There were no comeback quips on his tongue. He went out into the thin light, tramping the overgrown path to the compost heap at the bottom of the garden. A long cobweb swayed on the trellis separating the lawn from the vegetable patch.

The smell of wet earth and fetid damp curled around him.

He'd forgotten that smell, and now it released a memory as scent often does.

He was seven years old, skipping down the pathway after returning from Gala Day, a half-eaten toffee apple clutched in his fist. Stars glittered coldly overhead, and the moon hung plump and full. Excitement still fizzed in his veins, of watching the avifauna take flight, of flames scorching the dark, of the dancing pattern of fire...

When the bird dropped out of the tree in front of him, the toffee apple tumbled to the ground. He waited for the bird to move. He crouched and poked it with a finger. Its feathers were soft and glossy. One eye when he turned it over was clouded, as though what it had seen in its final moments was enough to take its sight. The other was a soft, summer-sky blue.

'Oscar, come in now!' His mother's voice from the doorway, a glass of wine in her hand, warm light flooding the path.

And he knew now what he'd seen on that night.

The bird was a young jackdaw.

CHAPTER THIRTY

By the time Jackdaw got back to the cottage, the afternoon light had smudged from a non-descript murk to a palette of yellow-tinged grey.

Warm, golden light spilled from within, and welcoming heat warmed his chilled skin as he shut the door behind him.

He still couldn't quite comprehend how his sight seemed to be perfect now.

'Hi, Jackdaw!' Callie's voice from the back room. 'I won't be long. I'm just packing boxes. It got too damn cold in the pot shed.'

'That's cool.' He forced his tone into something that sounded normal. A word that was beginning to twist in on itself like a snake in the grass.

He stumbled to the sink and splashed cold water on his face.

The uncanny light pressed against the window.

'Right. That's all I'm doing for now.' Callie's steps stopped at the fridge. A blast of cold air as she opened the door, the soft clunk of a ring pull. 'Do you want one?'

He glanced over his shoulder, saw a Diet Coke in her hand. Her brow creased as she studied him.

'Are you feeling okay? You look really pale.'

Jackdaw took the can and popped the ring pull, taking a long draught. Sweet fizz on his tongue. He wiped the back of his hand over his mouth.

'I'm never not pale,' he said. 'Vampire genetics.'

Her expression softened. She brushed a strand of hair from her cheek and perched on the edge of the table, sipping her own drink. A sigh followed.

'This show, Jackdaw. It couldn't have come at a worse time. Are you sure you're going to be okay?'

He waved a hand dismissively, fixing her in a focussed gaze.

'We've been through this before. I'm not a kid. And anyway...' He paused as the lie bloomed in his mouth. 'Oscar said he'd come and sleep over.'

A grin of relief lit up her face, and Jackdaw inwardly grimaced at his deceit.

'That makes me feel loads better,' she said, taking another drink. 'He seems really nice. Even if he is Elspeth's nephew.' She puffed out her cheeks. 'Sorry, that was unnecessary. She's just well-known for being obnoxious.'

'You can't choose family,' Jackdaw said softly.

Silence hung between them, then she reached across and placed her hand on his arm. 'I'm glad *we're* family, Jack Dawtrey.' A gleam of moisture glistened in her eyes. 'Now, I'm leaving first thing in the morning. At some point, someone will come over to pick up the cart. I still don't know what they want with it.'

'It's the history thing,' he said. 'People here seem to like that better than the present.' He paused, measuring his next words. 'Why didn't you tell me this used to be the hangman's cottage?'

She looked away, her shoulders hunched. Her throat rippled.

'I didn't want to freak you out. You'd just got here, and it's not the sort of thing you can drop in conversation over supper.' She raised her chin. 'It's why I got this place so cheaply. No one in the village would touch it, and it wasn't really advertised anywhere. It's not as if people died here, though.'

Jackdaw didn't know what to say.

Her words were all true, but still a few grains of apprehension prickled against his conscience. This would be a good time to tell her about last night, but there was no way he was mentioning that on the eve of her leaving. He'd told Oscar about it, and then everything had got messed up between them.

'Do you know anything about them? The family, I mean. If there was a family...' His voice tailed off. The thought of a hangman having a family seemed wrong, but back then it was just a job, like a blacksmith or a farmer.

'I never asked about it,' Callie said, finishing the last of her can. She tossed it in the recycling bag hanging on the kitchen door. 'It might be documented somewhere, but it doesn't matter. All that does matter is the here and now, and me and you, and planning for our future. The past is dead. We can't reshape it.'

She went into the back room and emerged with a large box in her arms. 'Can you help me pack the car?'

A line had been drawn under his tentative questioning.

After numerous trips back and forth, Callie declared that what she hadn't packed wasn't coming with her. The boot and the back seat of her little car were stuffed with boxes.

'I'm not driving all the way to London,' she explained as she slammed the boot lid down. 'I've got a friend near Maidenhead, and I'm leaving the car there. My agent's hired a van to take my work to the show.'

'Are you like really famous?' Jackdaw asked.

The notion hadn't even occurred to him before.

She laughed and the sound rolled over the cobbled yard, melting into the falling darkness. 'I am most definitely *not* famous. But a few people like what I produce, and they're willing to pay for it. Which is good for us. Otherwise we'd be living on baked beans and toast.'

As they walked back towards the cottage, Callie paused and stared towards the barn. 'I'm sure I bolted that door…'

'I'll go,' Jackdaw said quickly. 'Just in case something's got in that shouldn't have.'

He trudged across with his hands in his pockets. A square of yellow light spilled out as Callie opened the cottage door, and then it was gone.

Jackdaw took out his phone and flicked on the torch app.

The gloom inside the barn shrank back from the piercing light like a cornered beast. He could see his breath clouding as the damp cold enveloped him. He swung the light from corner to corner, hulking shapes taking form as it glanced over them.

The hayloft and its staircase. The old, rusted implements on the walls. The bales of mouldy straw. He angled the light to the rafters, narrowing his eyes to look for roosting birds. But all was quiet. Until a rustle split the silence.

A rustle that came from the back of the barn.

'Hello, tiny creature,' he murmured.

But then he remembered Ophelia and how the little girl liked to hide. Surely she wouldn't be out this late, though?

'Ophelia.' His voice was small, devoured by the shadows. 'Are you here? Come on, it's getting dark.'

A cold draught against his ear, brushing strands of hair onto his cheek. He turned, his heart in his mouth, his lips slightly parted. He turned towards the cart. For an instant, she was there, sitting on a collapsed hay bale, swaying her body from side to side.

His phone died in his hand, plunging the barn into pitch blackness.

'Ophelia,' he whispered. 'You need to go home.'

She laughed, a high, sweet tone that coated his skin with goosebumps.

'Silly boy, do you not understand? I am home.'

Something moved in front of him. Jackdaw felt the air shift before he heard the sound. The creaking of a rope.

His foot caught on his trailing trainer lace and he stumbled backwards, hitting the ground with a painful jolt that shuddered along his spine, his useless phone clutched in his hand.

Scrambling to his feet he ran for the door, panic nipping at his heels.

He left the door unbolted, just in case the conclusion he'd come to was complete insanity. Raking his hands through his hair he paced the yard, glancing at the barn door, willing her to come out and rib him for being so scared.

But nothing bled from the confines of the barn but forlorn darkness.

Because Ophelia was dead.

CHAPTER THIRTY-ONE

The moon hung plump and bright, rising through the bare branches of the trees, just as she had done on the night this all began. The man kept his eyes forward, his steps slow but solid. He knew where he was headed.

On his back was a hessian sack stuffed with what he would need. The awareness that this might be the last night that he drew breath thrummed in time with his heartbeat. But he was ready. He'd been ready all of his life. If he died here, he wanted no one to find him. He wanted the forest to devour him whole so that he would be a part of it for eternity. Peace had been made with the villagers who knew him. He didn't want them to come looking if he didn't return.

The glade stood silent in the thick, moonlit dark. No creatures rustled through the undergrowth. Not even a breath of wind stirred the treetops. Even his sticklings hanging from the branches were motionless.

Twig set his sack on the leaf-strewn ground. He sank beside it, crossing his legs with difficulty as his hips were stiff and worn. He laid the contents in front of him—the battered pewter plate, the tarnished silver fork with one tine missing, the flask of water drawn from the stream that meandered through the forest.

And here, in his hands, the bright-red fly agaric toadstools with their white, wart-like spots. This time, he had dug them from beneath the lonely silver birch tree. That was where he had gone with Maggie Moon and Naomi all those years ago—the time when he had felt the plates of centuries shift, the crack of an eye opening into the past, the tantalising glimpse of…

He studied his trembling hands, his knuckles misshapen with the blight of arthritis. How had he lived so many years when those who came before him had been cut down before they had a chance to bloom?

Because life is hard, and truth means nothing to those who hold the sword of power.

He broke the caps from the toadstools and slipped one of the stems onto his tongue. It grounded him to the land. Humming softly to himself, he crushed the caps onto the plate with the fork, adding splashes of water until he'd formed the lumpy paste to the correct consistency. He brought a forkful to his lips.

He paused a moment and lifted his head to the stars.

Somewhere deep in the trees, a crow cawed.

Gaze down at your servant and grant him sight.

A yearning burst inside him like a blister releasing its cushioning liquid, a yearning for knowledge, for just a glimpse of the boy whose goodness had been his downfall. The boy whose spirit wandered the land at this time. The boy who searched and searched for the one to make him whole again.

All this oblivion, all this grief and hope held high with gritted teeth. All this loyalty and sacrifice and suffering. They were only boys, caught in the snare of a man whose privilege had been gifted to him from the cradle.

He closed his eyes, emptied his mind of everything that was now. The brackish taste of the paste filled his mouth. His tongue began to lose all feeling, and as it did, a mist swirled behind his eyes.

This was the veil he had touched before.

If he could penetrate it, the past might bless him with the knowledge he had craved for decades. It was there, rippling behind the haze.

Sounds vibrated through his core.

The rhythmic gait of a horse's hoofs on grass.

Laughter.

The crack of a shotgun.

A boy screaming.

He wanted to plead for more, but numbness owned his limbs. Still the haze ebbed around him, ribbons of wavering light and misty shade.

I only want to see, he begged silently.

But even as he petitioned, he knew he wasn't worthy. He could feel his heartbeat skittering against his rib cage, a warning of his weak mortality.

Twig's bravery reached its zenith. *Has he not suffered enough?* He offered this plea for a lost boy.

The scent of pine and wet soil curled into his nostrils, along with a sweet, high rot. He opened his eyes, felt something there with him in the tree-laden dark—something that raised tongues of madness in his soul.

He wondered what death would taste like. He waited.

And then the spirit of the boy who had died over two centuries before told him what to do.

CHAPTER THIRTY-TWO

Jackdaw awoke in a cold sweat. He'd been dreaming about the cart, and in the very depths of his mind, he could hear its sturdy wheels trundling across impacted grass. He rubbed his hand over his face. Moisture coated his fingertips. He licked one finger and salt exploded on his tongue.

Sweat or tears? Either one wasn't welcome.

He glanced at his phone—4.44am. Three more hours, and Callie would be setting off on her trip. And then he'd be alone. The fact didn't thrill him. Honestly, if he really thought about it, he was scared. Scared that his reality was running away with him, that he was seeing ghost girls in the barn, that *something* had come into his room.

Far away, the sound of a crow shrieking split the night silence. Jackdaw scrambled across his bed and opened the window, grateful for the cool chill on his skin. The land beyond was dark, thick with shadow and indiscernible shapes.

Grey clouds scudded across the moon, and up on the hill, over the forest, stars glittered coldly.

The call came again, and this time Jackdaw answered, sending his own avian greeting into the darkness.

A high-pitched response… that sounded almost triumphant.

'You are really losing it,' he muttered, shaking his head.

He leant against the wide, cold sill, until his elbows started to complain. He was no further forward in unravelling the mystery of the journal. He had no fucking idea *how* to start. And he'd blitzed the only friend he could have had.

Loneliness pressed against him, sharp and bitter and greedy. He'd done this to himself by letting Oscar in.

By daring to hope.

Anger boiled through his veins, dissolving any chance of sleep.

Padding across the floor, he opened his bedroom door a chink and stared down into the dark maw of the staircase.

The light switch was at the bottom.

I can do this.

He rested his foot on the first step, his hand automatically reaching out to hold onto something. His fingertips brushed against the coarse rope as the metal rings clinked against the wall.

He yanked his hand back, cradling it to his chest as a grisly realisation settled. The rope made sense now he knew this used to be the hangman's cottage.

He edged down the stairs one at a time, staring into total darkness, his mind conjuring shapes and noises that weren't there. He skimmed his fingers along the wall when he reached the bottom, throwing the switch on the light. The living room came into focus, and he slumped against the wall with relief.

He eased through the kitchen door, closing it behind him as he didn't want to wake Callie. She had enough to worry about without finding him skulking in the kitchen in the middle of the night.

The fridge gave up a slice of cold pizza, and he was halfway through eating this when his gaze fell on his backpack still behind the door. He pulled out the journal and set it on the table where Callie had left a pile of last-minute labels, together with an assortment of sharpies and a pencil with a chewed end.

The warmth from the quarry tiles seeped into his bare feet as he opened the journal, scanning over the pages he'd read before.

Never forget. Never forgive.

Say his name.

Find his...

Was it all a joke? But yet, tracing his fingers over the old ink, he was certain that it wasn't.

Something had happened here. Something awful.

He turned the page over and found the harsh indentations that had bled through the thin paper. His gaze fell on the pencil, and a smile curled across his lips.

Scooping it up, he began to lightly scribble over the marks.

And letter by letter the missing word appeared, like an object from the mist.

B...o...n...e...s.

Find his bones.

Jackdaw sat back in his chair, drumming the pencil against the edge of the table. He chewed the inside of his cheek until a copper tang exploded onto his tongue. His knee began to tremble and he brushed his hair out of his eyes as he felt his reality shift again. It was so quiet here he could almost hear his own breath.

He turned the journal over and opened the back cover, looking for more clues. At first he thought the last page was blank, but as his eyes skimmed down, he found two words and a date printed neatly at the bottom.

Lonan Carter. 1805.

He stared at it until his vision became blurred.

Was this the boy who had written the journal?

The hangman's son?

Jackdaw's mind began to reel at the discovery. He could go to the library tomorrow. Surely there'd be historical documents about who had lived here. It would give him something to do and get him out of the cottage. Every time he came back, he was riddled with feelings he didn't understand, feelings that were stripping his skin away and revealing raw, open flesh.

If Oscar was here, he would tell him to lighten up. He'd shove him with his shoulder, his expression warm and playful.

Oscar made him feel safe.

Jackdaw didn't know how the hell to pick *that* apart. Maybe it was because Oscar had grown up here, that he was tied to the village in a way Jackdaw could never be.

He took a glass from the cupboard and went across to the sink, running the tap for a few moments before filling it. Movement in his peripheral vision, beyond the oak. There was something in the field, a pale shape. He narrowed his eyes, identified it as human, and as soon as that thought registered, he shrank back out of view.

After a few seconds he looked again, wondering if his brain was playing tricks on him. But no, now he could see the shape more clearly—a man, he was sure it was a man. He was just standing there, motionless, staring at the cottage.

Jackdaw's jaw stiffened.

He curled his fingers into his palms, striding to the door, opening it with a don't-mess-with-me flourish.

There was nothing to see. Only the tang of something he knew—leaf rot and dank earth, and something that turned his stomach inside out.

His head spun from all the chaos rampaging around his brain.

A breeze ruffled his hair and he turned towards it, his nostrils flaring. The whisper came out of nowhere, a low, breathy sigh that he felt vibrating against his ear drum.

Isaacrow…

Jackdaw's heart exploded into his throat and he wheeled around searching for a shape, the stranger, anything… the breeze died, soaking into the night as though it had never happened.

He formed the word on his tongue and whispered it.

Isaacrow.

Isaac Row? A name? A clue?

He chewed the edge of a thumbnail as he went back into the cottage, closing the door behind him, his heartbeat still lodged in his gullet.

But possibly the wildest realisation that settled on him as he stood in the quiet warmth of the kitchen, was that this place was changing him. He just wasn't sure into what.

CHAPTER THIRTY-THREE

Callie heaved her overnight bag onto the passenger seat. She hadn't slept, tossing and turning, caught between being scared of missing her alarm call and her constant worry about leaving Jackdaw alone.

He's more than competent. He's looked after himself for years.

This was what she kept repeating to herself even as she prepared to leave. It's not like she was fleeing the country, London was only a couple of hours' drive away. But the distance didn't matter.

In the few short days that Jackdaw had been with her, she'd grown so used to his company that she couldn't imagine living without him under the same roof. So much of her younger self was mirrored in him, and she wanted to protect him from all the mistakes she'd made.

When I get back, we'll plan his future.

As she walked across the yard, darkness still hovering on the edge of a sulky dawn, he was standing in the kitchen, looking out over the fields, his eyes almost invisible under a fall of hair.

'That's me all done now,' she said, as she closed the door.

The kitchen was warm and welcoming and *home*, and for a moment the last thing she wanted was to leave and go do adult things in London. But that wasn't an option.

She drained the last dregs of her coffee and grabbed her handbag from the table.

Jackdaw turned from the window, gifting her with a grin.

'I'll be fine,' he said, before she had a chance to say anything. 'I'll only have one wild party. It's not as if the neighbours will complain.' He gestured outside, where a thin light bled over the hill.

Her throat tightened and she opened her arms, drawing him close. This time, he allowed it without flinching.

'Call me if you need me,' she whispered fiercely against his shoulder. 'I left Maggie's number on the pinboard. There's food in the fridge.'

'Go.' His breath ruffled her hair. 'Rake in some cash so we don't have to live on baked beans.'

She laughed as she released him, blinking away the moisture in her eyes.

He walked with her to the car, leaning on the door as she climbed in and started the reluctant engine. Through the windscreen, the dark hulk of the barn loomed. She remembered what she'd sensed there—what she *thought* she'd sensed there?—and wanted to warn him about it, but the words died in her throat.

I mean, what could I say without scaring him rigid?

'Be good,' she whispered. Her hand reached for his, and then she closed the door, ramming the car into first gear. He stood watching as she drove away. Her gaze didn't waver from her rear-view mirror until he was lost from sight.

As she turned onto the lane and the sky lightened, a murder

of crows circled over the field. She hoped Jackdaw would remember to feed them. It was one of the bizarre aspects of the village she didn't really think about anymore.

Everyone always left food out for the crows.

She turned off the lane as she reached the bottom, avoiding the rain-filled potholes on the track that led to Maggie's cottage. It was early, but she knew Maggie rose with the dawn no matter what time of year. Truth be told, she hadn't even fully acknowledged that she was making this call, it just happened— so she ran with it.

Maggie opened the door as Callie unlatched the gate, golden light spilling from the kitchen.

'I can't stop long,' Callie said, with a sigh. 'I don't want to get caught up in too many traffic snarls.'

Maggie beckoned her into the hallway. She was dressed in an old pair of navy tracksuit bottoms and an Argyle sweater with pink and blue diamonds that had seen better days. Grey strands spiked from her knitted hat; Callie realised that she'd never seen Maggie without something covering her hair.

'I'll keep an eye on Jackdaw.' Maggie pushed a warm muffin wrapped in a napkin into Callie's hands. 'Although I'll do it from afar, as Lord knows a boy of that age doesn't want babysitting.'

'You're a godsend, Maggie.'

Callie's trepidation lightened a notch.

'God and me aren't on good terms,' Maggie replied, the lines around her eyes crinkling, 'but I'll treat the birds to a fat ball or two whilst you're gone.'

Over Maggie's shoulder, Callie could see the kitchen table littered with bowls and scattered seeds.

Callie chewed the inside of her lower lip. Maggie's answer didn't make sense. Why was feeding the birds so important? The question hovered on her tongue, but the longer she dallied, the more she was tempted to stay for a cup of tea.

Maggie's quiet scrutiny pulled her thoughts back into focus.

'Oscar is staying with Jackdaw so he won't be alone, but I'll tell you that finding out he was related to Elspeth was a shock. He definitely doesn't take after her.' She wound her scarf around her neck again and closed her fingers on the door handle. 'Call me if you need anything, however small.'

On the spur of the moment, she pulled Maggie into a brief hug. The older woman smelled of woodsmoke and pine, as though she'd been walking in the forest and had come home to a roaring fire.

'Drive careful.' Maggie's words followed Callie out into the chill of an early morning. 'There'll be eyes on Jackdaw.'

As Callie drove away, the muffin on the seat beside her, she pondered that Maggie's last words had been a bit odd, too. But then, sometimes Maggie didn't talk sense, like the language she knew was one only she was fluent in.

Yet another perplexing thing about living here.

The car passed through the sleeping village and climbed the hill at the other side, and it wasn't until the road curved and Callie could see it all laid out snugly in the valley, that she realised she hadn't mentioned Gala Day to Maggie.

Maybe Jackdaw would enjoy it? Callie had never been as it always seemed to be around the time of the show, and she wasn't even sure if she would have ventured out anyway because it wasn't really her thing. She found the whole idea of a celebratory event at the place where people died a touch creepy. And the paper bird thing. What was it with birds and this place?

That's what you get for living in the sticks.

The thought skipped across her mind in a blaze of truth.

The past can't hurt you, and it's up to you to decide the future— and that was what fuelled her resolve as the miles raced past.

CHAPTER THIRTY-FOUR

Maggie pushed through the heavy doors into the library.

A scattering of cars parked outside had piqued her interest, especially as it wasn't supposed to open until later.

For a moment she thought there was nobody there, until she heard a chair squeak along the wooden floor. Someone cleared their throat.

'If you're in here without permission, I'll be having words,' Maggie said, her voice full of authority.

'What makes you think we haven't got permission?' Elspeth's form appeared from behind a shelf of books in the corner.

'The fact that you're hiding away like mice instead of being out here in the open. Which is, quite frankly'—Maggie's gaze drifted across two battered leather sofas in the middle of the room—'much more comfortable.'

Elspeth's lips tightened into a grim line, her nostrils flaring.

Maggie unlatched the swing half-door by the library desk, straightening her spine as she met the attention of the others cloistered away.

Eleanor Farley, who ran the post office. Matt Coxall, who had a livery stable at the end of the village. Estelle Tudor, the headmistress of the primary school.

The self-proclaimed village council, purely because their families had all lived here for generations. Gossip was delivered to them by those who longed to be brought into their fold, but this was a tight-knit group who didn't trust strangers.

A group whose main purpose was to prepare for Gala Day and to make sure it all ran smoothly. Those who tried to add anything new to the festival day were shot down in flames.

It would run as it had always run, under the guise of tradition, the zealous devotion to a cause that would protect the village in the coming year.

The folklore of a place is in the earth beneath, in the twisted roots of the trees, in the water that runs through the land.

And this land had seen so much death—some deserved and some unforgivable. The story that had seeded everything came firmly under the latter. Whilst the particulars of it may have been tangled by many tongues and possibly enhanced, the foundation was sound. The hangman had lived in the cottage on the hill, and the gibbet, historically used to display dead or dying criminals, had been an execution frame.

There were those who whispered that the death of the traveller boy was the hangman's last duty. What happened afterwards left him destroyed, a shell of a man.

'Did my invitation get lost in the post?' Maggie graced Eleanor with a look that had made many quiver, but the postmistress merely laughed, a short, sharp sound with no humour.

Maggie knew so much about the council because a long time ago she had been one of their number. And these secret meetings were only held for something of supreme importance.

'Come and sit down, Maggie,' Matt Coxall said, pulling out

a chair. He was a softly spoken man who always smelled of peppermint sweets and manure.

Elspeth sighed, her gaze drilling into Maggie's back as she took the offered chair.

There was someone else hidden behind the shelf of books who hadn't made himself known.

Twig.

Maggie inclined her head as he shuffled into view. A hiked brow in greeting. Of everyone here, she trusted him the most. After all, he'd been with her that fateful night.

He settled on a chair, continuing to wind a strip of willow into one of his poppets. His silence spoke volumes, and Maggie stiffened in her seat.

'We were just going over the details for the parade and the avifauna,' Estelle said, pulling on the hem of her tweed skirt. Estelle's tone gave Maggie the impression that the woman thought she was talking to one of her school charges.

A clandestine hush fell upon the group, interrupted only by the sound of an occasional car on the road outside.

Maggie's gaze flicked around the gathering.

They all looked slightly dishevelled, their faces a little dingy, dark circles under their eyes.

Her brow creased.

This meeting had been going on for hours, possibly all night. What could be that important? Whatever it was, she didn't like the way her gut clenched at her introspection.

'I'm assuming everything will go ahead as normal?'

No one spoke for a few heartbeats, which only added to Maggie's suspicion.

'Everything will proceed as normal, except—' Matt's words were cut short as he glanced at Elspeth. His tongue moistened his lips.

'Absolutely as normal,' Elspeth said, fixing her gaze on Maggie, her eyes as sharp as flint. 'Why would we do anything different? It's tradition.' A glimmer of something that might have been triumph flashed in Elspeth's eyes.

Maggie folded her hands in her lap.

Elspeth was lying. They were all lying.

Dread curled around her bones. She looked at each of their faces in turn as the library clock on the wall ticked ever onwards, counting down to Gala Day.

CHAPTER THIRTY-FIVE

The cottage seemed eerily quiet when Jackdaw went back inside. He stood in the kitchen, his head cocked to one side, listening.

Listening for what?

The thought skimmed through his mind, his body reacting with a faint prickling of his scalp.

As he shoved bread into the toaster and made himself a coffee, he tried to make sense of the bizarre events of last night and the man in the field… and the name he had heard.

The toast popped up with a metallic clang, the unpredictable mechanism sending it shooting onto the worktop, and his heart notched up a gear. If he was skittish now, standing in the kitchen in daylight, what chance did he have when darkness fell?

He couldn't go to pieces. He *had* to get a hold of himself.

As he chewed he thought, not for the first time, how much easier this would be with Oscar.

'Stop it.' He slammed his palm on the table with more force than he realised, the sting making his fingers tingle. His jaw set in a firm line as he stashed his dishes in the sink.

And now, his default kicked into place for the first time since he'd arrived here. He made a mental list of what he needed to do before he left the cottage, going through each task methodically, pushing any other thoughts to the side.

He showered and cleaned his teeth, put on clean clothes, dropping the dirty ones in the laundry basket in the small back room with the clay-pocked sink.

It felt strange not to add putting in his contacts to his list. But he didn't need them anymore. That was a solid fact amidst all this uncertainty.

Today, he'd show everyone *exactly* who he was. The thought made him bite the edge of his lip, but it was also a little bit freeing—as though he was shedding a skin and starting anew.

And then he went out into the cold November morning, taking Callie's bike from just inside the barn. He didn't glance further into the darkness, didn't think about Ophelia.

The lane was dusted with glittering frost, so he dismounted and pushed the bike down the hill, wary of adding another accident to his tally. A few cars passed him, mainly with kids in the back on their way to school. He saw a milk float packed with bottles, stepped aside when a woman came out of her door wearing the high-vis jacket of a school crossing patrol. She carried a STOP sign with a silhouette of two children under the word, the neon colouring a stark contrast to the grey morning.

At the top of the high street, he paused.

The chill from the metal, peeking through the worn rubber of the handlebar grips, seeped into his skin. He had no idea where the library was. He took out his phone. A scowl furrowed his brow. Despite having an almost full charge, he had no signal. Callie had mentioned it. That the village rested between two hills and the nearest mast was miles away.

Reception was, at best, fretful.

At worst, non-existent.

He sighed. So much for technology.

'Shuffle along a little, young man.' A voice pulled him from his thoughts, and he turned to see a postman in a bright-red jacket and black trousers, an empty sack in his hand.

Jackdaw hadn't even noticed that he was standing close to a post box.

The man smiled, showing uneven teeth, but as his gaze swept over Jackdaw, the smile died, morphing into something Jackdaw thought might be surprise. But there was something else there, too—something sly.

Jackdaw stepped back, mumbling an apology. He kept his head down, sure that everyone he passed was studying him, acutely aware of being the stranger.

Of being an oddity.

He almost rammed into a sign at the edge of the pavement. But this time luck was on his side. It was a village map with points of interest stamped onto the wooden plaque. There were entries for the local pub, the church, a chemist, a school, a doctor's surgery, the post office and—his lips curled into a grin—the library, tucked away down a side street. He took a moment to look at the village as a whole. It was long rather than wide, resting in the palm of the valley. The hills rose on either side, a protective shield for all who lived here. But as his gaze skimmed across, it halted on the gibbet. He wondered what it had looked like with a body swinging from a noose...

He backed away from the board, the toast he'd eaten earlier

churning in his gut, and he wasn't really looking as he crossed the road. The blare of a car horn froze him to the spot, the vehicle passing so close that he saw the glare from the woman driving, open hostility in her eyes.

It was Elspeth.

With his heart still pounding in his chest, he wandered until he found the side street, which wasn't much more than a cobbled path winding behind the main road.

The library sat on its own, a small, squat building with arched windows and wide doors.

Jackdaw propped the bike against the wall and went inside, passing through another set of glass double doors with wire insets. The brass plates on the front were worn, dull from decades of hands.

A woman sat behind a desk, a pile of books at her side. The name plaque on her desk stated she was Clotilde Coughlan.

She glanced up, tortoiseshell-framed glasses perched on her nose. 'Can I help you?'

But even as these words left her lips Jackdaw could feel the same level of scrutiny as he had from the postman.

He straightened his spine. 'I'd like to look at some old local history books.' His chin jutted forwards.

Clotilde made a show of removing her glasses and polishing them on her scarf.

'It's a shame you didn't come in earlier,' she said, her hand rising to her throat. 'I'm afraid all the local history books are out at the moment.'

'All of them?' Jackdaw said. His tone indicated that he didn't believe her.

'Yes,' she replied. 'There's a project at the school about the village, and the children have stripped our shelves bare.' She motioned behind her.

All Jackdaw could see were rows upon rows of books.

'When will they be returned?' he asked, determined to get something out of this visit.

'Whenever the children have finished with them. We don't specify a time limit here. We like our children to understand their history, to be a part of it.'

She paused and picked up an object from the desk, expertly twirling small digits at one end.

It was a library book date stamp. Jackdaw had seen one on an old movie he'd watched, and he knew that method was outdated now. All libraries used a digital system for checking books in and out. Apart from this one.

He shook his head, frustration curling his fingers into his palms. One hand was on the door when he turned to her again.

'Does the name Isaac Row mean anything to you?'

He watched her visibly pale, watched as she licked her upper lip, pressing herself back in her seat as though he was a disease she didn't want to catch.

'I'm sorry, no,' she said, shaking her head.

Just for a moment there was a crack in her composure, and he knew as he left the building that she'd been lying.

He set off again, back along the high street, being ultra-careful about people and traffic. There was one other place he could go that might give him an insight into the history of this place, somewhere that couldn't hide its facts.

The graveyard.

CHAPTER THIRTY-SIX

Jackdaw reached the church without mishap—which he counted as a win, considering everything else that had happened to him here. He was slightly winded after pedalling uphill with no rest, and his breath ghosted in the crisp November air.

He rested his bike against the boundary wall and looked down at the village below, the houses nestled together as though they were keeping a secret. Wisps of smoke drifted from chimneys. He studied the landscape—from here, he could see Callie's cottage and, if he turned 180 degrees, the gibbet on the opposite hill. Both had such a terrible history and somehow he'd found himself caught up in it.

Jackdaw had always been nonconformist and independent—his upbringing had forced that on him. But standing here with a cruel wind making his eyes stream, he couldn't help but feel a little bit lost, like a tiny wheel that had somehow drifted apart from the large cogs that made everything else work.

He sighed and thrust his hands into his jacket pockets, passing under the moss-coated lychgate to reach the graveyard. The hairs on the nape of his neck rose as though someone was watching him, but when he glanced over his shoulder all he could see was the stark outline of the gibbet silhouetted against a sullen sky.

Isaac Row.

He repeated the name in his head as he trudged along between each gravestone. Some bore no inscription at all, the letters dissolved by weather and time, and some only had the faintest indentations. He crouched and ran his fingers over the marks, the encroaching lichen springy against his fingertips. Dates danced around his mind, some from as early as the 1600s, people who had lived and worked here, and were now crumbled bones under the earth.

But they weren't the bones he was looking for.

He flopped down on a bench, watching a crow as it hopped from grave to grave, digging at the moss for insects. It cocked its head to one side, preened a wing feather and shook itself. A throaty caw drifted across to him.

He replied with his own greeting, mimicking the bird as corvids mimicked human speech. It fixed him with a beady stare then flew off, landing on the path that led to the back of the church.

It waited.

'What do you want?' Jackdaw said, as though the crow could answer him.

It waited.

'I don't suppose you know where Isaac Row is buried?'

The question left his lips and he laughed, pretty sure that desperation was drip-feeding insanity into his veins.

Another caw from the crow, an impatient sound that had him on his feet as something brushed against his senses.

'Go on, then,' he said. 'I'll follow you.'

Part of him—the rational part—thought the crow would take off over the fields, and he'd be left standing alone. But it continued to hop along the pathway, sometimes finding a grub hidden beneath a pile of mouldering leaves.

The flagstone pathway snaked around the church, and there were other smaller tracks leading from it, made up of trodden-down grass that crisscrossed between graves. A huddle of yew trees stood at the back of the church, bright-red berries dotting the green-needled branches, boughs almost touching the ground. The graves here were smaller, some only marked by wooden crosses and makeshift monuments.

Jackdaw wandered between the gravestones, his eyes skimming over any names he could find, but nothing came close to the one he was looking for. Frustration throbbed behind his temple and he kicked at a loose piece of flint, sending it bouncing into the long grass.

The crow flew into the nearest yew and disappeared into its gloom-drenched heart, leaving him a solitary figure under a sky that was darkening by the minute.

Great.

Now he was going to get soaked as well as getting nowhere.

He kicked at another stone and watched it skitter across the pathway. It tumbled for a distance as the ground dipped, and Jackdaw's attention honed in on a larger grave right in the corner.

Something was off about it.

His mouth twisted to one side.

Not only did this look out of place amongst all the smaller graves, but what he was seeing didn't make any sense.

It was only when he was a few steps away that his mind decoded the confusion. The plinth of the grave had once been white marble, but now algae stains coated the stone, its green veins rampaging across its surface. There was a marker, but from this side no words were visible.

But what was causing Jackdaw's mouth to run dry was the angel that had once graced the top of the grave. It lay on its side in the dirt, its blank eyes coated in soil, its hands clasped together in an eternal prayer. A riot of thorny weeds had grown up through its fingers, anchoring it to the ground.

Yet this angel had no wings. Ugly gouges marked where they once had been and Jackdaw recoiled, instantly remembering the wings that had been nailed to the door. Why was something like this hidden away at the back of the church?

He edged around it, treading through a thick carpet of leaf mulch that submerged his trainers. A tumble of hair fell over his eyes, and when he glanced up through it, beads of moisture coated the strands. He looked back at the church, or rather, where the church had been, because now the building had all but disappeared—eaten by a swirling mist that had risen from nowhere. It clung to the old stones, as though the ghosts of the dead had all rebelled against their final resting places.

His fingertips began to tingle, and he was suddenly hyperaware of his own presence. He felt each breath of cold air as it rushed into his lungs, felt his beating heart as the rhythm drummed in his chest.

Jackdaw didn't have to crouch to read the inscription on the stone. It had been sheltered from the worst ravages of time.

Francis Henry Parnell 1765-1810

Who by his own hand delivered us into darkness.

Jackdaw tugged on his earlobe as he read the words, then read them again, a frown creasing his brow.

What kind of a messed-up inscription was this?

He pressed his fingers to his chilled lips, a dull ache throbbing behind his temple. He was no closer to finding the elusive Isaac Row, and now there was another name added to the tangle of bewilderment in his head.

For a few moments he just wanted to stress about school and parents like any normal kid. But he didn't have any parents, and he'd never really been normal, whatever that word came loaded with.

Mist drifted between the gravestones. A damp chill settled on Jackdaw's bones, and he hugged his arms around his body.

Everything is connected.

A phrase from his mother sprang up from nowhere— his eleven-year-old self, standing in her bedroom doorway, asking about the notes and scraps of paper pasted to the wall.

Back then he'd not given it much thought, it was just the odd way she talked. Now the phrase made perfect sense—but that was crazy, his mother had no connection to this village.

He huffed out a breath and left the grave, left the discarded angel shorn of its wings.

A sound reached for him through the mist, and he tilted his head to one side, much like the crow. It was a harsh yet rhythmic rumble, a rolling… wheels rolling… wheels rolling over grass…

The cart.

He stumbled forward, his foot catching on the edge of a grave half-buried in leaf drift. A simple wooden cross marked the spot, and by its base was a pink rose, its petals still vibrant as though someone had left it there recently.

He crouched to read the inscription.

God called her home.

The name was hidden by trailing ivy, and he brushed it aside with a trembling hand.

His breath caught in his throat, his vision tunnelling, shock numbing his senses.

Jackdaw knew that God had nothing to do with it.

Because Ophelia Carter was still here.

CHAPTER THIRTY-SEVEN

– One month earlier –

Francine Dawtrey knew everyone thought she was selfish and delusional. After all, she spent all her time holed up in the tiny box room of her house, pasting scraps of paper to the walls and joining them up with string. To an onlooker, it would have appeared that she was trying to solve a crime scene, a woman so entrenched in her own thoughts that nothing else mattered.

She had a daughter who had walked away to live her own life, and a son who would probably do the same thing.

The latter prospect gnawed away inside her mind, forcing her to forego sleep and food, to endlessly scroll websites and forums in the vain hope of finding something that would tie all her tattered threads together.

An incessant drumming throbbed in her brain, telling her that fate had linked hands with time—and a catastrophe loomed that she couldn't bear.

Because she had started it all.

Her fingers shook as she penned another note in her spidery scrawl. She could hear Jackdaw in the kitchen downstairs, the rough scraping as he rummaged in the iced-up freezer drawers for food.

Had she bought any recently? She couldn't remember.

Her heart ached and part of her wanted to go to him and take him in her arms, to cover his face with kisses and apologise for all her actions, all her neglect. But how could she tell him that what she was doing was all for him? If she could just find a way to pause what was happening, she could warn him—but warn him of what? Never to go to a certain place?

By her constant inattention she had forced him to be independent, to trust his own judgement. If something happened to her, that was her legacy. Her eyelids drooped, her head nodding, and she pushed up from her chair, her body weight slight, but still it felt like she was moving a boulder up an unrelenting hill.

The back door slammed shut, and she went to the window, twitching the curtain to see Jackdaw walking down the path to the gate, his slender shoulders hunched against the cold.

Snowflakes fluttered from the sky, feathered edges coating the golden leaves of the silver birch in the next garden. Flakes landed in Jackdaw's hair, so stark against his mop of black, and she stumbled backwards, collapsing onto the lumpy sofa she used as a bed because she never wanted to be away from the words on the wall.

It was too early in the year for snowfall.

She put her head in her hands, exhaustion etched along each bone of her body.

It had snowed that night it all began.

A dusting precious because of its rarity.

She remembered her face upturned to the inky sky in delight, catching each flake on her tongue. Her mind floated somewhere just out of reach, but the feeling didn't scare her. The rapturous joy of simply being alive fizzed through her veins.

She turned as laughter rippled across the glade, a man and a woman holding hands, twirling together faster and faster.

Love gripped her heart. Love for them both and each leaf on each tree, each snowflake as it kissed her skin and hair.

Her life beyond this forest meant nothing in this moment.

She was free. She was where she was meant to be. A soft palm against her cheek, and the woman with hair the colour of wheat in the sun pulled her into a warm embrace, lips seeking hers.

The man watched, his features soft, sweat glistening on his bare chest from their coupling. He whispered her name. A name she'd draped around herself when she'd arrived here, leaving her old one in the outside world.

Everything was beautiful and snow-kissed.

Until it wasn't.

A screech sounded from the trees, an ear-splitting ruckus as if a thousand birds had woken all at once. Branches bowed under the sudden weight of multiple avian bodies. A single, chilling caw split the night. Followed by another and another, until she had to put her hands over her ears to try to drown it out. She backed away, unable to tear her gaze from the obsidian mass of crows. Glossy eyes watched her every move, heads tilted to one side as if she was a grub wriggling on the ground. Her spine met the unforgiving trunk of a silver birch.

Fear shivered through her, any voice she had clogged in her throat, her limbs almost boneless.

The man fell to his knees, hands clasped in front of him, lips silently forming words.

She wanted to rage at him—*fight, fight, they're only birds!*

But part of her knew they were not simply gathered here by accident. Something they had done had angered them. She tried to dredge up the details of this night, but they were lost in an alcohol-fuelled haze of laughter and secrets and bodies wound together on the woodland floor.

This perfect glade set deep in the forest.

The woman with the sun-kissed hair shrieked, staggering back as she grabbed a shirt from the ground, holding it against her nakedness. And then she turned and fled.

A twitch of a bough as a crow took flight, followed by three more. They swooped low, wings beating the air, gaining on the woman who ran, her bare feet pounding the narrow track.

From her vantage point by the silver birch, she watched in abject horror as two of the crows barrelled into the woman's head, claws tangling in her hair.

A scream echoed across the glade, something so terrible that the man folded in on himself, his hands clasped over his face.

On the woodland track, golden hair turned to crimson as unrelenting claws and beaks tore across a scalp—reducing it to ruins.

All she could do was watch, as the undergrowth swallowed the woman who had loved her so softly. All she could do was wait, until the screams hushed and the bracken stilled.

And then she fled, deep into the forest. She ran and ran, towards the rays of dawn spiking the horizon. She stole back across deserted farmland, shivering with cold and fright, stealing a ragged jacket from a scarecrow to conceal her bare flesh.

Somehow she made it back to the cottage she had rented for the week. She stuffed clothes into a suitcase, her mind already trying to shut down what she'd seen.

She left the village by 9am, hands gripping the steering wheel, tears rolling down her cheeks.

By the time she got home, a dull ache had started in her stomach, and she barely made it to the bathroom to throw up.

Flecks of red stained the toilet bowl, and for a moment she thought it was blood.

She wrinkled her nose and leaned farther in.

The flecks weren't uniform in size or shape. She scooped one onto the tip of her finger.

It had a skin-like quality, and that's when awareness dawned.

It was a mushroom.

Something she had eaten from the palm of the man's hand.

But that wasn't the only thing Francine Dawtrey brought back from the forest.

CHAPTER THIRTY-EIGHT

A tractor stood idling noisily outside the cottage when Jackdaw arrived home. He'd sat on the bench in the churchyard for a bit, trying to come to terms with what he'd seen. The mist had cleared, leaving behind a stark, grey sky the colour of dirty snow.

A man jumped down from the cab, wearing an old waterproof jacket with patches on the elbows, dirty jeans, and mud-crusted Wellington boots.

'Elspeth sent me,' he said, his accent rich and drawling. 'Come to get the cart, I have.' His gaze drifted to the barn and Jackdaw didn't miss the way his posture stiffened.

Jackdaw deliberately made a show of messing with the zip on his jacket. He'd been here with Oscar when Callie said Elspeth could borrow the cart, but his mind was still unmoored.

And he still remembered the rumbling of wooden wheels vibrating through the mist.

It was a message, a caution, but it might as well have been in hieroglyphics. All he knew was that it didn't feel right.

'You'll need to get those doors open,' the man said, his gaze drifting from Jackdaw's head to his feet.

'I'll get the key.' Jackdaw edged past the tractor. The padlock didn't need a key, but he was playing for time. His pulse gathered speed, his heartbeat thudding in his ears.

Once inside the cottage, he let out a deep exhaled breath and rested his spine against the thick, wooden door. Maybe if he stayed here the man would just go away. But that would only be a respite—for some reason Elspeth wanted the cart and, if she came to the door and demanded it, he couldn't say no.

Jackdaw had always been a little afraid of people in authority. They left him feeling vulnerable, without any control, and he avoided them as much as he could. He'd gleaned that Elspeth was like a bloodhound—once she caught the scent of something, she wouldn't let go.

He snuck to the kitchen window and glanced out. The man was still there, stamping his feet against the cold.

Jackdaw bit the edge of his lip, the gesture ending in a grimace. He wished Callie would appear and take over but he was here on his own, like he'd asked for.

It was up to him to make the decision.

With his heart lodged in his throat, he opened the door and walked slowly across to the barn, pretending to unlock it. His fingers trembled—either from cold or uncertainty, he wasn't sure. He pushed the door open, and the darkness inside rushed over him and bled into the yard. It was close to freezing but the chill inside the barn felt glacial, or maybe that was just his heightened senses. He opened the other door, struggling as the bottom caught on clods of old straw.

Part of him wanted to run to the cart and splay out his arms, say *no, you can't take it, it belongs here!*

But what reasoning did he have? Only the one that sang inside his gut.

A loud chug and a belch of diesel as the tractor swung across the barn opening, its bulk blocking the thin light filtering in. Jackdaw stood shrouded in gloom, his palms slick with sweat. He edged towards the cart, stopping inches away. His head began to spin, and he thought he might throw up.

His eyes searched for Ophelia, even though he now knew the truth of her, desperately hoping she'd tell him what to do—but she wasn't here. His mouth formed her name, his brain still caught on the barbs of what she was. She was part of this story, another puzzle piece he couldn't fit into the whole.

Diesel fumes filled his lungs as the tractor backed into the barn, its dazzling reversing lights coming closer and closer. Jackdaw placed his hand on the cart, curling his fingers over the warped, ancient wood. Fear coursed through him, something real and thick and forlorn. His feet were on the ground but yet he was in the cart, his hands tied with rope, the shaking motion of the wheels tipping him off balance.

Isaacrow...

The whisper brushed past his ear, as gentle as a butterfly wing. The taste of sweet apples filled his mouth and he cried out, saliva exploding onto his tongue.

'You be sickening for something, lad?'

The man's voice snagged on Jackdaw's consciousness and plunged him back into the present. It took him a moment to decipher the meaning, and all the while, the man was looking at him as if he was something from an alien world.

'No, no, I'm fine,' Jackdaw said, although he was a universe away from fine.

He wanted to climb onto the cart and let it spin him away into the past—and he wanted to light a match and burn it to ash.

The man drew on a pair of thick gloves, and Jackdaw watched as he attached the shafts of the cart to the tractor, tying it securely with rope. Just before he climbed back into the cab, he paused, glancing back over his shoulder before heaving himself up. Whatever words he was going to say were lost in the roar of the engine.

Jackdaw watched helplessly as the cart slowly began to move, its wheels creaking in protest. Wisps of hay fluttered from its back. He walked alongside it, his fingertips hovering over the footboard. It felt like a funeral procession.

It felt like a betrayal.

He watched until all he could see was the top of the tractor cab moving steadily down the lane.

Had he imagined the urgent whisper, the name that refused to leave him alone? He didn't think so, but then all of his reality seemed to be skewed. He sighed, turning to look back.

The space where the cart had been wasn't completely empty. Jackdaw stared, his jaw slackening, knowing exactly what his eyes were seeing even as his mind faltered.

There in the straw-cluttered dust, growing from embedded dirt, was a scarlet flush of colour.

A host of fly agaric mushrooms.

CHAPTER THIRTY-NINE

Those that had lived in the village for decades could feel it.

That subtle shift in the air that settled on their skin and soaked through to their marrow, which had nothing to do with the chill of November.

Some said the knowledge was in their blood. It had been passed down through generation after generation.

They toiled away at the avifauna, fixing tiny avian bones to its webbed skeleton so that it rattled as it moved.

They hung woven willow poppets on their doors.

Anything to repel whatever might come looking. It was a sign to say they remembered.

And if they remembered… he would, too.

It was a pact they had made after that terrible day so long ago.

Strangers would utter noises of disbelief, laughing about the superstitious nonsense alive and thriving in this little rural community. But you could tell those who it had spooked, for they didn't go out in the dark and huddled closer together.

Others had tried to quieten this haunted spectre who roamed after Martinmas, sprinkling holy water in the forest, whispering prayers as the sun set behind the hill.

Surely their faith would save them?

But the land remembered, because it could still feel the footprints of two boys within its soil.

The wind remembered, because it still carried their laughter.

And the trees—oh, the trees.

They knew the secrets of their hearts.

Faith was a worthless word.

CHAPTER FORTY

Oscar sat sprawled on the offensive floral sofa in the front room, flicking through his phone, when Elspeth bustled through the door. He'd slept late, emerging into the kitchen with a yawn, fully expecting a dose of wrath from his aunt and a lecture about how he had frittered the best part of the day away. But the kitchen was immaculately tidy—and silent.

He hadn't slept well, waking more than a few times to what he'd thought was the sound of tree branches scratching against his window. That was an impossibility, as there was nothing remotely close enough. The memory of the dead bird kept brushing against his mind, as though it was pasted to the back of his eyes. It had to be because of Jackdaw.

And the fact that Gala Day was tomorrow.

He was toying with the idea of seeing what kind of mood Elspeth was in, and asking for a ride to the next village, to the train station, and just taking off for the day *anywhere* but here.

Elspeth marched through to the kitchen and filled the kettle, settling it on the old range. 'Did you have breakfast?'

Oscar took his feet off the table, something he normally got yelled at for, and studied his aunt.

A few things didn't make sense.

One, she'd gone into the kitchen in her shoes. Two, she was still wearing the same clothes as yesterday, which he'd *never* seen her do. And three, her mind was obviously not focussed on him and the list of things she always found fault in. Four, Oscar's plate sat on his lap, and she hadn't even noticed.

Had she stayed out all night? The sudden thought was so absurd that he almost choked on the disbelief that shot into his throat.

'I want you to go to the cottage,' she said, turning to finally fix him with a cool gaze. 'And make sure Jackdaw is safe.'

Oscar's brain stuttered and he had to catch his jaw before it fell open. Only last night she had warned him to keep away.

'I thought you said—'

'Forget that,' she snapped, cutting him off. 'It's only right that we look after him. Especially as his sister is away. He seems very vulnerable, a little skittish. We don't want anything happening to him...' Her voice trailed off as she poured boiling water into a teapot, her face vanishing in a cloud of steam, before adding, 'You'll be a good influence.'

Oscar's plans of spending the day away dissolved into ash.

'What do you mean?' he asked, and immediately wished he hadn't.

His aunt pressed her lips together, which was never a good sign. 'We all know that cottage has never passed any safety regulations, and as for the barn...' She tutted, tapping her fingers on the countertop. 'It's full of unguarded things.'

Oscar could have asked what she meant, but her tone clearly said she was done explaining—he was astute enough to know all the signs and react for the best of his health.

So he swallowed his curiosity and headed for the shower.

An hour later, he was standing outside the cottage.

He'd taken a shortcut over the field, the mist slowly dissolving as he walked. He saw Sam Marsden in his tractor chugging down the lane. Sam raised a hand and waved. Oscar found himself repeating the gesture. He hadn't lived here for five years, and yet people still knew him. Maybe part of him never left…

He was chewing over this crazy notion as he rapped on the door to the cottage, waiting for a few moments before banging against the wood with the flat of his hand.

'Jackdaw! It's freezing out here. Let me in!'

He stomped his feet just to reaffirm his words. Silence from within. Had Jackdaw gone out? But even as that thought settled, another fluttered down—where would he even go?

If Oscar had the whole house to himself with no adult interference, he'd probably stay in bed until midday, eat pizza until he felt sick, and game until his fingers ached.

Jackdaw didn't seem like that kind of a boy. He seemed fragile as though he was made of glass, but beneath that was a certain toughness, as though the whole world had battered him into a corner but he still had claws.

Oscar was about to give up when he heard the locks unlatch. *Of course, it's Martinmas.*

The door swung open slowly and Oscar pushed his way in, just in case Jackdaw slammed it in his face. Their last conversation hadn't ended well.

A muscle ticked in Jackdaw's jaw.

He lifted his chin, his eyes narrowing.

Oscar held his hands up.

'Hey, I'm sorry I was such a dick yesterday. I didn't mean to press your buttons or scare you. I was only trying to make you aware of how fucked up this place is. But then, I think you already know...' He glanced towards Jackdaw and prepared himself to be blasted.

Instead, Jackdaw wilted. His shoulders caved and his face softened. He bowed his head, hiding behind a fall of hair.

Common sense made Oscar stuff his hands into his jacket pockets. If anyone deserved a hug it was the boy in front of him, but he'd been warned before about being too outgoing. It didn't mean anything except *I'm here*, but Jackdaw had a cautious soul, and Oscar had already messed things up more than once.

Jackdaw leant his weight against a kitchen chair, his gaze fixed firmly on the quarry tiles. 'I let them take the cart,' he said softly. He raised his head and finally met Oscar's eyes. 'I didn't want to. It belongs here.' A shake of his hair and an exhaled breath. 'I'm going totally crazy.'

'Do you want my opinion?' Oscar asked, resting the heels of his hands on the countertop, aware that he was going to give it anyway. 'I think you've been thrust into this new place with new people. That the bits and pieces you've learned have disturbed you because they don't make sense. You're not going crazy... this place doesn't follow any normal rules.' He graced Jackdaw with his best reassuring grin, known to get him out of the stickiest of situations. He really wanted it to work this time. 'How about you feed me, and we can start over?'

'Are you always hungry?' Jackdaw asked, his stance relaxing for the first time. He went across to the freezer and peered inside. 'What do you like?'

Oscar turned to look out of the window. A line of crows sat on the lowest bough of the oak tree. One threw back its head, a deep caw coming from its throat. A shiver rolled down Oscar's spine.

'Anything. You choose.' He hoped Jackdaw didn't hear the note of trepidation on his words.

His gaze flicked past the oak to the gibbet on the hill, a stark silhouette against the grey sky.

Down in the village, lights already glowed. Lamps were lit early because November's dusk came thick and swiftly. He pushed away the thought that it was Martinmas, and he was here with a boy called Jackdaw in the hangman's cottage.

And the legacy of its walls.

CHAPTER FORTY-ONE

They ate far too much pizza, then flopped down on the lumpy sofa in the back room and played with two retro handheld games Oscar had brought with him. Jackdaw was surprisingly good, beating Oscar's score time and time again. Now it was full dark, and Jackdaw knew this idyllic afternoon would end. He'd be left alone with his own gyrating thoughts. Going over and over all the things that defied logical thinking.

'Hey.' Oscar snapped his fingers in front of Jackdaw's face. 'I've just beaten you hollow on this round. You don't have to pity me that much.' A grin followed, as warm as sunlight, and Jackdaw had to look away.

Oscar was so capable and easy-going. He had his whole life planned out. A sliver of jealousy slid between Jackdaw's ribs. It made him feel queasy, unless that was the pizza.

Oscar's phone rang in his pocket.

He grimaced as he answered it. 'My aunt.'

He's going to go home. The thought stung, and Jackdaw wondered how he had gone from the boy who didn't need any friends, to the boy who craved this friendship as if it was air and he was drowning. It opened up a gaping vulnerability in him, one he had buried up to now, because no one had ever understood him or treated him as an equal.

'She's coming to pick me up in ten minutes.' Oscar's voice cut into Jackdaw's pensive thoughts. 'Will you be okay? I can ask if I can stay if you want?'

Yes, please stay.

'I'll be fine,' Jackdaw said in a voice that didn't sound like his own. 'But come over tomorrow?' He hoped it didn't come off as desperation.

'It's Gala Day tomorrow. It's not as lame as it sounds, and it's something to do. I know all the stallholders, so we can blag food without paying.' That grin again. 'They light a huge beacon when it gets dark, and…' He paused, and a shadow fell over his face. It was gone in an instant. 'I'd never tell anyone about it where I live now, but here…' He paused again but this time for effect. 'It's a Big Thing.'

'But why do they do it?' Jackdaw's brow creased. It sounded like something out of an offbeat movie.

'Tradition,' Oscar said, tipping the remnants from a bag of crisps into his mouth. 'It's to appease any wandering spirits, to show them we still remember.'

A shiver tripped over Jackdaw's skin. *It's only superstition.*

The crunch of tyres on gravel outside, and they both stood and went out into the kitchen. Oscar glanced to the window. 'I'd better head off. She hates being kept waiting. And I don't want to upset her or she'll have me running around tomorrow doing chores, and that I don't need.'

Jackdaw didn't move. He wrapped his fingers around the back of a chair, clutching it so tight that his knuckles whitened.

Don't go.

Oscar opened the door, leaning against the jamb for a moment. Cold air rushed in greedily and the room chilled. The light from Elspeth's headlights cut into the dark, illuminating Oscar in a golden glow.

'I can see now,' Jackdaw blurted out. 'I mean, I don't need the contacts. I don't know why.'

As soon as the words left his tongue, he wanted to scoop them back in and swallow them whole.

He looked away as Oscar's lips parted.

What a stupid, stupid thing to say.

'I'll see you tomorrow,' Oscar said softly. 'We can talk more.'

And then he was gone, leaving Jackdaw alone.

Jackdaw checked every window and every door twice to make sure they were locked. There was no way he was going outside until dawn broke. He mused that he was being too skittish, that there were reasons for the strange things that had happened.

The mushrooms in the barn? Fungi grew in dark, damp places, and he just hadn't looked under the cart before.

Perfectly credible.

He went through to the back room and lay on the old sofa, flicking through the channels on Callie's ancient TV. All he could find was a black-and-white movie and a news programme about farming forecasts for the year. She didn't even have a streaming service, and this blew his mind for a moment until he remembered that she probably worked most nights.

Didn't she get lonely? As soon as that notion hit, Jackdaw squirreled it away. Of course she didn't get lonely. She'd grown up just like him. Independent. Comfortable with her own company.

And that's exactly how he'd been—until Oscar. Jackdaw had read before about connections, how you could meet someone and bond with them immediately, as though you'd known them in a previous life. He'd always scorned the concept.

Or maybe he was just clinging on to Oscar because he was real and warm and safe, and Jackdaw was spiralling close to the edge of a cliff there was no coming back from.

His phone rang, and he snatched it from his pocket.

'Hi. I'm just doing the annoying older sister thing and checking up on you.'

Callie's cheerful voice made his throat close up.

'Jackdaw?' A note of concern.

'I'm good,' he said quickly. 'The signal isn't great here.'

Despite everything, he smiled. *She cared.*

She made a noise that could have been a laugh or a snort.

'Tell me about it. I'm at the hotel in London, and my phone has suddenly remembered that it can do more than one thing at once. Did you eat?'

Jackdaw's smile broadened. 'Of course I ate. With Oscar, if you must know. There'll only be crumbs left when you get back.'

'My poor bank balance.' She laughed for real this time. 'When I get home…' Her voice tailed off. 'Oh, sorry, Jackdaw, I've got a call coming in from Adele. I'd better take it. Tell Oscar I said hi. Be good, little brother.'

Jackdaw stared at his phone when she ended the call.

She still thought Oscar was staying over because Jackdaw

hadn't told her otherwise. Guilt lined his throat, his shaky emotions making tears well at the back of his eyes.

Little brother.

When he'd first arrived, he'd worried that she would try and be a replacement mother. He didn't need that. He'd survived without his first one. Neglect rips away your skin layer by layer until all that's left is raw, oozing flesh. Jackdaw had built a new skin, one tough enough to withstand the years of fending for himself at home and fending off others at school.

He was a one-boy army, dodging shrapnel and trying to win the war. Now the battleground had changed and he was lost.

He checked his phone again. 10.30pm.

A gust of wind rattled around the eaves, and somewhere outside a gate banged against a post. He went through to the kitchen and checked the door again. The heavy latch was strong and secure. He filled a glass with water, staring at the darkness beyond. Shapes moved in the oak tree.

A single caw split the night in two. The birds were here and Jackdaw didn't know if that was a good sign or not.

Sleep. He desperately needed sleep.

He climbed the stairs, his feet heavy on the wooden treads, avoiding the rope slung through the iron rings.

Night flooded through his window, a single shaft of moonlight arrowed across his bed. He sat the glass on his nightstand and flicked on the lamp, ready to curl under the covers, his eyelids already drooping.

He was too exhausted to notice that emerging from a crack on the beam above his bed was a tiny red-capped mushroom.

CHAPTER FORTY-TWO

'Are you listening, Oscar?'

Elspeth's words cut into Oscar's thoughts as they drove away from the cottage. Jackdaw's last comment hung heavy in his mind. It was all too bizarre. In fact, most things that had happened since he'd arrived back here had been… his mouth twisted to one side as a word punched through. *Unnatural.*

'Oscar!'

'Oh, sorry.' He shook his head and shifted in his seat to look at his aunt. She had that expression on her face he remembered from when he was a kid. The look that said she disapproved of the fact he wasn't giving her his full attention.

'I was asking if Jackdaw had told you anything…' She paused as she slowed down to pass a cyclist. 'Out of the ordinary.'

Oscar gritted his teeth before words flowed from his mouth. There were plenty of weird things Jackdaw had said, but something made him swallow them unvoiced. The more time he spent with this vulnerable boy, the more Oscar realised that he wasn't making any of this up.

Unless Jackdaw was having some kind of psychotic episode, which would totally be valid given everything he'd gone through. And why did his aunt even care anyway?

It made zero sense.

Some part of him couldn't wait for this week to be over so he could go home and forget he'd ever been here.

The pointed glare from the driver's side told him he hadn't answered her question.

'Nothing, really,' he said, trying to sound nonchalant. 'We just ate pizza and hung out.'

He wanted to ask why she had pushed them together, when only last night she had warned him off from getting too close because of Jackdaw's "misfortune."

'I need you to help with arranging things in the village hall so we can get an early start in the morning.'

Oscar suppressed a groan. He'd learned that it was better to do what she asked than argue. That always ended badly. No one argued with her, not even his father, who wasn't the most patient man on earth.

Now that she'd made her demand, the conversation lulled. Oscar stared through the windscreen, watching the dark mass of trees and hedges blur past. The lights from the village became stronger and he turned in his seat to look out of the back window—the single porch light on the cottage blinked on and off as the road dipped and climbed until, at last, it faded from view.

Elspeth pulled into a prime spot right outside the village hall. It was empty despite cars being parked all along the street. It had been left for her.

The village hall was a low, rectangular building with the entrance at one end. It had double doors leading to a small, square foyer where the toilets were, then another set into the hall itself.

They pushed into a bustle of people, some stacking cans and bottles into boxes. Others were busy labelling plastic trays containing cakes and scones or carrying taped-up cartons from the storage room on the left hand side of the hall.

'Go and check on the avifauna,' Elspeth told him, her mouth turned down, as laughter rang out from the back of the stage. 'There are newcomers here this year, and I don't want any disrespect.'

Oscar scooted off quickly.

A few people raised their hands in greeting or smiled at him, and he went through the motions of being civil.

He edged through a narrow door that led him to the side of the stage, leaping up four steps to the room that was hidden behind.

'What the hell...' A voice from beyond a thin curtain at the far side of the room. 'Would you look at this thing?'

Oscar passed a woman with a black marker pen in her hand and a small child with a half-eaten lollipop clutched between sticky fingers.

'Mine,' the child said, ramming the lollipop into a mouth that had only just learned words but had already mastered the art of ownership.

Oscar pushed aside the curtain to find two men, heads bowed, scrolling their phones. They glanced at him without interest.

Suspended from the ceiling was the great bird, the avifauna. The one they lit on Gala Night to guide a spirit away from the village. It was over two metres in height, a giant construction of willow framing and stretched paper.

A bird's skull lay at its throat like a macabre necklace, the hollow eye as black as pitch. Small bones nestled against its skeleton. Wings hung motionless at its side, but tomorrow, when a lantern lit it from within, they would be raised to the night sky, raised to the darkness.

One of the men poked the bird with his finger. It swung on its hook, the paper rustling like dry leaves along a woodland path. The bones clacked together in defiance.

'Don't do that.' Oscar found his voice, and behind it, an anger rose for their scorn. They didn't understand. You had to be born in Combe Hurst to understand. 'You shouldn't be back here.'

The taller of the two men looked like he was going to argue until a loud wail pierced the standoff. Oscar wheeled to see the kid with his face turning red, little fists clenched at his side.

The lollipop lay stuck to the dusty, wooden floor.

Chaos erupted as the woman tried to comfort the boy, his fury the kind only a two-year-old can produce. The men sidled away, but not before giving Oscar the dirtiest of looks.

He watched as the woman guided the child through the door, as its wails decreased to a sob.

Behind him, the avifauna still swung like a piece of meat on a hook. The edge of a wing brushed against his shoulder and he turned slowly, raising his head to look into its face. The formed, strong beak tapered to a wicked point.

A crow's beak.

And the hollow, lightless eyes perfectly mimicked the skull hung at its throat.

A chill shivered through him, insectile feelers across his skin. He had the strangest impression the bird was sentient, that although it didn't have any eyes, it was watching him.

Which had to be the most fucked-up thought of his life.

He took a step back and saw the avifauna through the eyes of a stranger. How Jackdaw would see it.

CHAPTER FORTY-THREE

It was the stench that woke him. A rich, damp rot that spoke of autumn and death.

Jackdaw rubbed his eyes and raised himself up onto one elbow. He reached across and flicked on the light.

Or tried to. The rocker switch clicked but nothing happened.

Just great. A blown bulb. A confused irritation gnawed at the edge of his grogginess. Now he was awake, he really needed the bathroom. His feet hit the wooden floor and shockwaves vibrated up his legs. The bare boards were freezing. He padded across to the door, his arms around himself, teeth chattering, his brain trying to come up with some reasoning as to why it was so cold.

He paused at the top of the stairs and stared down into the inky blackness below. He eased down two steps, the stench becoming stronger as he descended. Itchiness clawed at his throat and he coughed, the sound rolling into the deep gloom.

Something gritty lay on his tongue. He swept his fingers over it, felt that same grittiness on his fingertips, the smell curling into his nostrils.

Earth. The scent of freshly turned earth after a rainstorm.

His heart beat a rapid staccato behind his rib cage.

Something brushed against his thigh and he swerved away.

The sound of metal clunking against the painted walls.

He needed light.

The desperate urge quicksilvered through his veins and he half-ran, half-stumbled down the rest of the stairs, his fingers blindly searching for the light switch at the bottom.

A sob of relief as his fingers found the old toggle and flicked it. Nothing.

He repeated the action, the click ringing out sharp and lonely, the sound like a stricken morse code in the absolute black. Jackdaw couldn't see anything, not even the shape of furniture, and a helpless fear trip-hammered through him.

What if I've gone blind?

It was a logic borne from the fact that his eyesight had sharpened over the past few days. What if that had been taken away?

He stood in the dark, his arms outstretched, and forced his feet towards the kitchen. The stove would be lit. It was always lit. The kitchen would be warm. He could get a glass of water and rinse out his mouth and everything would be okay…

His fingers combed over the kitchen door. Had he shut it? He didn't remember. But the latch was on the left. He knew that. He'd caught the sleeve of his jacket on it too many times.

Except the latch was now on the right.

He dug his fingers into his hair, pulling on the roots, hanging on to the sting as he spiralled. The door creaked open and his breath hung in his throat.

A low glow came from the stove, and he wanted to bow down in front of it. Yet it didn't seem quite right. The stove was too wide, stretching along most of the wall adjacent to the window.

Earth on his tongue again. Revulsion wrinkled his nose as he spat on the floor.

The window, the window.

He crept towards it, saw the thin, pink glimmer of light on the horizon as dawn washed over the land. His fingers curled around the sink edge, finding wood, not porcelain. The single tap was set into the wall. A drip of water fell against his wrist. Ice cold.

A tremor ran through him as his chest heaved.

He jumped back as a chaos of sound came from outside.

The barn door creaking open. Raised voices. The rhythmic clatter of a horse's hooves on hard ground.

The barn was locked. He'd done it himself and checked twice.

His hand flew to his mouth, and he bit down on his knuckle until the metallic tang of blood coated his tongue.

Wooden wheels moving, a rattle he'd heard before more than once. It was impossible.

They'd come for the cart yesterday, but yet here it was, being harnessed to a thickset horse by someone Jackdaw had never seen before. He wore shapeless trousers stuffed into boots and a waistcoat over a pale shirt.

This can't be happening. Jackdaw rubbed his eyes again, both grateful for the gift of sight but still rigid with shock of what was unfolding.

'What about Lonan?' The boy harnessing the horse addressed someone Jackdaw couldn't see.

The barn door jarred on the ground as it was closed.

A man's voice.

'Leave him. He cannot see this. He needs to sleep.'

A surge of energy spun through Jackdaw as though someone had electrified his veins. He ran for the door and tried to slide the bolts back, but they refused to budge. He pulled on the handle, then beat his fists against the wood, desperate to stumble out into the yard to… what? To see if this was real?

The voices continued.

'I do not like this.'

'It is a sorry state. We will feel God's wrath, believe me. But Parnell will not hear of a pardon. He says the boy is guilty, and this will send a message to all of his kind.'

Parnell. Parnell.

Jackdaw had seen that name before… in the churchyard.

He slumped to the floor and folded his arms around his knees, his fractured mind spinning into a bottomless void.

He was either going steadily crazy or he was seeing events from the past.

Lonan.

The boy who had written the journal.

The boy who had lived here.

It defied logic—but if he didn't unravel this bewildering, fragmented puzzle, it would haunt him for the rest of his life.

Yet the thought terrified him.

He needs to sleep…

The words fell again, hot and heavy, and Jackdaw shot to his feet, skidding across the kitchen floor and mounting the stairs two at a time. He stumbled into his bedroom, sure that he'd see another boy sleeping—but the bed was empty. He went across and lifted the scrunched-up pillow, still damp from his sweat.

The stench that had woken him had dissipated into nothing,

its job done.

A sharp cry fell from his lips as a tumble of black feathers fluttered to the floor at his feet. They'd been under his pillow.

He staggered back until his spine hit the unforgiving wall, his fist pressed to his lips, his heart pounding fit to burst. His shoulder caught the edge of the mirror. Instinctively, his hand shot out to steady it.

A face gazed back at him, pale and fevered and haunted.

But it wasn't his own.

CHAPTER FORTY-FOUR

Jackdaw spun back from the reflection in the tarnished mirror. He looked again and saw only his own face, mouth open in terror, his bright-blue eyes wide, pupils enlarged with fear.

For a moment he'd seen another boy, one with blond hair and anguished eyes. For a moment Jackdaw had felt that anguish seeping into his own bones, the torment reshaping the core of who he was.

He forced himself away from the mirror and scrambled over the bed, hands grasping for the window latch. Chilled night air rushed over his clammy skin and he sucked in great mouthfuls, willing his pounding heart to settle.

He wasn't sure what was reality and what was delusion.

What he'd seen and heard outside didn't feel like the latter— it felt like truth.

A creaking in the oak tree as four crows settled. He could see them all despite the blackness of the night, lined up on the bare branches, watching.

Desperation chewed through him with steel fangs as he raked his hands through his hair.

'What do you want from me?' He screamed the words into the night, and a barrage of caws answered. He'd always prided himself on being able to mimic birds, but what good was that when he didn't understand their language?

On the hill beyond, the moon slipped out from behind a bank of wispy cloud. It hung above the stark silhouette of the gibbet, a silver coin ripe for the plucking.

The cart I heard outside. It's going to the gibbet.

The thought was a sucker punch to his stomach and he doubled over, fingers clawing at the wide windowsill.

Jackdaw flopped heavily onto the bed, his mind frantically trying to dredge up all the details he had heard.

Lonan.

The name ripped through him.

He turned and stared at the mirror.

Is that who I saw?

It made zero sense, but yet it made all the sense in the world. He remembered what he'd read about Martinmas, about the time when spirits wander. Another memory itched at the back of his mind. He closed his eyes and willed it to surface.

He was seven years old, climbing the stairs with a mug of tea in his hand, tongue poking out of the side of his mouth in concentration.

'Mum,' he whispered at the door.

It was closed. It was always closed.

He called again and wondered if she was sleeping on the battered sofa. He wondered if she'd died there amongst all of her notes and strings and desperation.

Putting the mug on the floor, he twisted the round doorknob and peeked inside. The curtains were half-drawn and a wan light speared through the gap, arrowing across the worn carpet.

His mother was curled up on the sofa, tangled greying hair fanning over her brow, her perpetually frowning face softened in sleep.

He retrieved the mug and placed it on the desk amongst a pile of open notebooks with scribbled findings.

MARTINMAS.

The word was scrawled across a page, and he remembered his childish brain trying to work out who Martin Mas was and why he was so important.

There were more words underneath, some separated by blank lines, but the handwriting was indecipherable.

'Spirits wander when trauma still ties them to this world.'

Jackdaw spun around, eyes wide. His elbow caught the mug of tea, sending hot liquid slopping across the desk, soaking the notebooks.

Panic seized him and he tried to mop up the spillage with his jumper, but he only succeeded in spreading the mess further.

'Get out,' his mother said, through clenched teeth. 'You were never meant to be here.'

Back then, he always thought that she meant there in her room, but now... now he wasn't so sure.

What if she meant here in Combe Hurst?

What if she meant something else?

It was just another layer of confusion to add to the thick mud clogging his mind. If this was a book, he would discover the missing thread tying all these things together and would come out triumphant. Unless it was a horror story. A grimace settled on his lips.

A feather drifted across the floor, caught on a draught from some gap in a wall or floorboard. He bent down to pick it up, running his fingers along its edges, smoothing the vane back and forth.

A howl split the silence, the sound rolling through the dark from the forest. The branches of the oak shivered as the crows took flight, a mad frenzy of beating wings and hoarse cries. They soared into the sky as one, wheeling and diving as if connected by a single mind. Jackdaw watched the corvid murmuration, a black undulating shadow against the moon, the dance unshackled from any rules, driven by something wild and fierce.

Some part of him knew that crows didn't do this and certainly not in the middle of the night, but another part understood its significance, and he was both terrified and awestruck.

The howl came again, this time closer, and the birds dissolved into the night as though they'd been dismissed.

The gate creaked and banged back against its post.

The kitchen door opened, the bolts sliding back with a clatter.

Jackdaw stopped breathing.

He was going to die.

The scent of fresh-turned earth and moss and organic decay drifted under his bedroom door.

He pressed himself against the wall, the chill from the plaster leaching into his spine, the feather still clutched in his hand. His held breath escaped his lungs in a ragged sob.

The overwhelming sense that he wasn't alone crawled over his skin. His eyes raked the shadows in the room, heavy in the corners, distorted by the moon glow through the oak.

'Lonan?'

The name was a gasp through trembling lips.

An intense chill grazed across his cheek, spreading to his jaw, travelling to his lips. His mouth prised open.

A cold tongue slid across his chin, moving oh-so-slowly towards his throat. It halted at his racing pulse, at the warm life within his flesh. He squeezed his eyes shut.

If he died tonight Oscar would be the one who found him. Their deepening affinity would be severed, and the memory would haunt Oscar for the rest of his life.

'All I ever wanted was a friend,' Jackdaw whispered, as blackness took his sight.

CHAPTER FORTY-FIVE

The tennis ball bounced off the wall again and again. Oscar had thrown all his focus behind the repeated action, his jaw clenched. Something was off, and Elspeth was acting oddly. All the time he had known her, he had never seen her so preoccupied. He'd even left his towel on the bathroom floor, and she'd just picked it up. He sighed as he caught the ball with his right hand.

'Oscar!' His name from the bottom of the steps. 'Are you doing this to deliberately annoy me?'

'Sorry,' he yelled back, bouncing the ball one last time. He was definitely doing it to annoy her.

He checked his phone. 9.20am. His message to Jackdaw an hour earlier had gone unread.

He's sleeping, he reasoned. *Hell, I'd be sleeping if I wasn't here.*

But something niggled against him, like a small stone in a shoe.

'I'm going out to check people know where they're supposed to be.' Elspeth's head appeared around his door and Oscar's heart leapt. He hadn't heard her on the stairs. 'When I get back, I'll need you to load the car for today.'

Oscar glanced outside. It was bright and clear with a hint of wispy cloud.

Gala Day.

'Have you spoken to Jackdaw?' Elspeth paused, her hand on the door jamb. 'Make sure he comes with you today.'

'Why do you care about him so much all of a sudden?'

The words raced from Oscar's throat and they carried more than a hint of defiance.

Elspeth's brows shot up. Her tongue ran over her upper teeth.

'I'm just being welcoming,' she said. 'Since he lives here now, he needs to know about our traditions.'

She went downstairs, and Oscar waited until he heard the front door slam. He pulled on a thick sweatshirt and stuffed his feet into a pair of old trainers, galloping down the stairs as an idea loomed. His common sense warred with a growing unease.

She will ground me forever if she finds out.

I can be there and back in twenty minutes. She'll be longer than that. Last minute over-checking is totally her thing.

Oscar made his decision, grabbed a jacket and a scarf, and bolted out of the back door.

In his hand were Elspeth's car keys.

He crawled along the back lanes leading to the cottage, his heart in his mouth every time another car came towards him. The gearbox crunched as he changed into second for the steep incline. He didn't even have his provisional licence, and his only experience was driving around a supermarket car park in a friend's car with acres of space around him, which was nothing like this. His fingers were white-knuckled on the steering wheel, his stomach aching with stress.

This was so not a good idea.

As he turned onto the track that led past the barn, sheer relief made his hands tremble. He drove through the open gate, his gaze already skimming over the cottage.

He jumped out of the car and ran across to the cottage door, banging on it with his fist. There was no answer. He scooped a handful of gravel from the drive and peppered Jackdaw's open window, chewing the edge of his lip.

Sunlight winked from the glass and then faded.

The sky darkened and Oscar looked over his shoulder.

The earlier wispy cloud had morphed into sullen steel-grey, lying heavy along the horizon on the opposite hill. From here, he could see the stark outline of the gibbet that would play a starring role in tonight's festivities.

Festivities.

The word felt wrong, like a square shape being forced into a round hole, its edges sheared away, masking what it really was.

Already he could see the pale, ghostly shapes of half-erected marquees. A rhythmic thumping sounded over the fields, posts being set into the ground. In a few hours, the hill would be teeming with people.

He glanced towards the forest and narrowed his eyes.

Soon the children would be gathering wood for the beacon. He remembered doing that same thing, thrilled that this was a holiday from school and somehow aware of the importance of the task.

He pulled his phone from his pocket and rang Jackdaw's number. After a few seconds a ring tone sounded in the cottage.

He pounded on the door again.

'Jackdaw! Get yourself out of bed!'

The longer he stood there, the more panic rippled in his throat. Jackdaw had been scared yesterday when Oscar left. He should have stayed.

He looked up at the window and huffed out a breath. A row of crows sat on the gutter edge, their eyes following his every move. He felt like he was a specimen under a microscope, that somehow the knowledge in those glistening eyes was so terrible that a human mind couldn't grasp it without losing its grip on reality. He gave himself a mental slap-down.

His hand closed over the doorknob. The metal was ice-cold in his grip and he gasped. But the door opened to him—and now he was truly afraid. If Jackdaw hadn't locked the door—and he had bolted it yesterday—anyone, or *anything,* could have got in…

Oscar sprinted across the kitchen, grabbing a carving knife from the knife block as he passed. He thundered up the stairs, hoping to scare anyone that might still be inside, even though that thought made his heart skitter in his chest.

Jackdaw's bedroom door was shut.

Oscar clicked the latch and put his shoulder against it. It swung back and hit the wall with a loud crash.

And then he stopped dead in his tracks.

Jackdaw was lying on the floor on his side, his face paler than milk. The room was freezing, the kind of cold that burned your skin. Condensation coated the walls, and Oscar could feel it dampening his hair. An earthy, rotting smell clung to the room, like something had been buried and then dug up.

A quivering exhale left his lips—the beam above Jackdaw's bed was covered in tiny, red-capped mushrooms…

A high-pitched whining sounded in Oscar's ears, but his brain somehow found the connection to his nervous system, forcing his feet forward.

He sank to his knees at the prone boy's side, trembling fingers reaching out to Jackdaw's neck.

Please, please, don't let him be dead.

Oscar didn't believe in a higher power, but right now he was willing to believe in anything just to find a pulse.

CHAPTER FORTY-SIX

Jackdaw's eyes opened. His eyelids felt like they'd been dipped in concrete and the lining of his throat hurt like hell. He tried to swallow and winced. Hazy images flashed through his mind, the stuff of nightmares, and for a moment, he wondered if this was just another page in a dream because Oscar was looking down on him, his green eyes heavy with concern.

'What...?' Jackdaw squeaked out a word. His brow creased as he tried to unjumble why he was lying on the floor and why Oscar was here.

'Did you fall?' Oscar's cool hand slipped behind Jackdaw's neck, his other clutching Jackdaw's forearm. 'Because this floor doesn't look like it would be the best place to sleep.'

Jackdaw allowed himself to be hauled into a sitting position. The room began to spin and he grabbed hold of Oscar's hand. Nausea flooded his throat.

'Going to throw up—'

He had two seconds to turn onto his side before the bitter gorge erupted from his mouth, spattering the floorboards. He closed his eyes and groaned, heaving another surge of watery vomit. It pooled across the boards, seeping down through the cracks.

'Sorry,' he muttered. This was vulnerability. And the last thing he wanted was Oscar's pity. His recollection of the night before seemed like it was stirred into a sea of mud, and he was dimly aware of Oscar's steps echoing across to the door, then thundering down the stairs.

Don't leave me.

The thought speared through him, hot and sharp and desperate. But what did he expect?

His stomach cramped, sour bile coating his tongue. He wiped the back of his hand across his mouth. His skin was clammy, but now, as awareness seeped back into his consciousness, he realised that he was freezing.

A loud bang jump-started his fight-or-flight instinct and his head snapped up. Daylight flooded through the window— the *open* window. It swung slightly in a breeze, the old wood creaking as it was forced to move.

Did I open it? He bit the edge of his lip, using the bottom of his bed to haul himself semi-upright.

Birds. They'd been in the tree last night. Birds watching him.

'Here, let's get you cleaned up.'

A hand on his shoulder, a warm, damp towel pressed against his face. *You came back.* The small act of caring formed a lump in Jackdaw's aching throat. He buried his face in the towel, wiping away the strings of vomit from his chin.

'What the fuck did you eat?' Oscar said.

Jackdaw lowered the towel. 'I don't remember eating anything after you left,' he croaked.

'Well, you must have done, because I had the same as you and I'm fine.' Oscar flopped down on the bed, the old box-mattress springs complaining.

A flash of another night and another weight. But the springs had been silent then… Jackdaw shivered.

'I hate to break it to you, but whatever you ate was definitely red. And there were no carrots.' Oscar's words held a note of humour. It vanished in his next sentence. 'Jesus, Jackdaw, you scared me, lying on the floor like that.'

'Sorry,' Jackdaw mumbled again.

His hand trembled as he clutched the towel.

'Feathers,' he said, turning to Oscar. 'There were black feathers under my pillow.'

Oscar's brow hiked. 'Under your pillow?' He reached across and lifted it. A single white feather floated in the air. 'There's nothing black here, Jackdaw. Did you dream it?'

Something indefinable crossed Oscar's face, something that made Jackdaw's heart ram against his rib cage.

He wanted to tell Oscar about the mirror and the cart, about Lonan, about hearing a conversation in the yard that happened centuries ago. That something unearthly had come into his room and touched him. But that would make Oscar flee for good, and Jackdaw wouldn't have blamed him.

I'm delusional, he thought. *And if I'm not, I have to face whatever this is alone.*

'Could you get me a glass of water?' he asked. 'All I can taste is puke.'

'On it.' Oscar graced him with an off-balance grin, his eyes crinkling at the corners. He scooted across the floor then pulled himself back, hands clutching the top of the door frame. 'You do realise that you left the door unlocked last night, don't you?' The grin faded for a moment. 'Not that there's likely to be anyone wandering about here in the dark.'

Jackdaw waited until Oscar's feet hit the bottom of the stairs, until the tap started running in the kitchen sink.

He unclenched his right hand which had remained tightly shut. Crushed into his palm was the unmistakable form of a red-capped mushroom.

The red flecks in the cold vomit on the floor.

Oscar let the tap run into the sink, his scattered thoughts buzzing around his head like a swarm of wasps.

The stench in the room even though the window was open.

It's from the fields, he reasoned. *Farmers spreading liquid manure.*

The wrong time of year, another voice whispered.

The freezing temperature.

From the window. It's November.

The black feathers Jackdaw had mentioned.

He couldn't find a reason for those, apart from the crows on the gutter.

Jackdaw had left the door unbolted, and Oscar had palmed him off with a comment meant to reassure… but it was Martinmas, and everyone in the village locked their doors at Martinmas.

Something was truly out of kilter and Oscar couldn't work out what it could be.

Another worry surfaced. It poked him. Hard.

Elspeth was probably back now.

An inward groan as his gaze settled on the car outside, weak sunlight glinting from the windscreen. He was so dead.

His fingers began to numb from the cold water running over them. He shook his head and refocussed his thoughts.

Get Jackdaw cleaned up.

Get them both to Gala Day.

Survive Elspeth's wrath.

HAVE SOME FREAKING FUN!

Today he'd have a heart-to-heart with Jackdaw, find out how he could help him.

You know you'll be leaving in a few days, don't you? An inner voice delivered a harsh and unwelcome truth.

Oscar mulled it over as he took the glass of water back upstairs. Jackdaw was sitting on the bed, his knees pulled up to his chest, his face buried, his jet-black hair a stark contrast against his pale arms.

Despair radiated from him in waves.

A crawling shiver passed over Oscar's skin, something so visceral that he felt it run across his chest and trip down his spine, curling around his limbs.

A lone bird cawed in a nearby tree.

He padded across the room and leaned his weight against Jackdaw's shoulder, pressing the glass into his hands.

The gesture said *drink.*

But beneath, it also said *I'm here.*

CHAPTER FORTY-SEVEN

'Eat.'

Oscar put a plate of scrambled eggs on the kitchen table as Jackdaw came through from the shower, towelling his wet hair. The hot water had been almost painful on his skin, but at least he felt vaguely human now.

How could I have been so stupid as to eat that mushroom? He flayed himself with his own foolishness. Hell, he knew how toxic they were. How they could cause breathing difficulties and nausea. Inwardly, he grimaced. Yeah, that was a definite. Ten out of ten for being decidedly not cool.

'I'm not hungry...' His stomach cramped at the sight of the congealed eggs.

Oscar steered him across by his shoulders, pulling a chair out by hooking a foot around a rung. He pressed him into the seat and stuck a fork into his hand.

'The first few mouthfuls are the worst. Once you've swallowed those, you'll be fine,' Oscar said. 'It's going to be a long day. I don't want you keeling over on me.'

The toaster popped, and Oscar flung out an arm and caught the slice as it was ejected forcefully. 'See? I remembered that your toaster is bad-tempered. I'm like an honorary houseguest.'

As Oscar set to slathering an insane amount of butter onto the toast, Jackdaw watched him through a curtain of damp hair. Oscar was just so capable, and he always knew what to say to make everything feel better.

Exactly what Jackdaw couldn't do.

Oscar slung the toast onto a side plate and deposited it in front of the eggs. Jackdaw gazed at the oozing butter and his stomach spasmed.

'Too much?' Oscar said, his mouth twisting to one side. 'Just eat the eggs then.'

He grabbed the toast and bit into it, the melted butter running over his fingers. 'Are you sure you don't want this? It's seriously good.'

Jackdaw forked a little egg and brought it to his lips. He sniffed it, well aware that Oscar was watching every move.

'I swear to God, Jackdaw, if you don't eat some of this I will feed it to you like you're a toddler.'

A laugh burst from Jackdaw's lips at the imagery, and Oscar swept his hand through his hair as though he was doffing a cap. It was such an old-fashioned gesture, and Jackdaw's expression must have said that.

'Hey, my mother is a history professor. I know the most random junk. And I was brought up here. We practically had lessons in all that ancient stuff.' Oscar licked a run of butter from his wrist then quietened, retreating into his own thoughts for a moment.

Jackdaw nibbled at a shred of egg and then swallowed. His stomach didn't rebel so he tried a little more, tentatively chewing just in case.

Oscar studied him. 'See?' The grin was all triumph edged

in relief.

A shard of guilt poked Jackdaw in a tender place. He didn't want to be a burden to Oscar.

'You always seem to be rescuing me,' he said, looking down at his plate and stirring a circle through the eggs. 'I'm really grateful.' He glanced up for a moment to find Oscar with his chin propped up on his hand, his head tilted to one side.

'You don't have to be grateful, Jackdaw,' Oscar said, his voice soft. 'I'm your friend. That's what friends do. They look out for each other.' A moment of silence passed between them before Oscar rolled his eyes and grimaced. 'Believe me, it's going to be your turn soon because I borrowed my aunt's car to get here… and I don't even have a licence.'

Jackdaw felt his jaw slacken, and he almost spat out what he was chewing. His eyes widened. 'You did what?' He didn't think he'd ever broken a rule, unless flying under the radar most of his life was an offence.

'I was worried about you,' Oscar said, tracing a line of toast crumbs on the table with his forefinger. 'What you said before I left yesterday… you seemed scared.' His voice trailed off as he turned to meet Jackdaw's gaze.

Jackdaw had to rummage around in his memory of yesterday to find out what he'd said. And then he remembered. He'd told Oscar about his eyesight, that he didn't need the contacts. He didn't even know how he was supposed to explain that. His cheeks flushed.

'So, you can see fine now, for real?' Oscar came to his rescue. 'Maybe you just outgrew the need for your contacts? I mean, it's not unheard of for your eyesight to change.'

'Maybe,' Jackdaw said with a shrug. 'But I can see really, really well now, like my sight has been supercharged.'

Oscar reached across to the fruit bowl and snagged an apple. He bit into it, the crunch loud in the small kitchen. Jackdaw watched him, although he was very close to burying his head in his hands. *Supercharged?* He swallowed a groan.

'There's probably lots of reasons an optician could give,' Oscar said, wiping a line of apple juice from his chin. 'But why worry? You can see now, so that's all that matters. Just roll with it.' He made a fist and punched Jackdaw's shoulder gently.

A wave of warm intensity surged through Jackdaw. Maybe it was relief. Or maybe it was just the joy of finding someone who accepted him for exactly who he was, with all of his quirks and awkwardness.

A ringtone interrupted his introspection.

Oscar pulled his phone out of his pocket and winced. He angled it towards Jackdaw. Elspeth's name lit up the screen. They both watched until it cut off, the *missed call* symbol appearing at the top of the phone.

'That would be the call to say that I'm grounded for life,' Oscar said. He bit the edge of his thumbnail. 'Should we run away together now?'

It was a flippant comment but Jackdaw's heart leapt. He would do that in an instant.

'Okay.' Oscar tossed the apple core towards the kitchen bin. It hit the flip-top lid and disappeared. 'Go grab some warm clothes, and I'll turn the car around. I've never reversed before, but how hard can it be?' One corner of his mouth curled in a wry smile.

Jackdaw stood and slid his plate onto the kitchen worktop. Clearing up could wait. He was going to spend the day with Oscar. His steps lightened as he padded through to the stairs, taking them two at a time. His jacket was slung over the bottom of the bed and he had to sidestep the towel covering the mess he'd thrown up. His nose wrinkled.

The mushroom sat discarded on his nightstand.

Now he was level with the mirror, and if he turned his head… *no, no, don't look.* A thought burned through him then, digging its way into the soil of his mind. What if he'd only imagined he'd seen Lonan in the mirror? If he'd already eaten some of the mushroom, he could have been hallucinating.

That was pure logic.

But still he didn't turn to look at his reflection.

The sound of a car engine coughing to life came from outside. Jackdaw scrambled across his bed and looked out of the window. The gearbox squealed as Oscar tried to put it into reverse, the noise making Jackdaw's teeth ache. After a few botched attempts Oscar finally succeeded, and the car slowly moved backwards towards the barn. The yard there was large enough for him to be able to turn around to face the lane.

A smile broke on Jackdaw's lips, and the gesture made him sigh. Then something caught his eye in the sky above. A whirl of dark shapes rising and falling against the clouds. He narrowed his gaze and found two crows locked in battle, wings flapping furiously, claws extended. Loose feathers fluttered down, dancing in the breeze.

More swooped in from the left, joining in the fray, taking turns to attack.

Were they defending their territory? Crows did this if an outsider tried to intrude. Or maybe it was a young crow trying to nudge itself up the hierarchy?

The screeching became louder, more insistent, and Jackdaw glanced down to see Oscar staring up through the windscreen.

Another assault, and now Jackdaw couldn't decipher which bird was which, because it was all a manic circle of feathers and wings and savagery.

An avian scream tore through the air and Jackdaw flinched. He watched in horror as one bird fell like a stone, hitting the windscreen with a sickening thud. Jackdaw was immediately flung back into the lunchroom—on the day the bird had hit the window. The day his mother died.

His throat closed and he grabbed the windowsill for stability, his gaze fixated on the car—on the long, red smear painting the windscreen. The bird slid down until it was resting on the wiper blades, one wing hanging at an obscene angle. Then the engine roared into life, a harsh metallic disharmony clunking from the gearbox, and the car shot backwards so fast that Jackdaw didn't have time to react, he could only watch in horror.

The car crashed into the barn doors. They buckled under the impact. Wood exploded, sending splinters high into the air, then a wheezing rush as steam poured from the gaps around the bonnet as the radiator gave way.

Jackdaw waited, his limbs jellified.

He waited for Oscar to climb out.

But he didn't.

Oscar stayed slumped over the steering wheel, motionless.

CHAPTER FORTY-EIGHT

Jackdaw flew down the stairs as if all the hounds of hell were on his heels. His foot slipped on the last step, sending him sprawling against the wall, the metal rings that held the rope banister clanging against the plaster. A sharp pain exploded through his shoulder girdle, but he was off running again before it had truly registered.

Please let him be okay. Cold fear sank its talons into his flesh.

As he hoicked open the cottage door his vision tunnelled, and all he could see was the twisted wreckage of the car. A slat from the barn door hung askew, the tip of it scraping across the car roof in the breeze. The noise it made grated against his bones.

Oscar hadn't moved, and Jackdaw realised with a bolt of panic that he hadn't worn his seatbelt—because he'd only intended turning the car around.

A loud cheer echoed over the field and Jackdaw wheeled, his eyes searching for the source. Out on the hill, by the gibbet, a large, pale shape had taken root. A marquee for the festivities. Tiny people scuttled around it, some banging posts into the ground to hold the guy ropes secure.

Ropes.

A shiver ran through him as his mind spiralled for a moment, before he hauled his focus back to what was important. He ran across the yard to the car and grabbed hold of the door handle, yanking it, but it wouldn't budge. The whole back end was shunted, a mass of twisted metal and wooden splinters, the car itself embedded into what was left of the doors.

He banged on the window with his fist, hoping against hope that Oscar would move. Through the glass, Jackdaw could see the distorted shape of the dead crow, gore streaked across the crazed windscreen.

One summer–blue eye stared lifelessly back at him.

The dead bird wasn't a crow intruder—it was a young jackdaw.

His knees gave way and he sank into a crouch, his heart thudding so hard he could barely draw a breath.

Focus, I have to focus…

He cupped his hands over his nose and mouth, forcing himself to inhale shakily, then exhale. It was a method he'd found on YouTube a few years ago when panic attacks were a constant in his life, the act slowly regulating his heart rate.

Gradually, his thoughts cleared.

He ran around to the passenger side and tried the door there. It was stuck fast.

Break the glass, break the glass…

He frantically searched the yard for loose bricks or broken flagstones, but everything was too small. He needed something with a sharp edge.

The barn, there'll be something in the barn.

He hadn't ventured in since the cart had been moved.

What if moving it had caused the shifts in his reality? Caused this accident? But he couldn't let his thoughts dwell there.

He stepped back a few paces then ran at the car, launching himself towards the roof. A moment where his hands slid across the metal, desperately searching for grip, and then his feet found purchase on the rubber at the base of the windows and he scrambled up.

He slid across, his feet extended, kicking away the debris. Slats of wood gave way under the impact, and it felt good to be doing something constructive when everything up to now had felt like he was being hauled along, in some kind of ocean current, powerless and terrified.

He used his heels to drag himself forwards, his hands raised to brush away shards of sharp wood, until he was far enough in to push himself off the car.

The dark interior of the barn licked around his limbs.

His feet landed with a thud that echoed around the rafters. A stench arose that he instantly recognised. Damp, rotted leaves and wet soil, but with something else, something musky. Sweat beaded on his brow, his tongue darting across his lips.

What he needed was on the opposite side of the barn. That was where all the old farming implements were hung. Jackdaw knew that they would still be sturdy enough to break glass.

But that would mean he would have to walk into the thick, inky shadows. The muted light from the opening he'd made didn't stretch very far, and his phone was in his jacket pocket in the cottage.

Just walk.

He straightened his spine and gritted his teeth. A dull ache pounded in his shoulder where he'd hit the wall. He hung onto the pulsing pain as he forced his feet forwards.

One step.

Two.

Three.

To his side was the forlorn space where the cart had stood. He turned his head for an instant. Somewhere in the barn, something rustled.

His foot came down on a soft mass half-buried under a pocket of straw. It splattered under his sole and his upper lip curled in disgust. The sickly sweet aroma of a rotted apple rose to greet him.

He remembered the maggot-ridden apple in the orchard on the day he'd found the stick figures hanging from the trees. Something told him that it was all connected, that everything that had happened were spokes on a giant wheel, forever turning until…

The barn wall loomed before him.

Now his eyes were accustomed to the gloom and he could pick out shapes hung from wooden brackets; a hay pitchfork, a rake, a broom, and then his gaze alighted on something that glinted—an axe.

He grabbed it from its perch, surprised at the weight as gravity swung it towards the ground. A stack of old sacks rested on an upturned barrel to his right. He took one and wrapped it around his hand, hefting the axe to his chest as he turned.

A creaking came from above his head, from the rafters.

He lifted his face and gasped.

Ophelia sat, her booted feet dangling, long, dark hair framing her pale face as she stared down at him. An instant where he wanted to cry out that this was too dangerous… and then the cold, hard realisation doused him in ice. It didn't matter, because nothing could hurt her anymore.

A frosted fist opened in his gut. 'Tell me what to do.' His voice was small and shrill in the vast space.

She opened her mouth and words formed, but he couldn't hear what she was saying. It was as if she was looking through a window, and he was on the other side.

'I can't hear you!' Frustration exploded through his veins.

The minutes were ticking by. Oscar needed him.

An instant where the shape of the little girl flickered in and out like a radio signal. Her hand came to her chest over her heart, and her lower lip trembled.

And then she was gone.

CHAPTER FORTY-NINE

Jackdaw's grip loosened on the axe as he stared at the place Ophelia had been only moments ago. He hadn't seen her for a few days, and he didn't know whether that was a good sign or not. What had she been trying to tell him?

But there wasn't time to wonder about that. He had to get Oscar out of the car.

Jackdaw sprinted towards the doors, clutching the axe to his chest. He leapt onto the car, using the rear bumper as leverage, and scrabbled down to the yard. A quick glance through the window showed Oscar still in the same position.

He hefted the axe up, both hands on the haft—he'd dropped the sack he meant to use to protect his fingers somewhere in the barn—and swung it from shoulder height. The blade hit the passenger window side-on, the glass crazing slightly. A jarring vibration travelled from his wrists to his shoulders and he flinched at the spark of pain.

He swung again, this time putting all his weight behind it. The edge of the blade hit dead centre, and the glass shattered, fragments flying into the car and the yard. He threw the axe on the ground and reached through the shattered window, his fingers searching for the door release.

A creaking groan from the hinge as it opened—Jackdaw flung himself onto the passenger seat, tiny pebbles of glass biting into his knees.

'Oscar?' He shook the other boy's shoulder.

If he doesn't wake up… the thought leeched the breath from his lungs and panic clawed at his throat. The dead jackdaw with its lifeless eye was an omen he couldn't ignore.

He brushed Oscar's curls away from his face. His brow was resting on the steering wheel, his hands limp at his side.

'Please wake up.'

The plea trembled on Jackdaw's lips. He clutched one of Oscar's hands, blinking back the hot well of tears.

A slight twitch of a finger in his palm. A groan followed by a mumbled word that made no sense at all.

Relief zinged through Jackdaw's veins, a surge of giddiness dissolving his fears. Oscar slowly raised his head, turned his face towards Jackdaw. There was a lump on his temple, and he'd bitten his lip when he hit the steering wheel, but he was breathing…

Jackdaw dropped his chin to his chest for a moment then lifted it again. 'Fuck. I thought—' He couldn't finish the sentence.

Oscar pressed his fingers gingerly against the pink swelling. He grimaced, then stared through the cracked windscreen at the dead bird. Recollection slackened his jaw, and he swore under his breath.

'The birds were fighting…' He shrugged, glanced down at the gearstick. 'I don't even think I was in reverse, so how did I end up like this?'

Before Jackdaw had a chance to chew over what he could say that would make a fragment of sense, Oscar groaned again.

'I am deader than dead this time. Not only did I borrow the car without permission, I've totalled it.' He hissed through his teeth, and Jackdaw wondered if it was because something hurt or because he was imagining what Elspeth would say to him.

'Do you think you can manoeuvre around and climb over this seat?' Jackdaw slid back until he was standing in the yard.

He'd seen too many movies where the car suddenly bursts into flames, and he wasn't taking any chances.

As Oscar contorted himself to get out, Jackdaw found his gaze settling on the dead bird again. The jackdaw had been an intruder and had been dealt with swiftly. A deep shiver rolled through him.

'Hey, are *you* okay? You've gone paler than even you normally are.'

Oscar stood in front of him, leaning against the car. There were blood spatters on his sweatshirt, and he'd raked his hair back from the lump on his temple. It altered his face shape, made him look older somehow.

'I… don't know,' Jackdaw blurted. How could he even begin to tell Oscar half of what had happened? That only minutes ago he'd been talking to a little dead girl in the barn?

Oscar's hand came to rest on his shoulder and Jackdaw leaned his cheek towards it. He slid his hand to the back of Jackdaw's neck and pulled him close for a moment. 'You've been through a lot,' he whispered. 'And we need to talk, okay? But I have to turn up for Gala Day, otherwise my aunt just might slip a noose around my neck and haul me onto that gibbet.'

A laugh followed, the breath ruffling Jackdaw's hair. It was a throwaway remark, meant to lessen the unspoken seriousness of what was suspended between them. Both of them had secrets they didn't know how to voice. Because how can you even explain the impossible?

Oscar didn't see the way Jackdaw screwed his eyes up tight or feel the paralysing fear that his words had birthed. When Jackdaw finally opened them, Oscar was staring off into the distance, towards the marquees and the stalls and the groups of children running from the forest with their arms full of sticks.

Heavy cloud brooded over the hill, sullen and silent, and the sun was just a flicker of brightness high in the west. Birds soared in the sky, crows and hawks and red kites—just specks to a human eye, but these were the avian watchers playing their part as they always had.

A cold wind knifed over the field, gathering fallen leaves into its clutches before spitting them out. It tore through the almost-bare branches of the oak, and the old tree groaned. This was its time to prepare for sleep. But yet it knew, as all things in this swathe of land knew, that there was a price to be paid for past sins.

And this year, that price was high.

CHAPTER FIFTY

They sat side by side in the cab of the old tractor as it rumbled down the lane, the noise from the diesel engine making communication impossible. Oscar had made a call to his aunt, asking for a lift from the cottage to Gala Day. He didn't mention the car, and she didn't either, and he guessed she was saving that wrath up for when the celebrations were all over. He'd suggested he and Jackdaw go over the field to the church and then climb the other hill to get there, but Jackdaw had firmly shaken his head and said he didn't want Oscar keeling over, which was a fair point. Oscar didn't think that would happen, but his head did ache a bit, and he'd already scared Jackdaw enough for a lifetime.

We're doing that to one another, he thought, as Jackdaw caught his eye and smiled. *Finding each other in situations where our hearts are in our mouths.*

Something niggled at the back of his mind but when he tried to grasp for it, it faded like the sun disappearing behind a bank of cloud.

Sam Marsden was wearing ear mufflers, and as the huge wheels rumbled over a gravel trackway, turning to climb the hill, Oscar understood why.

Jackdaw sat with his fingers intertwined, his pale face staring up the hill at the gibbet. Growing up here, Oscar just thought of it as part of the landscape—but to a newcomer, the stark sight of it and its history must be unnerving.

Especially considering where Jackdaw lived.

Oscar leant his shoulder against Jackdaw's, which was easy to do as the tractor lurched its way slowly towards the Gala Day festivities. It was a scrap of comfort for them both.

As they drew closer people stopped to stare, then darted their gazes away, as though they'd been caught in a sinful act. Jackdaw stiffened beside him and a surge of protectiveness flooded Oscar's veins.

The superstition in this village was insane. They might as well have been waving banners saying *Here comes the stranger. He brings evil and uncertainty.*

The tractor came to a shuddering halt. Oscar waved a hand in thanks to Sam and opened the door, jumping down onto the grass. Jackdaw followed, his gaze focussed on the gibbet rising behind them, its silhouette harsh against the cloud-drenched sky.

Rows of small marquees dotted the hill, some with bunting flapping in the breeze. People carried boxes from cars, hammered guy ropes into the ground to secure tents.

The rich scent of roasting meat floated in the air—in the centre, by the largest marquee, a man was basting a whole suckling pig over a fire, the metal rod slicing through the animal from mouth to rear.

Children ran past, some trailing small paper birds on a string. Their faces were flushed, and they didn't pay any attention to the pig or its fate.

I was like them. This was all just normal.

Jackdaw clung to his side like a shadow, his summer-blue eyes nervously flitting from side to side.

'And you thought this place was weird before?' Oscar laughed and nudged Jackdaw's shoulder. 'Don't worry, once people realise that you're not bringing a plague they'll focus on someone else.'

It was meant to be an offhand comment to ease the tension, but the shocked expression on Jackdaw's face told him that he'd taken it very much to heart.

'Come on, let's eat. I'm starving.'

Oscar grabbed hold of Jackdaw's sleeve and dragged him towards a canvas gazebo, where a woman with a round face and ruddy cheeks was stacking iced buns into a tray. 'Hi, Mrs. Higgens. Any broken ones going?'

The woman stopped what she was doing, a smile crinkling the corners of her eyes, her short white curls tousled by the breeze.

'Oscar! I heard you were back.' She pulled him towards her in a tight bear hug. 'What a sight for sore eyes you are. But it looks like you've been in the wars.'

'This is Jackdaw,' Oscar said, extracting himself from her embrace and side-stepping her scrutiny. 'He's with me.'

What could have been called a shadow passed over her eyes, but it was gone in an instant.

'Here, dig into this box. These were the ones that collapsed when I iced them.' She pointed to a plastic container behind the table.

Oscar walked over and flipped off the lid, taking a couple of buns. 'Thanks, Mrs. Higgens.'

He pressed one into Jackdaw's hands.

They were a few steps away before she called to him.

'Take care, Oscar. Remember your schooling.'

Jackdaw looked at him as they walked off, the bun still cradled in his hands.

He's holding it so tenderly. Like it's something that will disappear if he makes a wrong move.

'What did she mean?' Jackdaw asked.

They both stepped aside as two small girls swept past, holding little figures woven from willow.

'I've no idea,' Oscar said, stuffing half the bun in his mouth at once. He winced as it bypassed his swollen lip. *Remember my schooling?* He scratched his head with his bun-free hand.

Jackdaw's gaze followed the two girls. 'I've seen those figures before, in the woods.'

'Yeah, Twig makes them. He'll be here somewhere, you can't miss him. He lives in the forest at this time of year and looks a bit weird, but he's harmless,' Oscar said through a mouthful of bun.

'But why?' Jackdaw asked, looking up through a fall of hair. 'Why does he make them?'

Oscar had never really thought about the why. It was just something he'd grown up knowing. He considered the question, brushing the back of his fingers gingerly over his lips. Twig made the figures throughout the year and hung them from the trees. Then, on Gala Day, the kids were allowed to play with them. Only when the beacon was lit were the willow figures thrown into the fire.

A burst of laughter as the girls gathered with a group of others. They put the figures on the ground and joined hands, dancing around them in a circle.

Blackbird, blackbird, hear this song
Dead boys can't speak but you did no wrong.

It was a rhyme, a stupid playground rhyme. It punched its way into Oscar's memory—he'd sung this, too, only he'd been chasing other boys and tagging them. The one who'd been touched had to play dead until someone else took his place.

Jackdaw sagged beside him, the bun tumbling to the ground. His fingers were still splayed as though he was holding it.

Images flooded Oscar's mind, freeze-frame snapshots of his childhood here, of the customs he'd observed, of the way the gibbet had been part of every day of his life.

He glanced towards it. Two crows sat on top of its crossbeam, their heads tilted, watching.

'Oscar!'

His name rang out, and he wheeled to find his aunt standing in the doorway of the large marquee, her arms folded, her lips set into a thin line.

'Here we go,' he whispered to Jackdaw. 'Don't go far. I'll come and find you soon, yes?' He looked back over his shoulder as the light began to fade.

'Jackdaw, don't go into the forest.'

CHAPTER FIFTY-ONE

Callie had almost forgotten how different London was. It wasn't just the buildings all crammed together, or the constant surge of humanity every time she stepped outside her hotel. It was something too difficult to put an actual name to, or maybe it didn't even have a name, it was just a feeling…

She'd spent last night walking by the Thames, the glittering lights of the city reflected in the water. People bustled past her, heads bowed, lost in their own worlds. Her thoughts were never far away from Jackdaw.

November sun beat through the glass of the studio where her show was to be held. It was a converted warehouse in Lambeth, across the river from the Tate Britain. The gallery occupied the entire roof space, an airy rectangular room with huge skylights.

Footsteps struck the reclaimed wooden floorboards and Callie stopped in her unpacking, the floor around her strewn with bubble wrap and tissue. Adele threw her arms around Callie, kissing her cheek fondly. Adele's many bangles jangled in Callie's ear, one snagging in her hair.

She extracted herself with a slight grimace—this always happened, and Adele never seemed to notice—as Adele launched into a flurry of examining pots and holding them to the light.

'Exquisite work, Callie, darling. You know if you ever have enough for more than one show, you just have to breathe in my direction.'

'And you know you're my first port of call,' Callie said, laughing. Adele was a woman filled with colour and light, her fashion sense eclectic to say the least. Today she wore an orange and gold kaftan that swirled around her ankles, Doc Marten boots in a shade that could only be called puce, and a heavy gold necklace with an eye of the sun disc hanging from it. She was the polar opposite of Callie, but Callie adored her.

'I thought we could display the smaller pieces here.' Adele drifted away to rustic shelving set against the wall. 'And your others here.'

More shelves occupied the prime space in the gallery. They'd been sliced from vintage beer barrels, a nod to the brewery which used to exist a few streets away, and were intersected by horizontal ledges. Spotlights in the ceiling were angled to flood them with light and show whatever was displayed to full advantage.

Callie busied herself arranging bud vases and ceramic butterflies on the first set of shelving, standing back occasionally to move an item slightly to the left or right. These were her bread-and-butter pieces, the most affordable ones, all in her distinctive style.

'You must come to London more often,' Adele said, as she plucked a vase from its tissue blanket, gushing over a stark image of a winter tree painted on the side.

'My brother lives with me now.' Technically, Jackdaw was

her half-brother, but he was family she'd never known she had, and that was all that mattered.

'That's fabulous.' Adele beamed at her, her necklace catching a glint of sun from the window. 'Is he arty? Please say he is. Another Dawtrey following in your footsteps would be magical.'

Callie was about to say that she didn't know if Jackdaw was arty at all. He'd only lived with her for less than a week, and most of that time she'd spent holed up preparing for the show. A wave of guilt settled, clammy and insistent. When she got home, she would direct all her attention to him. He deserved nothing less.

'How many people are we expecting later?' Callie asked, expertly changing the conversation.

'I limited the invitations to fifty, but you know we could accommodate double that. Everything will be sold.' Adele's matter-of-fact comment was so sure of itself, but each year, Callie had a niggle of doubt that maybe this would be the year the bottom fell out of the demand for her work.

'Diego phoned me this morning.' Adele nudged Callie's arm, a bright smile lighting up her face. 'He says he already has a place in his home ready for your *pièce de résistance*.'

'He hasn't even seen it yet,' Callie said, but she couldn't stop her own smile curling on her lips.

'He doesn't need to see it. It's a Callie Dawtrey.'

Adele gifted her with a knowing nod, then tapped Callie's hand. 'Now come and have coffee with me before things get ridiculously manic. What are you wearing? Don't tell me, it's black. You know I would adore you in colour, darling, not that I don't adore you anyway.'

The gallery darkened as Adele walked towards the door and Callie looked up, expecting to see grey clouds obscuring the sun—a sudden gasp as her fingertips rose to her lips.

On each of the five skylights running the length of the roof, birds were gathered, their heads tilted towards her. This was London, no stranger to the pigeon population, but there were no pigeons looking down at her. They were all crows.

Combe Hurst and Jackdaw and the ways of a small country village had followed her here.

Callie stood in the ornate bathroom, breathing in through her nose and out through her mouth. Her plain, black designer dress clung to her figure. It was the one she wore every year because she figured nobody would remember that it was the same, and even if they did, it was tough—because she wasn't a clothes horse.

Adele had insisted that Callie borrow the eye of the sun necklace, and even though it was something Callie wouldn't have chosen in a million years, she had to admit, as she looked at her reflection in the Art Deco bathroom mirror, that it set her dress off to perfection.

She grasped the edge of the sink and lowered her head, taking another deep breath.

'Okay, Callie, showtime.'

A spray of perfume and a slick of lipstick.

Jackdaw hadn't answered her call when she'd tried to ring him back at the hotel.

He's just busy with Oscar. He doesn't need me checking up on him all the time. Give him some space… The anxious thoughts rampaged around her head, refusing to fade.

She pushed the building apprehension into the back of her mind and walked into the spotlights.

CHAPTER FIFTY-TWO

Maggie pushed her way through the crowd, the letter stuffed into her pocket. The words, when she'd read them, had gnawed at her consciousness, picking at old scabs. She was a stupid old woman for not piecing it together before, but then no one could have foreseen all of the cogs that had to fall into place to turn the wheel full circle.

Superstition has a way of nourishing a land. When kernels of truth mingle with hearsay, the results fading down through generations, all that's left in the soil is the truth—and that's what refuses to be silenced.

Lonan Carter had been the hangman's youngest son. He had lived in the cottage on the hill. His blood ran in the earth and in the water. But his spirit was at war.

And now a new boy lived in the cottage and the cycle had turned again.

A shaggy dog ran past her, its tongue hanging out, chased by a small girl wearing wellingtons and a pink, padded jacket. A woman toasted marshmallows on an open fire, handing out long sticks to the children so they could toast their own.

The rich aroma of suckling pig and sticky toffee—a banquet for the senses.

Ribbons of light meandered up the hill, villagers carrying lanterns to celebrate.

Or to ward off whatever lurked in the darkness.

And at their head, the wraithlike shape of the avifauna suspended from a makeshift cradle, the puppeteers beside it, dressed top-to-toe in black.

The crowd grew still in reverence. A breeze ruffled over the avifauna's paper skin, turning its head in her direction, and she shivered as the hollow eyes raked across her.

She hurried on, catching a glimpse of Oscar, his fair hair a smudge of light, Jackdaw at his side, and she didn't know whether to be grateful or alarmed.

Boys should not form friendships here.

Because at Martinmas, it drew Lonan too close. The boy who'd had a bond severed so brutally was always looking for companionship.

Her eyes scanned the hill, finding the ominous form of the gibbet. A constant reminder of this village's brutal past, a constant reminder of prejudice and the whims of the privileged.

Francis Parnell's grave was tucked away in the corner of the churchyard, conveniently forgotten. There were those who visited it at night and spat upon its stones. Those who knew, like she did, that Parnell had been the worst kind of man—rich, powerful, and without an ounce of empathy.

But without him, where would this village be? Cast adrift in a modern world that cared nothing for history and heinous sins—and boys who could not rest.

Yet keeping its yesteryear alive preserved the village's prosperity. The sacrificial blood, the lighting of the avifauna.

Here is our offering, our penance. Here we remember the bird that should have been set free…

And the village did prosper. The surrounding farms produced healthy livestock, grew bountiful, disease-free crops. Children thrived. The old remained hale and hearty. Visitors came and lavished their money. Combe Hurst had been showered in manna from heaven.

But beneath this blessing was a sordid, maggot-ridden truth.

No one wanted Lonan to find peace, because then all this would be at risk.

That was what she and Twig and Naomi had been trying to do on that long-ago fateful night. Trying to reach back into the past to see what had truly happened.

But there had been a lie there, too, no matter how pure their intentions had been.

Because Naomi hadn't been Naomi at all.

Her fingers clutched the letter in her pocket, the thin paper crackling against her palm.

'Maggie.' A familiar voice at her side.

She turned her head to gaze up into Twig's wrinkled face. His eyes were still the same pale silver-grey as they'd been that night.

'Look at how they all watch him,' Twig said. He didn't need to explain.

'It's because they're all atwitter with what Elspeth has fed them,' Maggie snapped. 'He's just a boy.'

'Hmnn.' The noise Twig uttered spoke volumes. 'He's *the* boy, Maggie Moon. We both know that.'

'Can we help him?' Her voice rose an octave, her fist tightening in her pocket. 'We have to help him.'

'You know we just have to let it all play out. He's here because he needs to be here. The land demands it.'

Maggie couldn't argue with that logic, especially considering the contents of the letter. Should she tell him? And if she did, what good would it do? Would he think any differently?

She watched as Oscar disappeared inside the marquee, Elspeth standing sentry at the tent flap, disapproval shimmering from her in waves.

The rumble of wooden wheels on grass sounded from behind her, and she turned to see Matt Coxall leading a black horse through the crowd. Behind it was the cart from Callie's barn.

'Why now?' she murmured, more to herself than to Twig.

Stupid, stupid question. You know why.

She wasn't the only one watching it. Jackdaw, too, had his gaze firmly fixed in that direction.

Oh, my sweet, sinless child. Her heart clenched in her chest.

Yet the blood that ran in Jackdaw's veins was tied to this land. Even if he didn't know it.

'I can feel the veil thinning, Maggie Moon,' Twig said. 'I almost saw behind it a few nights ago, but I couldn't keep the paste down. My body is too old for this hallowing.'

'One of these nights you'll do that and not wake up,' Maggie said. She was well aware that every time he absorbed more of the fungi into his bloodstream, the more he was dicing with death.

'I can't die yet,' Twig said. 'Not when I'm so close to seeing.'

She wanted to say that death didn't care if he was close or not, that it would come for him in its own time.

A drumbeat pounded into the falling dusk, and all eyes turned towards it.

'Don't interfere, Maggie,' Twig said, as he drifted away into the throng. 'What will be will be.'

Maggie watched him limp away, his normally tall stature bowed over as if the constant absorption of toxicity was dissolving his spine.

She drew the letter from her pocket, reading the scrawl upon it. A letter written quickly. A letter written because the author didn't know how much time she had left.

I'm so close, Maggie, but there's a shadow stalking me. I see it from the corner of my eye, and I'm afraid. Not for me, but for Jackdaw. I'm sorry I left without a word that night. I'm sorry that I didn't stop to check if you were okay. I just had to get out.

And I've spent all my time since that night trying to piece together those shreds of history and hearsay that we tried so desperately to unravel.

I feel Lonan, too, especially at Martinmas. He comes to me in my dreams and he wails, tearing at his hair. What they did to that boy was unforgivable.

*There are birds everywhere I go, black birds mainly,
but sometimes tiny sparrows and wrens. I find feathers
in my bed, in my shoes.*

*I've completely distanced myself from my son, because
if he looks at me he'll know where he came from.
I called him Jack, but he goes by the name of Jackdaw
because his hair is thick and black and messily beautiful,
and his summer-blue eyes are bird eyes, all-seeing and
haunted and confused.*

The cruel irony of this pierces my soul.

*He'll find his way to you, I know that. Please take
care of him as much as you can. I know he's there for
a reason. I know he's there to finish what we couldn't
on that summer night.*

I don't have to tell you whose son he is.

*Yours, in love and sisterhood,
Francine (but always your Naomi)*

Tears burned at the back of Maggie's eyes. She folded the letter
and stuffed it back into her pocket.

CHAPTER FIFTY-THREE

Jackdaw watched Oscar disappear into the marquee with his aunt. He stood with his arms hugging his body, aware of all the eyes that had wheeled in his direction now that he was alone.

It's just because I'm new here, he told himself. But underneath he faced the sobering fact that wasn't the only reason.

It was because he was a boy who lived in the hangman's cottage. Just like Lonan had. He knew Oscar wasn't telling him everything—he blew out a breath and scuffed his toe against a clump of grass.

Well, he wasn't telling Oscar everything either. Because... because he was scared that, if he did, Oscar would look at him like every other kid had.

That this fledgling friendship they'd formed would be stamped into the ground.

He glanced at the sky. Dusk was falling fast, and with it the energy around him seemed to crackle in the fading light. The nape of his neck tingled and he turned to see a tall, thin man watching him from the edge of the unlit beacon. He was sure it was the man he'd seen a couple of nights ago, when he'd heard the whisper again.

Isaacrow.

It *had* to be a name. Isaac Row.

But who had he been, and what ties did he have to Lonan and Iza?

A sudden creak vibrated through the air, then the unmistakable rumble of heavy wheels on grass. Jackdaw spun, his gaze fixing on the space between two tents. A man led a horse through the gap, and behind it was the cart—the cart that had been torn from its resting place.

The horse didn't look like it should be pulling a cart. It wasn't sturdy or shaggy. Its dark coat was covered in a sheen of white sweat, and as it tossed its head from side to side, Jackdaw felt that it didn't want to be here any more than he did.

He imagined himself riding it, digging his heels into its flanks and speeding away. A wave of disorientation spiked through him, and for a moment he *was* astride the horse, feeling its pulsating power as it galloped, its hooves thundering across the ground. But he wasn't alone. A warm body was pressed against him…

A sharp jab in his ribs rocketed his thoughts back into focus, but the bewilderment still hung at the back of his eyes.

'See, still alive.' Oscar stood before him, a twisted grin on his face. 'But it was a close one. She read the riot act to me about taking the car without a licence. "How could you be so stupid, Oscar?"' He mimicked his aunt's voice so well that Jackdaw couldn't help smiling.

'Short story is that she'll have to tell my parents and that won't be fun, but it's strange.' Oscar paused, chewed over something before voicing it. 'She seemed like she was just going through the motions, like she had something much more important on her mind than me totalling her car.'

'I guess this Gala Day thing is really significant for her,' Jackdaw said. 'Luckily for you.'

Oscar cuffed him lightly on the back of his head. Jackdaw pouted, delight shining in his eyes as they fooled around. He swerved as Oscar raised his hand again, then stopped dead in his tracks. The gibbet loomed in front of him. His stomach went into free fall.

'Hey,' Oscar said, resting his hands on Jackdaw's shoulders. 'That's not the original gibbet, you know. That one was struck by lightning years ago and taken away. No one knows where. Maybe they burned the damned thing. This one is a replica.'

Oscar was trying to soothe his unease but still the sight of the ominous structure so close, replica or not, made Jackdaw feel nauseous.

A sudden drumbeat resounded over the hill and everyone stopped what they were doing. The beat struck again, a solid, deep boom that Jackdaw felt behind his rib cage.

'Showtime,' said Oscar. He grabbed hold of Jackdaw's sleeve and steered him towards the other side of the marquee. A tall maypole stood in the ground, black and white ribbons wrapped around the post. The edges slapped against the wood, snapping in the wind.

'I thought maypoles were for, well, May,' Jackdaw said.

And they should have brightly coloured ribbons.

'Not here.' Oscar tugged him along, and now they were part of the crowd all surging forward. Men and women and children, their faces flushed, all drawn to the same point.

At the rear of the marquee stood the unlit beacon.

The haphazard collection of sticks and branches that the

children had gathered were stacked against slats of wood surrounding a stout pole.

The drum sounded again and a deathly hush settled.

Jackdaw leant into Oscar's weight at his back.

An ache throbbed behind his left temple.

Heads turned, and Jackdaw followed their gazes.

Elspeth appeared from the crowd, holding a lit torch high above her head. Smoke curled into the ever-darkening sky. She turned to face them all.

'And so, we are here at this hallowed time to celebrate our Gala Day. We remember our history. We remember those who were wronged. We ask them to bless our land as we give them part of ourselves.'

She bent low and touched the flame to the kindling, walking around the beacon and repeating the action. Small flames burst into life, the crackle of dry wood, the scent of pine taking light. Within a few minutes the whole bonfire was ablaze, a beacon on the hill for miles around.

Jackdaw turned to the gibbet, heard the creak of a rope that wasn't there.

Now the children moved towards the pyre, the smaller ones guided by adults. They clutched the stick figures tight before throwing them into the flames. Their faces were cloaked in shadow but their eyes were bright.

'Why do they do that?' Jackdaw asked, his voice barely a whisper.

'It's a ritual,' Oscar said. 'It ties them to the land, to the forest.'

Jackdaw's next words caught in his throat.

What kind of a place marks its children like this?

He was suddenly acutely aware that Oscar had done this very thing. That Oscar had been marked.

And that everyone here, no matter how old they were, had gone through this ritual.

And that he, by virtue of being the stranger, was marked in a very different way.

CHAPTER FIFTY-FOUR

The tall, thin man broke from the throng. Jackdaw watched as the crowd parted as one. The frenetic energy around him raised goosebumps along Jackdaw's arms. He swallowed the coat of unease lining his throat.

The flames from the bonfire painted the man's face in fluttering ghoulish shadows. He wore a half cape of black feathers around his shoulders. They glistened in the burning light, and Jackdaw was aware of multiple gazes settling upon him. He wanted to fade into the night, wanted to run home and bolt the doors and pray for morning.

But he knew that wouldn't help him. He'd been drawn here for a reason, all the terrifying happenings pointing to one thing, and one thing only.

Find his bones.

But how was he supposed to do that? And why?

The man—*Twig*, Oscar had said his name was Twig—drew a butcher's knife from a belt around his waist. The wicked blade glinted in the fire glow and Jackdaw's heart began to gallop in his chest.

'It's okay,' Oscar murmured behind him, and Jackdaw clung on to the reassurance.

His panic was a feral creature, padding across his skin, its jaws drooling. Nausea rose in his throat and he swallowed the bitter bile. He was freezing cold and burning up, and his limbs had all but turned to jelly.

'We offer blood for the land!'

Twig's voice ricocheted across the hill, and just when Jackdaw was certain that *he* was the sacrifice, a small girl stepped forward, carrying a woven willow basket with a lid.

Twig opened it and pulled out a squawking chicken. He held it up by its feet, its wings beating once then stilling. One amber eye settled upon Jackdaw.

Sweet fuck… it was the chicken he'd seen with the little girl coming out of the church. His mind skittered to a halt, and he had to dig his fingernails into his palms to stop the bombshell revelation when it hit him. They had blessed the chicken in the church so they could kill it. Everything about that was wrong.

One quick swipe of the knife across the chicken's throat. The crowd that had been holding its breath let out a collective gasp. Jackdaw wanted to look away, but he couldn't.

Twig grinned, dipping his forefinger into the blood and painting his lips. He began to swing the doomed bird, the blood dripping from its throat arcing as the motion grew stronger. Then he spun in a circle. The blood sprayed into the crowd, most of it landing on the row of children at the front.

Jackdaw expected screams of horror, but the expression on their faces was pure joy. Triumph.

Parents gathered them into their arms. Hugs and kisses and proud smiles. It was a celebration.

Everything around him became a blur and he was barely

aware of Oscar's arm around his shoulders, of being led away to a quieter spot on the hill, of being pulled down onto damp grass.

'I'm sorry,' Oscar said. 'I should have warned you.'

'That was...' Jackdaw inhaled a shaky breath. 'Fucking awful.'

Oscar stayed silent for a moment, and Jackdaw understood that he was choosing his words carefully.

'It's an offering to the land,' Oscar murmured, tugging at a strand of long grass near his feet. 'To say that we still remember.'

'Remember what?' Jackdaw wanted to retreat inside his own skin and never come out.

'Okay.' Oscar blew out a breath. 'Remember when we had our disagreement, and I said I wanted to show you where the stories all began?'

Jackdaw grimaced. 'I thought you were messing with me.' He paused and picked at a thread in a rip in his jeans. 'Because that's what everyone has always done.'

Oscar nudged his shoulder. 'With hindsight I could have phrased that better. You were scared that day. I understand why you told me to fuck off.'

'I think I said *fuck you.*' Jackdaw's lips twisted to one side. 'Not my best moment.'

Oscar stared into the distance. A muscle twitched across his cheekbone. 'You already know about who lived in your cottage. Back then, execution was a profession. If you were a son, you followed whatever your father did.'

Jackdaw shivered.

'Yeah, I know.' Oscar sucked his bottom lip. A curl fell across his temple, the dappled blue of a bruise stark against his fair skin. 'We know from census records that the hangman, Jacob Carter, had three sons, and a daughter who died from scarlet fever. The sons all took part in the executions to some degree. But it's the youngest who's remembered on Gala Day.'

Jackdaw's shoulders caved. *A daughter who died from scarlet fever? Ophelia.* He knew she was dead, but somehow, hearing it from Oscar made it too real.

He pulled his thoughts back to Oscar's words about the hangman's sons. 'Lonan,' he said softly. He could feel Oscar scrutinising him, wondering how he knew.

'Anyway, because Lonan was the youngest and Jacob Carter wanted him to have some kind of an education, he was sent to the village school. Being the hangman's son, you can imagine how that went down.' Oscar shook his head. 'Kids acted like kids even back then. We think this is where he made a friend. Another boy who was an outsider. His name is on the school records, but only for a few months.'

Jackdaw hung onto these details, drinking them down as if he was the drought and they were the rain. He tried to piece together what he knew and what Oscar had just told him, but there were still chinks where his understanding struggled in a quagmire of uncertainty.

'What has that got to do with the forest?' Jackdaw said.

Something in his blood told him that this was important, that this could be the missing fragment.

The drumbeat sounded again. Once. Twice. Then it began to pound in a rhythm that sounded like a heartbeat. It swallowed Jackdaw's question whole.

Oscar stood, holding out a hand to pull Jackdaw up.

'It's the avifauna,' he said, his voice tinged with excitement. 'Come on, we have to get a good spot.'

He dragged Jackdaw across the field to the point where the incline became steeper. Where the hill led to the gibbet.

People ran past, lit torches held high, smoke curling into the dark. They gathered on the edges of the hill, leaving a pathway in-between.

Oscar pushed through them, climbing onto a grassy knoll. Jackdaw was a shadow at his side. He was tangled up in knots, fearful of what was about to happen, fearful of knowing anything else in case that knowing shredded the last of his sanity.

The drumbeat was making it hard to focus on any kind of coherent thought.

A loud cheer went up from the crowd.

Jackdaw stared through the masses. People hoisted small children onto their shoulders so that they could see better.

He caught a glimpse of something pale soaring above their heads.

And then it appeared. A huge, gangling paper structure spread across a willow skeleton. It was lit from within and operated by people head-to-toe in black, their arms moving the wings so that they rose and fell, manipulating the head so that it tilted to gaze left and right. The click-clack of small bones rubbing together was its menacing soundtrack.

A corvid beak opened and closed, and Jackdaw found his own mouth mirroring the actions. He'd seen it before, only he hadn't known what it was, the day of the accident when Oscar had taken him into the village hall.

It was both grotesque and mesmerising, and as it climbed up the hill, Jackdaw's panic scored through his veins like liquid poison. Now it was level with him and it stopped, the puppeteers turning the head so that it was looking straight at him.

The drumbeat stopped suddenly.

The echo drifted into the dark.

The avifauna opened its beak, and from somewhere a shriek blared across the hillside.

The few people in front of them stepped aside.

Jackdaw shrank back.

'Whoa.' Oscar's breath ruffled his hair. 'You've been chosen.'

CHAPTER FIFTY-FIVE

Callie mingled with her guests, smiling and making polite conversation, thanking them for their generous support of her work. She'd had no time to oversee the placement of her prime pieces, but she trusted Adele to have displayed them to their full advantage.

Through the gaps in the crowd, she could see a smattering of red stickers on the shelves, red stickers that meant a sale. The jug and the tiles she had specially crafted for Diego weren't on public display. Adele had spirited them away to a side annexe.

'Absolutely stunning, Callie.' A woman in a black tuxedo suit and large gold earrings touched her arm. 'I had to buy *The Mother and Child.*'

Callie took a sip from her champagne flute. The bubbles tickled her nose. The woman kissed her on the cheek and drifted away, a waft of expensive perfume in her wake.

Callie hadn't always named her work but Adele, wondrous agent that she was, suggested it—because she had told Callie that pieces with names sell better. The owner can drop it in conversation to others. Exclusivity is an aphrodisiac for the rich.

Adele caught her eye from the other side of the room, and Callie saw the edge of a leopard print jacket disappearing into the side annexe. She exhaled softly, her heart beginning to thud. The other pieces were her bread and butter, but the ones cloistered away out of view were her caviar pearls. With these sales, she could afford to plan Jackdaw's future.

She cut through the pressing crowd, soft jazz playing through the gallery speakers, making her apologies as people tried to engage her in conversation. The heavy door loomed and she pushed it open, stepping inside the room. It shushed closed behind her, muting the outside noise.

Diego Acala stood beside Adele.

He towered above her, his close-cropped black hair catching the light from an overhead spot bank. A pillar blocked her view of what he was scrutinising. Her palms began to sweat, and she wiped them down her dress.

'Callie.' He turned and walked towards her with a broad smile, taking her hands in his and squeezing them. 'I am in shock. What you have crafted here is nothing like I have ever seen before from you.' He shook his head, his thick, dark brows rising, lips parted.

A long moment where Callie wanted the ground to open up and swallow her.

This is it then. The year I totally fucked up. He hates everything.

Somehow she forced her feet forward, keeping her eyes lowered until she was in front of the display stand. The tiles she had crafted with the feathers forming the torn wings sat against pegs that showed the full artistry of her work. Here, exhibited in the right light, she couldn't help but feel a swell of pride. The subject was macabre yet stunningly beautiful. *Inevitable.* She concentrated on the name inked on a small rectangular card, felt her mind curl in on itself.

Her gaze rose to the next shelf where the jug sat, its avian spout curved downwards in disapproval, the eye almost three-dimensional in the light, the colour the exact shade of Jackdaw's.

Her heart clenched. *Why hadn't he answered his phone?* A noose of unease tightened her throat.

Diego was saying something about the jug, gesticulating wildly. She willed herself to focus, a smile plastered on her face.

'I am in love,' he said, his hands rising to clasp his cheeks. He stepped to the side. 'See how the eye follows me around? It is exquisite.'

Relief flooded through her as Adele clapped her hands in excitement.

'But you truly excelled yourself in this, Callie.' He withdrew slightly so she could see the edge of another stand, hidden behind a pillar.

Confusion muddled her mind. He had seen the only pieces she had marked for him.

He led her around the pillar. Something dangled from a hook. It drifted slightly in the currents of the air-conditioned room. Her jaw slackened.

A small willow figure swung freely. The thread attaching it to the hook wasn't string or ribbon or twine—it was a thin, twisted rope. The figure had been pressed into wet clay, then removed, so that the clay formed the meat of the body with the willow bones outside. A reverse skeleton.

'If you are changing mediums, I am fully behind you,' Diego murmured. 'This is inspired.'

He stepped back and whispered to Adele—the price he was

willing to pay. She didn't even confer with Callie, just nodded, her hand lifting to cover her mouth.

Callie stood in the side annexe, accepting the praise lavished upon her. Praise for a piece that wasn't meant to be here. She'd thrust the figure into leftover clay in a flurry of annoyance.

Let's see you get out of that.

Somehow, it had followed her.

Her gaze swung back to the figure. Adele and Diego didn't seem to have noticed that the rope wasn't attached to the top.

That it was threaded around its neck.

As they discussed payment, Callie drew her phone from the slim bag over her shoulder. She called Jackdaw, hoping against hope that he'd answer this time. Nothing.

She tried Maggie's number, her heart thudding in her ears. It rang and rang, each passing second building an agitation that made her fingertips tingle.

She was here in London, in a place full of overly rich people fawning over her work. Her dress was suddenly too tight, her shoes nipping her toes. She wanted fresh air on her face and the warmth of her cottage.

She thought about the crows on the roof earlier. Of the birds that had gathered more so than usual since Jackdaw had arrived. She thought about Gala Day, and superstitions, village gossip, and snippets of conversation.

No good can come out of a boy in that cottage.

Dread formed a lead weight in her gut, her breathing becoming shallow and rapid. The room swam before her eyes, the spot bank blurring into a bright, vicious light.

Her knees buckled and she was dimly aware of Adele by her

side, of Diego striding towards her.

'I need to go home,' she said, her hands clutching Adele's forearm, multicoloured bangles biting into her fingers.

'My brother's in danger.'

CHAPTER
FIFTY-SIX

Jackdaw was pressed so tightly against him that Oscar could smell the fragrance from whatever shampoo he'd used in his hair. Everyone was looking at them.

The avifauna stood as still as stone.

A hush descended like the silence after snowfall.

It was an honour to be chosen. It meant that you'd done something positive for the village. That you were important. He remembered as a child, waiting and waiting, his breath held, waiting for the avifauna to decide.

But why had it chosen Jackdaw? A niggle of doubt squirmed in his gut.

His aunt had told him not to get too close—that she didn't want Jackdaw's misfortune, whatever that was, rubbing off on him. And then she'd changed her tune, had more or less pushed him into seeing Jackdaw again because she didn't want anything happening to him. It just didn't make sense.

The avifauna raised its wings and the drumbeat sounded again.

'You have to step forward,' Oscar whispered against Jackdaw's ear. 'It's okay, I promise...' His words trailed off as a loud rumble vibrated along the hill.

He turned, looking over the heads of the crowd, saw Matt Coxall from the livery stable, leading a horse up the incline. Behind it was the cart, the cart that had sat in the barn by the cottage for over two hundred years.

The jingle of a harness rattled above the lumbering of the cart wheels as the horse side-stepped, shaking its head so violently that Matt was almost pulled off his feet.

As the cart came to a halt in front of them the horse's eyes rolled back, the whites glistening, and a shiver ran from its withers to its flanks. Its black coat was covered in sweat, despite the chill of the night.

Oscar's brows knitted together. This was totally off. Gala Day ran on carefully orchestrated rituals. This wasn't one of them.

Elspeth stepped from the crowd and walked to the back of the cart, flipping down the rear flap. The light from myriad torches threw flickering shapes across the scene, elongating shadows, casting haunted guttering light across faces.

'I think they want you to get in the cart,' Oscar said. His heart had ramped up a gear. Jackdaw hadn't said a word since the avifauna had chosen him.

'I can't...' Jackdaw said, turning to look at him. 'That's the cart they used...'

He didn't need to continue because Oscar knew in a blinding flash of understanding.

That's the cart they used for the hangings.

He wanted to take Jackdaw and run, but his feet were rooted to the spot.

'You can't say no,' he whispered. 'Just do it.'

But he didn't want Jackdaw to do it... everything about it

felt wrong.

He'd been brought up here and never questioned anything, but now, returning, he could sense something dark and rotted beneath the surface.

And this deviation from the normal scraped along his instincts like a rusty nail against glass.

The air of expectation thickened around them.

He nudged Jackdaw gently. 'Come on, I'll walk with you.'

Jackdaw's shoulders slumped, but he let himself be led to the rear of the cart, every eye on the hill fixed upon them.

Oscar's head spun with his own thoughts, hyper-aware that what he felt here wasn't right. But powerless to stop it.

Jackdaw stood behind the cart, his legs shaking. His throat had closed up so much that even breathing became a gruelling act. He tried to hold onto a shred of common sense.

It's just a cart.

What harm can come to me? There's all these people here.

But underneath he knew, he knew that they'd do whatever they needed to.

His hand reached out to grasp the cart, his fingers brushing against the old wood.

Fear blazed through him. Something hot and thick and overpowering. But it wasn't just his fear. His stomach heaved and he barely stopped himself throwing up. Faces blurred together in a murky soup, melted with flame and darkness. He could sense

Oscar close, and he hung onto the security. But whatever he did now, he'd have to do alone.

Somehow he forced his legs to climb into the cart.

The gibbet loomed before him, a stark silhouette painted in flame. He squeezed his eyes shut, but he could still see it imprinted against his retinas.

The cart lurched as it began to move and he almost fell, reaching out to steady himself on the sides. From here, the ripe smell of the horse's sweat rolled over him, along with the stench of the manure it had just dumped on the ground.

It knows, he thought. And even though that sounded impossible, it shone against his mind's eye. *It can feel what the cart was used for.*

The avifauna led the way, its pale wings rising to meet the star-drenched sky. A chant flowed from countless lips, something filled with the wild, something devout and all-knowing.

And throughout it all the drumbeat sounded, echoing across the hill like a death knell.

It was a slow climb to the gibbet, as the incline was sharp and the cart was heavy. Jackdaw couldn't help but imagine a body swinging from the structure, legs kicking uselessly as life was throttled away.

He closed his eyes again.

Lonan, please help me.

He didn't know what else to do but put his faith in a long-dead boy.

The cart swayed to a stop.

Two men unfastened the rear flap, reaching to haul him out. They were anything but gentle. Jackdaw wheeled around, almost certain that someone would be coming for him with a rope.

His teeth chattered in his jaw, his muscles locked tight.

Someone stepped from the crowd, holding not a noose, but a lighted torch. They thrust it into his hand.

Hot wax spattered onto his wrist and he hissed at the pain.

The puppeteers beneath the avifauna stepped out. They took hold of the wings and lifted it into the air. Without anyone to control it, its head hung almost to the ground.

Dead bird. Dead bird.

The thought rampaged across his thoughts.

'Set it free, set it free.'

Another chant began, gaining in volume as other lips responded until the whole hill mirrored the words. He looked at the flaming torch in his hand.

They want me to burn the avifauna.

He didn't know why. He didn't know what kind of superstition he was playing with.

A dangerous one, came the reply.

But he had no choice.

With his heart pounding against his ears and fear running roughshod through his veins, Jackdaw stepped forward and touched the lighted torch to the avifauna's tail.

CHAPTER FIFTY-SEVEN

'I need to go home,' Callie repeated. The words nested in her ears, small and still, and she was acutely aware of the miles separating her from Combe Hurst.

The miles separating her from Jackdaw.

'Callie, what's wrong?' Two faces swam before her vision, which had tunnelled to a point of bright light reflecting from the polished wooden floor of the annexe.

'My brother.' She managed to form two simple words.

Words that were her whole family.

A loud knock on the door and Adele rushed over. Through the crack, Callie could see people craning their necks to see what was going on beyond it.

Have we been here so long?

A murmur of voices. The scent of expensive perfume.

Somehow she managed to corral her thoughts into action. She grasped Diego's jacket, the nap of the leopard-skin velvet soft beneath her fingertips. 'Did you come by car?' There was a note of hopeful pleading hanging on her question.

She remembered a conversation with him the previous year, when he'd told her that he never used the Tube because he had a fear of being underground. She remembered the glint of an immaculately polished black car as it pulled up outside the gallery, the streetlights reflecting from its paintwork.

He nodded, his brow furrowing before the meaning behind her question hit home. 'Yes, yes, of course, you must take the car,' he said, pulling his phone from his pocket, his fingers darting across the screen. 'Victoria is an excellent driver. She will get you where you need to go.'

Relief zinged through Callie's veins before awareness choked it into submission. 'It's nearly two hundred miles away.' She glanced at her phone. 9.24pm. 'We won't get there until gone midnight.' That one fact hit like a cold hard rock, and she drew in a breath sharply.

She found Maggie's number and called it, pacing around the annexe like a beast in a cage, willing her friend to answer.

'Come on, come on!' Irritation flared, and she had a sudden urge to swipe all of her work from the stands and send it crashing to the floor.

Her call went unanswered.

Diego took her arm and steered her towards the back of the room. 'This way,' he said, pushing through an emergency exit door in a rear corner.

The green fluorescence from the sign bathed his face in a ghoulish glow before they were both through and rushing down the back stairs. Their footsteps echoed on the stone steps before they passed through another door, which led to a back alley.

The rush of cold air against Callie's skin brought her muddled thoughts into focus.

I'm overreacting, she told herself. *What harm can come to him in a small village?*

Gala Day. Gala Day. An event she'd never been to as she had no interest in old superstitions. But she remembered then—as Victoria stepped from the car, resplendent in a tailored black suit, as Diego told her the plan—she remembered that she'd researched the village before moving there, that Gala came from the Anglo-Saxon word *galga:* or Gallows.

Gala Day was the celebration of a hanging.

Her breath clogged in her throat.

Her phone rang and she grabbed it, hoping against hope that it was Jackdaw or Maggie, but Adele's name lit up the screen.

'Don't worry about things here, darling.' Adele's capable voice sounded against her ear. 'I've told everyone that you're not feeling well and needed to leave. Every piece has sold anyway, so I'll just let them drink all the champagne, then push them out of the door.' A slight pause, and Callie wondered if the call had cut off. 'I hope everything is okay at home, Callie. Please ring me when you get there.'

'Thank you.' They were the only words Callie could manage.

Diego opened the rear door of the Mercedes, and Callie climbed in.

'Adele gave me your address. Victoria estimates it will take just under three hours, but it depends on traffic getting out of London.'

Callie nodded, panic vibrating through her core.

Nearly three hours. She needed to be there NOW.

'Take care, Callie,' he said, touching her shoulder. 'Vaya con Dios.'[†]

---

†- GO WITH GOD.

He closed the door and Callie was immediately cushioned from the sounds of the city. The tinted windows blocked the glare from the streetlights and oncoming traffic, the rich earthy-sweet perfume of sandalwood curling around her. It was a protective womb from everything.

She clenched her fists, her nails digging into her palms, her breathing rapid and shallow.

'Seat belt, please.' Victoria's calm voice from the driver's seat.

Callie clicked it into place, and the car moved off from the kerb smoothly.

The last thing Callie needed was mundane conversation, and she was hugely relieved that Victoria wasn't in the least bit chatty.

The roads were snarled with buses and angry taxis, pedestrians taking their lives in their hands dodging in and out of the evening chaos.

Callie closed her eyes, tried to find a shred of composure. She couldn't get to Jackdaw any quicker.

At least they were moving, turning left onto Piccadilly before driving down Knightsbridge, Harrods lit up in a golden, opulent glow. Across the Hammersmith flyover, passing the airport signs for Heathrow before merging onto the M25. Mercifully, the traffic was flowing, but each mile dragged by with the urgency of a sloth. Callie dug her fingers in the soft leather of the upholstery and stared out of the window.

Life passed her by. Normal people on their way home to undisturbed sleep. They knew nothing of her fear for Jackdaw's safety, her panic that something awful had happened to him and she hadn't been there to prevent it.

She thought about the barn and the oppressive atmosphere, of her apprehension and then the terror when her fingers grazed *something*… she shivered, flaying herself with regret.

It was a sign, she thought, *and I didn't listen.*

The temperature in the car notched up a few degrees as Victoria deftly changed the settings on the air con.

They finally turned onto the M3, and the car accelerated to the maximum speed limit. But 70mph had never seemed so slow. Callie watched the miles ticking down on the sat nav, pressing her sweating palms together in a semblance of prayer.

Red brake lights pierced the darkness up ahead.

The windscreen wipers swiped over the screen in a smooth arc as drizzle fell from the sky. The car began to slow—and Callie wanted to scream.

'Roadworks,' Victoria said. 'Traffic shouldn't be this busy at this time of night.'

They approached a steel gantry, where the illuminated warning signs showed a maximum speed limit of 30mph. But that wasn't what brought the ripe tang of fear flooding into Callie's mouth. It was the row of black birds perched upon it, their focus firmly set upon the car.

And she knew then, as they ground to a halt, she knew that something was stopping her from getting home to Jackdaw.

CHAPTER FIFTY-EIGHT

The flame accelerated. Jackdaw watched, transfixed, his hand still clutching the torch, as the paper began to burn. Ash rose, stinging his eyes, and he stepped away.

The puppeteers waited until the tail of the avifauna was ablaze before releasing it. The paper bird broke from its willow skeleton and soared into the sky, a pale ghost against the inky night. It rose like a phoenix, in flames and finally free.

Until a gust of wind sent it spiralling towards the gibbet. It wrapped itself around the cross beam like an ardent lover.

A murmur came from the crowd but, unlike before, the sound was filled with unease.

Jackdaw turned and gazed at all the faces surrounding him. He'd done what they asked, and he just wanted to go home.

'Look!' An alarmed voice from the crowd. 'The gibbet. It's burning!'

Jackdaw wheeled, dropping the torch on the ground. The smell of scorching wood reached him, and his jaw slackened as the flames took hold of the structure.

Something flickered in his memory, a fragment of speech from Oscar earlier. *That's not the original gibbet. That one was struck by lightning years ago and taken away. No one knows where.*

A cry formed at the back of Jackdaw's throat as a terrifying awareness ran rampant in his veins.

If stone was supposed to hold memory, what about wood?

He knew then that the beam in his room was the original gibbet, the one the hangman used.

He'd been sleeping beneath the final gasps of the dead.

His mind untethered and he felt as stretched and ensnared as the avifauna had on its way here.

'Make him ride.'

Three words drifted towards him from a face he couldn't see. The crowd took up the chant. First one voice, then two, until all the lips spoke in unison. The children's chant became fast and fevered, their faces flushed. Gone was the jovial mood of earlier, the laughter of a celebration. Now the tone was much, much darker, savage and feral.

Behind him, the whole gibbet was now alight, a backdrop of dancing flame and crackling wood.

He realised that it was more than an historical landmark—it was a lifeline for those who lived here, almost an altar.

And he had destroyed it.

People broke from the mass and came towards him. He darted forward, side-stepping grasping hands, his feet slipping on hillocks of tufty grass. He fell but was on his feet in an instant, fear driving his limbs to *run, run, run.*

But he was one boy and they were many.

Two men tackled him to the ground then hauled him upright, their fingers digging into the flesh of his arms.

The drumbeat began again, somewhere close. The vibration echoed through his chest and he hung his head, gulping in ragged breaths of smoky air.

They dragged him down the hill towards the bonfire, and for a few heart-stopping moments he thought they were going to throw him into the flames. Instead, they forced him to his knees and others congregated, forming a ring. They began to circle him, their arms interlocked, until all Jackdaw could see was a blur of limbs and bodies.

Blackbird, blackbird, hear this song
Dead boys can't speak but you did no wrong.

The rhyme pounded in his head as he desperately tried to untangle all the threads floating untethered in his mind.

Blackbird, blackbird.

Was he the blackbird now?

Dead boys can't speak but you did no wrong.

He remembered what he'd heard in the yard last night when time had cracked open and thrust him backwards.

'It is a sorry state. We will feel God's wrath, believe me. But Parnell will not hear of a pardon. He says the boy is guilty, and this will send a message to all of his kind.'

Could it be…? His heart skipped a beat. They'd taken a boy to the gibbet all those years ago and murdered him even though he wasn't guilty?

He rose to his feet, summer-blue eyes narrowing. He looked at each of the impassive faces in turn and even though his knees were quaking, he thrust out his chin.

'Isaac Row,' he said. 'Was that the boy they hanged here?'

A collective intake of breath from those encircling him,

a murmur of apprehension.

'What do you know of Iza?'

Elspeth pushed her way through the wheel of bodies. Her eyes scrutinised him, her whole demeanour demanding an answer, but Jackdaw said nothing. His head was spinning. *Iza?* The name he'd heard was Isaacrow, and he'd pulled that apart to be Isaac Row. It made total sense. But what if...?

Iza.

A shiver ran through him like a frosted blade.

It wasn't Isaac Row.

The name had been Iza all along—Iza Crow.

All of this time, the birds had been trying to tell him.

'I know that he was hanged here,' Jackdaw said. 'And that he wasn't guilty of any crime.' Before he could decide if he should say the next words forming on his tongue they spilled out, defiance on every syllable. The effect they had was like a whiplash to Elspeth and those surrounding her.

'Lonan told me.'

It wasn't strictly true, but Lonan had been trying to tell him something.

Find his bones.

Lonan had been Iza's friend, and there'd been no grave to mourn by.

'Where did they bury him?' Jackdaw said, his voice sharp and clear.

Uncertainty flickered across their faces and he was convinced, for an instant, that they were afraid of him.

No one answered.

He wasn't sure if it was because they didn't know... or if they told him something awful would happen.

A whicker sounded nearby, and Jackdaw turned to see the horse that had pulled the cart. Its harness was gone, all it wore was a halter—Oscar stood by its side, one hand clutching a short lead rein.

Jackdaw met Oscar's gaze and his head tilted. For one excruciating second he wondered if Oscar had been in on this all along, but as he looked into the other boy's eyes, all he saw was a plea—a plea that said *trust me*.

'Make him ride!' Oscar demanded, his words spiralling into the crowd, and the mass took up the chant again. He thrust his fist into the air and guided the horse towards Jackdaw. The animal was still skittish, although not as much as it had been when pulling the cart. It danced alongside Oscar, its ears flicking backwards and forwards, its nostrils flared, foam dotting its muzzle.

And Jackdaw knew, as Oscar came up alongside him, that Oscar was giving him a way out. He remembered the disorientation from earlier, where he'd felt himself astride a powerful horse, and even though he'd never been on one before he let himself be lifted onto its back. His fingers grasped hold of a handful of coarse, black mane.

The horse quivered, a sensation that flowed through Jackdaw's whole body. It stamped one foreleg on the ground, tossing its head from side to side.

When Jackdaw looked down, Oscar had disappeared.

He looked for him in the crowd, his pulse quickening. He licked his dry lips.

Tasted smoke—and the sweet tang of apples.

CHAPTER FIFTY-NINE

Jackdaw clung to the horse's mane as it side-stepped, almost bouncing on its hooves. The coiled strength of its muscles rippled through his body, his common sense screaming that this was probably the most stupid thing he'd ever done.

Trust me. Oscar's silent plea.

But Oscar was nowhere to be seen.

The crowd pressed close, lit torches held overhead, smoke curling into the flickering shadows. Behind them on the hill the gibbet was truly alight, a blazing beacon of heat and rage and madness.

The chant began again, underwritten by the repetitive beat of the drum.

'Make him ride! Make him ride!'

Why is this important? Jackdaw racked his memory for any clues but came up empty.

Elspeth's face swam into view, a solemn mask, her lips pale and tight. He knew then she had planned this, that asking to borrow the cart was all part of her goal. She was always going to get the avifauna to choose him. She was always going to force him into a cart that had taken an innocent boy to the gallows.

She was reenacting history.

The fact hit him in the gut like a wrecking ball and he hunched over, a sharp pain knifing through his body.

The mass of people gathered behind him, until he was a terrified Pied Piper leading a chanting army of rats across the hill. The horse had begun to sweat again, its ears flicking back and forth, its head pitching from side to side—Jackdaw was sure his arms would be torn from his sockets. They approached the still-blazing bonfire and the animal shied away, nearly unseating him.

In front was total darkness. In front was the forest, wild and unforgiving and bathed in its own hellish narrative.

That's where they were driving him.

A log exploded in the bonfire, scattering cinders and catapulting ash high into the air. The horse reared slightly and Jackdaw's hands clutched its mane so tightly he could feel the coarse hair strangling his fingers. A single moment where he thought he was going to fall, where everything was fire and fear and the bitter tang of bile in his throat.

The feeling of power gathering its might beneath him.

This is it. This is when I die.

A shadowy form broke from beyond the bonfire, shrouded in smoke and ash.

His name yelled by a voice he knew. Oscar sprinted towards him. His hand was outstretched and Jackdaw reached his own, more in blind faith than a conscious decision.

Oscar leapt as the horse took off. A scrabbling nightmare moment of floundering limbs and searing pain as Jackdaw bore the other boy's full weight. And then Oscar was behind him, his hands clutching Jackdaw's waist.

Wind tore at their faces and savaged their hair as the horse galloped into the darkness. The metrical pound of hooves on grass, the scent of musk and sweat, all-consuming panic and triumph flooding their hearts.

And behind them, the piercing scream from Elspeth's lips.

It rose into the night, a sound that spoke of a plan that had gone hideously wrong.

Jackdaw had no idea how to stop the horse. All he could do was cling on and hope that it tired, hope that it didn't fall and send them both hurtling onto the unforgiving ground.

They gave themselves to the rhythm, gave themselves to the magnificent power of an animal in flight. They were both riders and observers—tied to this shared moment as the dark danced around them.

A slight easing of Oscar's weight against his back and then a loud, rebellious yell echoed into the night.

'Fuck, yeah! We did it, Jackdaw, we did it!'

A smile broke on Jackdaw's lips, easing the taut coil of tension across his shoulders. Whatever Elspeth's endgame had been, they had disrupted it. But yet, the crowd had been forcing him towards the forest. An instinctual shiver ran down his spine as the horse slowed a little. Whatever was in those trees, they wanted him to meet it.

And that meant Oscar would be in danger, too.

A line of woodland rushed towards them, a solid weight in the thick darkness. Jackdaw ducked just as the horse threw back its head. The blow caught him like an open throttle. An agonising shooting pain ricocheted behind his eyes. A crack of bone and a torrent of blood.

He felt his grip slipping as his vision hazed and then Oscar's arms were around him, the other boy's fingers clinging to the mane, holding them both in place. Branches tore at their hair, thrashing their faces, filling their heads with the feral scent of the forest.

The trees slowed the sweating horse to a trot. It snorted, sending spray from its nostrils, its flanks heaving with exertion.

'Let it take us,' Jackdaw mumbled, his mouth full of blood.

His head lolled back against Oscar's shoulder.

Pain snared against his heartbeat.

Something drove him forward, drove him into allowing fate or destiny or whatever the fuck people called it, to take over. He'd been placed here for a reason. A long-dead boy had been trying to communicate with him, because another boy had died in the most appalling way.

Francis Parnell had been culpable. This village was culpable because it replayed the horror every single year.

He had to set this right.

He had to help Lonan. Because he knew if he didn't, he would never have peace.

Find his bones.

Jackdaw had never been brave, not really... he'd just been tenacious because he'd had to be. He hadn't stood up to bullies, he'd just removed himself out of their way, happy in his own company.

Blood clogged his throat, his palms slick with sweat, but

Oscar's hands holding his said more than any words.

This was the time to stand up and face whatever horror was coming his way.

Find his bones.

The three words clung to him like a shadow.

And Jackdaw thought he knew how to do that now, although the idea terrified him.

Because there was a huge chance that he'd die in the process.

CHAPTER SIXTY

Jackdaw's blood dripped onto Oscar's hands as he clutched the horse's mane to keep them both astride. The forest breathed against them as the horse slowed. The animal seemed to know exactly where it was heading—and as long as that wasn't back to the livery stable in the village, he was fine with that.

His aunt had used him to get Jackdaw to Gala Day, he knew that now. She was always going to send Jackdaw into the forest, the place they'd been warned against going as children. Unless it was on Gala Day to gather wood for the bonfire.

Oscar wondered now, as the horse veered slightly left and he fought to keep them on its back, if that was because the forest and the unquiet spirit that dwelt there could somehow mark each child, add them to its tally of human disciples.

He winced as a low-lying branch swiped across his cheek, as if the trees were fighting back and punishing him for his thoughts. A muttered profanity left his lips. They hadn't reckoned with the fact he'd been away from here for five years, that in those years he'd cleansed himself of the beliefs that hung like dense fog over everyone and everything.

The village gave thanks on Gala Day and pledged their allegiance to the past with blood sacrifice and celebration, and in turn, the forest and what roamed there granted them health and prosperity.

'Oh my God, Jackdaw,' he said, as something that had been bothering him slipped into place like a key into an oiled lock.

Jackdaw lifted his head from Oscar's shoulder. 'What's wrong?' His voice was thick, nasally.

'Nothing's wrong, you idiot,' Oscar said gently, and then laughed, because what in the hell was right about any of this? 'I've just realised why you can suddenly see without your contacts.'

Jackdaw raised his hand to brush away a clot of blood on his chin. It slid off the back of his fingers and fell into the thick undergrowth. *Blood sacrifice.*

'The forest always grants everyone who lives here something special. A gift. It gave you back your eyesight.'

Jackdaw didn't say anything for a few moments. His face tilted to look up into the bare branches of the trees above them. Oscar followed his line of sight, drew in a shaky breath. In every tree there were crows, lined up or in pairs. Moonlight silvered through the drifting night cloud, painting the birds with a ghostly hue.

'Iza Crow,' Jackdaw whispered. 'That was the boy who died on the gibbet. The crows are his, and I'm the jackdaw. We're all part of the same family.'

A few days ago Oscar would have made a joke out of Jackdaw's words, not because he was cruel, but because it sounded, well, unhinged.

But now, with everything that had happened, he could sense all the puzzle pieces fusing together. What he didn't know was what happened next.

The horse slowed to a walk as they entered a glade carved from a stand of silver birch. Shards of moonlight arrowed through the gaps in the canopies, washing the pale bark to a glistening bone white.

'Here,' Jackdaw said.

The horse stopped and snorted, its ears flicking back and forth. The chilled air quivered with static electricity. Gooseflesh crawled along Oscar's arms. A tingle across his scalp. He blew out a breath. An owl hooted deep in the forest, and a fox barked in reply.

The rustle of something small in the undergrowth.

He swung his leg over the horse's back and slipped to the ground, his legs trembling from the manic ride. Jackdaw slid down beside him, and they both stood silently watching the breath from the horse's nostrils ghost into the air.

'I've been seeing things,' Jackdaw said quietly.

Oscar kept one hand on the horse's flank. A shiver ran through him — because whatever Jackdaw said next was going to turn Oscar's world inside out, and he wasn't sure whether he was ready for that.

'Well, not just seeing things… experiencing things that happened long ago.' Jackdaw hesitated and looked up into Oscar's face, his nose swollen, dried blood painting his lips. 'I know it sounds crazy. I'll understand if you want to go. You've done so much for me already.'

'I think I burnt the bridge of going back when I helped you escape.' That last word stung Oscar's tongue. What kind of fucked-up place had he lived in, where escape was the only option? He squeezed Jackdaw's shoulder. 'I'm not going anywhere.'

A lone crow cawed in the trees. Oscar didn't know if that was a blessing or a warning.

'I'm listening,' he said.

'I found a journal under the floorboards in my bedroom.' Jackdaw paused, his face solemn, his eyes never leaving Oscar's. 'It had a list of dates and names, which I think were a tally of the people who were hanged. At the end was a single scrawled line. *Find his bones.* I didn't know who that referred to, but I do now. It's Iza, and the boy who wrote it was Lonan.'

Oscar absorbed each word, and as they fell, his heart began to pound. Lonan was the one he'd been warned about since childhood. *Don't go into the woods at Martinmas or the hangman's son will get you.*

'How exactly are you supposed to do that?'

'I tried to find out,' Jackdaw said. 'But there's nothing in the churchyard about him, and the librarian said all the books on local history had been taken out.'

Oscar nodded. That made sense. The village was ultra protective of anything to do with its past, particularly when an outsider was asking.

The horse wandered away, its tail flicking, hoof beats muffled by the undergrowth.

Now they were truly alone.

'When you found me on my bedroom floor...' Jackdaw hesitated. A beat of silence. 'I know what I ate that made me sick. It was in my hand all along.'

Jackdaw's eyes flicked from Oscar's face to the surrounding

glade. He was looking for something. 'There,' he said, pointing.

Oscar trained his gaze. At the bottom of a twisted silver birch stood a clump of red-capped mushrooms. His eyes widened. 'I saw those on the beam in your room. Fuck, I'd forgotten about that.'

'It's the original gibbet, Oscar. The one they used for Iza.' Jackdaw's throat rippled as he swallowed. 'Callie told me that years ago they'd done some renovation work in my room.'

'So you're telling me that you ate those?' Oscar's voice rose an octave. His brain was tripping on the fact that Jackdaw had been sleeping under *that* beam. 'Aren't they poisonous?'

'Yes, they can be,' Jackdaw said. A flicker of fear passed over his face. 'But they're also hallucinatory. I think I can see what happened to Iza if I eat some more.'

'Woah,' Oscar said, holding his hands up. 'You're asking me to stand by and watch you poison yourself?' His heart was in full race mode now. 'That's what Twig does. He's been trying to see for decades. Everyone thinks he's slightly crazy.'

'I'm asking you to stand by and be my link back into now,' Jackdaw said. 'If I do somehow manage to see what happened in the past, I don't know how I'll get back.'

'This is batshit crazy, Jackdaw, you know that?' Oscar's thoughts hurtled through his brain at a thousand miles an hour.

'Iza was innocent. I think his death was the catalyst for all of this. And until we find where he's buried, everything will continue. And that's wrong, Oscar, that's wrong.'

Oscar hung his head. He had no comeback, because what Jackdaw had just said was the truth. What if he could somehow end the hold the forest had on the village?

'Where does Lonan come into all of this?' he whispered—because even now saying his name, especially in the depths of the forest in the dark, seemed like tempting fate to an idiotic degree.

'Lonan was his friend, and he's still suffering because of what took place. You told me that at Martinmas people are afraid. They lock their doors and windows, bad things happen. What if that's not Lonan looking for blood, it's Lonan looking for Iza?'

Oscar pressed his fingertips to his lips. Maybe he was trying to hold back the words that had formed on his tongue. Everything he'd ever been told here attested to the hangman's son having a vendetta against the village.

But what if Jackdaw was right?

CHAPTER SIXTY-ONE

Jackdaw saw the moment his words landed with Oscar. The other boy's face slackened slightly as he gnawed at the edge of his thumbnail.

Fear still burned through Jackdaw's veins, but there was another unfamiliar feeling riding on its back. Oscar believed him. Oscar wasn't running away.

Friendship. The word appeared in front of his mind's eye, bringing with it a warm blast of courage.

Oscar's gaze flicked over his shoulder, moonlight burning a path behind him. 'They're coming.'

Jackdaw wheeled to look towards the hill. In the far distance, only slightly visible through the trees, were tiny moving flares of flame.

He steepled his fingers against his lips, a torturous ache throbbing in his nose. He hadn't counted on the villagers coming looking for them. He'd thought that once they reached the confines of the forest, they'd be safe. Or as relatively safe as they could be, with the ghost of a tormented boy walking in their shadows.

Jackdaw hung back as Oscar's fingers brushed his sleeve.

An awareness prickled against his senses, an awareness that

became clearer with each heartbeat.

I've been in this glade before.

The day he'd first seen the willow figures dangling from the trees.

He turned slowly, his gaze fixing on a ramshackle structure almost invisible against the vegetation. He sprinted across, his mind snatching for snippets he'd learned—Oscar had said Twig ate the mushrooms. This had to be where he stayed.

Ducking under the low-lying roof, he was instantly bathed in inky darkness. His hands reached out blindly, his hearing kicking into gear. He tilted his head, bird-like, found the edge of a wooden chair, the cold slippery texture of plastic. His shin met the edge of a metal rail and he hissed at the sharp sting.

And then he stopped dead, stared into the thick, damp blackness at the rear of the shack.

Something was breathing, soft and shallow.

He inhaled through his mouth and caught the taste of rotten apples. The breath painted itself against his lungs and he held it.

'Lonan?' he whispered, his voice trembling. 'Please help me.'

He held out his hands, palms upwards in a plea. All of his instincts told him to run, run, and never look back.

But he stayed his ground.

The weight in the darkness shifted and freezing air shivered over his skin. Heavy pressure congested in his ears. The rattle of something metallic and the cold solidity of an object pressed into his hands. A bone-numbing chill as his fingers were curled around a utensil.

They were close now, these boys separated by centuries, close enough to kiss.

Or to kill.

What if I misjudged everything? he thought. *What if I've called him to me, and I am the sacrifice?*

His heart raced like a cornered animal, his sinuses screaming as the pressure against his ears slowly suffocated reality.

Something soft stroked against his cheek, brushed upwards towards his eyes. He closed them, his teeth clamped together in rigid fear. A ghost-like graze across his eyelids, then the sensation of something threaded behind his ear.

'Jackdaw, come on. They're getting closer!'

Oscar's form filled the door and instantly whatever had been in the shack disappeared. Jackdaw dragged himself back into focus. The compression against his ears popped like an overfilled balloon as he ducked through the door. Oscar caught him as he stumbled, and they both ran out into the glade.

The torches were closer now, the smell of melted wax drifting in the air. Their names echoed into the night.

'You found something in there?' Oscar said.

Jackdaw looked down at a battered metal plate in his hand. His other clutched a tarnished fork, one of its tines missing. He looked back at the shack, at the spectral world he'd left there. It dissolved with the desperation of Oscar's next question.

'Where the fuck do we go?'

A loud caw sounded from the bare branches overhead.

The thin bough bounced as a single crow took flight. It glided above their heads so close that they both ducked instinctively, before it landed in another tree just beyond the shack.

Jackdaw remembered the bird leading him in the woods…

'Let's follow it,' he said, grabbing hold of Oscar's hand.

They sprinted across the glade as the first line of villagers reached the outskirts of the forest. Darkness swallowed the two boys as they passed behind the shack. The undergrowth was thicker here. Years upon years of twisting bramble and wild branches tangling together, nature's defence against intruders—until now. Jackdaw took the lead, his gaze fixed on the crow as it darted from tree to tree. Slivers of moonlight tinted the path, such as it was, and they clung onto each faint shard.

'This isn't even a proper track,' Oscar said, as they paused for a moment. His breathing rasped with exertion.

'I think it is,' Jackdaw said, watching the crow. 'I just think it's a track that hasn't been used for a very long time.'

'That doesn't make me feel any better,' Oscar said softly, shaking his head.

They both knew what Jackdaw meant was that this track hadn't been used since Lonan and Iza roamed here.

'How do we know that we're not going round in circles?' Oscar pushed a particularly vicious barbed bramble out of the way with his elbow.

'We don't. We just have to trust.'

Oscar made a noise somewhere between a laugh and a snort. 'We're trusting a bird... you do realise that, yes?'

The dried leaves rustled up ahead and they both turned their gazes towards it, any words dying on their lips. They pressed closer together, stared into the nocturnal throat of the forest.

Jackdaw brought his hand to his ear. His fingers closed around something with a sharp point. He pulled it free.

It was a feather. A black wing feather from a crow.

A gift from a long dead boy.

He held it out in front of him like a talisman.

'Iza Crow,' he whispered.

The rustling stopped.

He could feel Oscar jammed tightly against him, his uneven breathing against his ear.

'We've come to help you. We've come to give you peace.'

Jackdaw had no idea if the words he was speaking were the right ones. But they'd got this far, and he knew that the forest—and Lonan—would have stopped them if they were in the wrong.

He held the plate against his chest like a shield, slipping the fork into his pocket.

The air around them became charged with the sharp, pungent zing of ozone, a tingling electricity settling on their skin. Jackdaw's ears began to ring. He reached behind him and found Oscar's hand.

They stepped forward, pushing through the dense vegetation, stumbling out into another smaller glade.

It was completely encircled with trees, packed so closely together that the track they were on was the only entry. The branches fanned overhead, forming a natural canopy of protection. Thin wheel marks pocked the ground, the remnants of an old campfire in the middle. Stout upturned logs served as seating.

Close by, the burble of a stream.

There was something otherworldly about it, something that prickled under Jackdaw's skin, filling him with an intense sense of purpose—underwritten with wretched terror.

They advanced cautiously, testing each step, both of them

silent, wracked with awe.

Jackdaw's gaze became fixated on a wild spread of copper bracken just beyond the campfire. A twisted silver birch grew in its centre. He pushed the fronds aside to find the base of the tree—and a clump of red-capped mushrooms.

A small noise vibrated in his throat and he crouched, plucking two from the mossy ground, before returning to Oscar. He held them out, his summer-blue eyes glistening.

'Fuck, fuck, fuck.' Oscar raked his hands through his hair. He met Jackdaw's gaze and smiled, a little wobbly. 'What do you need me to do?'

Jackdaw sat on one of the upturned logs. Damp seeped through his jeans, the physical sensation unsettling his focus. He deployed his default, mentally setting out what he needed to do—resting the plate on his knee, retrieving the fork from his pocket.

'Can you get me some water?' he asked. His mind plunged back to the other time he'd asked this of Oscar—it was only this morning, but it felt like a lifetime ago—when he'd first eaten the mushrooms and been violently sick.

Oscar's throat rippled and he glanced away. Jackdaw wondered if he was going to refuse, but he nodded and disappeared in the direction of the stream leaving Jackdaw alone.

But was he alone?

He turned and gazed around the clearing, needing to feel the reassurance that what he was about to do was the right thing.

Yet nothing stirred.

His throat ached with suppressed tears as he began to mash the mushrooms onto the plate.

CHAPTER SIXTY-TWO

Oscar limped back from the stream, water cupped in one of his trainers. The sight of Jackdaw sitting forlornly on an upturned log with the plate on his knee sent a dull ache through his core.

All the logic in his body was screaming at him, all of his medical knowledge—*don't let him do this. It's suicidal.*

Yet somehow his feet took him to Jackdaw's side. He dripped the water onto the mashed-up mushrooms, unspoken words clogging his throat.

'You can still go,' Jackdaw said, looking up at him. A shard of moonlight back-lit his hair, streaking the black with pearl.

Oscar crouched and took hold of Jackdaw's wrists.

'I'm not going anywhere.'

They both turned as their names rang through the trees, and the breath Jackdaw exhaled was the breath for both of them.

'I need you to feed me,' Jackdaw said softly. 'And if I throw up, keep feeding me.' A tremble of a smile. 'You're good at that.'

Oscar stuffed his hands into his pockets. It was the only way he could stop them shaking.

'How do you know this is the way?' he asked, despair hanging on each syllable.

'Because I've been seeing the mushrooms everywhere.'

Jackdaw stirred the mush with the broken fork. It was grey and lumpy and the smell which rose from it triggered Oscar's gag reflex. He swallowed and tried to calm his racing heart.

'They were under the cart when they took it away. Growing on the beam.' A pause then as Jackdaw met Oscar's gaze. 'Growing on the beam that Iza died on.'

'Can I remind you that you were violently sick the last time you tried this?' Oscar said. 'Most sane people would take that as a sign.' He nudged Jackdaw's knee with his fist before standing.

'Yeah, I guess.'

The unsteady smile on Jackdaw's face was the saddest thing Oscar had ever seen.

'Feed me, and then be here for me. If you're my mooring, I'll have something to grab onto to get me back.'

Oscar took hold of the fork. A pocket of the grey slime gleamed on the tines. He lifted it to Jackdaw's chin, and for a moment his whole world tunnelled into this sepulchral space in the forest with the moonlight as their witness.

The fork slipped between Jackdaw's lips and Oscar watched as he chewed, imagining how vile it must taste.

Jackdaw swallowed and almost immediately he doubled over and heaved onto the grass, saliva dripping from his mouth.

'Again,' he said, through gritted teeth. 'Give me more.'

And Oscar did, forkful after forkful, which came back up again, until one finally stayed down. A sheen of sweat glistened on Jackdaw's brow, his black hair plastered to his temple, blood coating the inside of his nostrils.

'Oh, fuck,' Oscar whispered as he dropped the plate on the mossy ground. Jackdaw's eyes were milky and unfocussed, his lips slightly parted, his breathing fast and ragged.

Oscar knelt in front of him and took hold of his hands.

'I'm here, Jackdaw, I'm here.'

And that's when he smelled it.

Smoke.

He turned his head, and the sight which greeted him hijacked all the feeling from his body.

There, somewhere far beyond, a tall flicker of flame in the solid darkness.

The forest was alight.

Jackdaw was floating, his mind untethered. He couldn't sense his body or his limbs. Everything was pale and wisp-like, drifting patches of fog sweeping past his mind's eye. There was a silence here that he craved, something so peaceful that it made sound seem like a factor of reality that shouldn't be there at all.

He wanted to curl into a foetal ball and sleep here, just drift away into oblivion.

The harsh caw, when it came, tore through his consciousness.

Soft feathers against his face.

The sting of sharp claws pricking his neck.

The patches of fog grew farther apart. Jackdaw narrowed his eyes as glare speared through the mist.

A jolt as he spun earthward, like falling in a dream. Wind in his hair, a vile taste on his tongue. A juddering sensation quivered through him as every nerve in his body spasmed in unison.

He raised his hand to block out the watery sun.

He was present on a hill that he recognised, standing by a young oak tree, looking at the cottage he now lived in.

A chimney puffed smoke into a pale sky.

The stone walls glistened in the sun.

His gaze cast outward. There was the barn, newly painted. There was the cart standing outside—the cart he had ridden in a few hours earlier. But now it was sturdy and undamaged, the metal wheel hub reflecting the lazy sunlight. A tuxedo cat weaved through the spokes, pausing to stretch its spine.

The cottage door opened and a boy ran out into the yard. A boy with messy blond hair, loose trousers stuffed into old boots.

Lonan.

'You had better hurry, boy.' A shout from the other side of the yard where a dark-haired youth, older than Lonan, was forking manure into an aged wheelbarrow. 'Go learn all those fancy words so you can run away and send your money back to me.'

It was a good-natured jibe and Lonan waved a hand dismissively, a grin lighting up his face. The other clutched a cloth parcel, tied at the top.

He hopped over the fence into the field and ran down through long grass and wildflowers. The sound of droning bees, drunk on pollen. Overhead, swallows darted in the sky, catching insects on the wing. The view was one Jackdaw instantly recognised, the church on the hill virtually unchanged. But as Lonan climbed towards it and crested the rise, his gaze flicked to the gibbet, tall and imposing.

I need to know what he's thinking. The thought settled in Jackdaw's mind. 'I don't know how to do that,' he murmured.

Pressure against his fingers as somewhere far away another boy waited.

'Oscar,' he said dreamily.

Lonan turned and gazed right at him, his collar length blond hair caught by the wind, and Jackdaw wondered for a moment if he was visible or perhaps even a ghostly image. But Lonan only shrugged, passing through the churchyard before continuing on down the hill that led to the village.

It was a vastly different place with fewer cottages, and the road was only packed dirt. Fields bordered the outskirts, black and white cows grazing, their tails swishing to keep away flies.

Lonan turned into a gateway. Railings surrounded a brick-built building, a clock tower at one side.

It's a schoolyard, Jackdaw thought. And as it settled, the harsh ringing of a hand bell assaulted his ears.

'One of these days, Master Carter, you will arrive after the bell and be punished.'

A thin woman wearing a long black skirt and a white blouse with ruffles at the collar scrutinised Lonan through thin-framed glasses balanced on her nose.

Lonan's gaze dropped to the ground as the woman stepped back and ushered him inside.

The heavy door slammed shut and Jackdaw was left standing in a schoolyard in a different century, with no idea of what he was supposed to do now. And no idea if he'd ever be able to find his way back.

Maybe this is what ghosts are, simply lost time travellers?

Something tugged at him from another place. Something that seemed urgent.

Jackdaw resisted because, if he tumbled back to Oscar now, he wasn't sure if he'd be able to stomach eating the mushrooms again. But how long could he stay here? Did time move in the same way? Surely he couldn't be anchored here for months or even weeks. He had no idea how long Lonan and Iza had been friends before Iza's young life was cut short.

Something moved at the corner of his vision, and he turned to see a crow perched on the railing. It rubbed its beak against the metal, uttering a sharp caw as it gazed at him.

It can sense me, he thought. What *had* he been sensing? *Apples, why have I been smelling apples? Find a point, skip towards it…*

The scent came back to him in a torrent, sweet and crisp but also high and rotten. He gagged, swallowed down the reflex to throw up as the maggot writhed in his memory.

The edges of his reality buckled into a distorted haze. His gut lurched as saliva flooded onto his tongue, before dropping freefall into a new scenario.

Now he was watching Lonan as he sat under the shade of a cherry blossom tree, picking at a meagre lunch, the cloth laid out beneath. Sunlight burned against the back of Jackdaw's neck. Other children played in the schoolyard, but none came close.

Turn around, Jackdaw urged, because he could feel something crucial hovering just out of sight. His breath stuttered as Lonan bit into an apple and slowly pivoted to look through the trailing branches of the tree.

Another boy stood there, leaning against the rails of a wooden fence. He was slightly taller, with dark hair that curled around the collar of a homespun shirt. His breeches were almost threadbare, the toes of his boots scuffed, shoelaces made from string.

Iza.

Jackdaw watched as a shrill whistle fell from Iza's lips, and then the sound of hooves thundered across the grass. Two bay mares pulled up sharply at the fence, jostling each other for Iza's attention. He stroked their muzzles, brushing away the persistent flies that tried to gather by their eyes.

A sharp crack as Lonan's foot came down on a dry windfall branch. Iza spun around, his eyes narrowing, found Lonan in his line of sight.

'If you are not eating that, give it here.' Iza's voice held a lilting brogue as he pointed at the apple. The syllables flowed together almost musically, and Jackdaw witnessed, transfixed, as the two boys met each other for the first time.

Lonan handed over the apple. Iza dug his fingers into the flesh, separating it into two. He fed a half to each of the mares, then licked the juice from his fingers.

'Iza Crow, traveller of the isles.' He held out his hand.

Lonan took it, and Jackdaw felt the warm sticky heat against his own palm.

'Lonan Carter.' A pause before adding, 'The hangman's son.'

Iza's dark brows shot up. 'Well, Lonan Carter, looks like we should watch each other's backs, given that we are both outcasts.'

Something broke inside Jackdaw's chest, something that shifted his sense of existence even more.

This was how it began.

With the scent of apples and a handshake and cherry blossom petals drifting on the wind.

CHAPTER SIXTY-THREE

Callie perched on the edge of the plush leather seat, willing the car to go faster. Familiar roads and landmarks swept past in the pressing dark, but Victoria's driving never altered from the smooth, professional piloting she'd employed all the way here. She probably thought Callie was insane living in a place where there hadn't been a street light for miles, where the potholes were, at best, liable to break an axle—and at worst, could easily swallow a car whole.

They passed the sign for Combe Hurst and Callie wanted to scream with relief.

'Straight on,' she said, hoping the urgency in her voice didn't make her sound as unhinged as she felt. 'Then take a right and follow the lane.'

It was a journey Callie had done too many times to mention, and normally she would have admired the cluster of roadside cottages and the lack of light pollution, but tonight, everything was tainted.

Because something was wrong and Jackdaw was in trouble.

'There's something alight on the hill,' Victoria said, in a ridiculously calm voice. Callie wondered if all chauffeurs who drove rich people around had to pass this test, if nothing at all ever ruffled them, be it nose to tail traffic or three feet of snow.

Her gaze swept over the roofs of the cottages on her left and the blood iced in her veins. Blazing at the top of the hill was the gibbet, a frenzied framework of flame. To the right of it was a smaller patch, as though the gibbet had spawned an offshoot.

The bonfire, she thought. *Maggie told me about the bonfire.*

The car veered right and began to climb the hill, and Callie was torn between asking Victoria to detour to the Gala site or continue on the journey home. But she had to check if Jackdaw was safe in the cottage with Oscar. That would make perfect sense, right? Then she could wave Victoria off, hug her brother, and go and rock in a corner—because this night had seriously frayed every nerve ending she possessed.

As the car rolled to an even halt, Callie was out of the back door like a lit firework. She paused for a second as Victoria lowered her window.

'Could I ask for one more favour? Can you just stay whilst I check the cottage?'

She didn't even wait for Victoria to answer, just turned and—

Her frantic gaze found the wreckage of the car embedded in the barn door.

'No, no, no!' Images of both boys slumped and lifeless stung her mind as she stumbled across. The security light sprang to life, accenting the car in a sharp, cold beam. Fragments of glass gleamed in the yard.

When two radically different emotions met in Callie's already frazzled mind, a kind of fusion happened, where she knew what she was seeing but also couldn't believe it. The sense of relief at not finding either boy behind the wheel made her knees buckle, but the sight of the twisted, bloody jackdaw smeared across the windscreen was an omen that hollowed out her soul.

What if they were in the barn? *What if what if what if—*

She threw herself against the door, tearing at the splintered wood. Shards of ragged timber raised welts against her flesh as she forced herself through a gap that pared the skin from her knuckles.

Complete and utter darkness enfolded itself around her.

She reached for her phone, then realised she had left it on the back seat of the car.

'Jackdaw? Are you here?'

Her voice rang out into the unwelcoming, inky space.

'Oscar?'

From the back of the barn came a harsh and chilling sound.

The creaking of a rope with a weight attached.

A sudden beam of light caught her in its glare and she wheeled, her heart doing cartwheels in her chest.

'Is everything okay here? I saw the car.' Victoria stood with a stout torch angled towards Callie.

Callie tried to speak, but the words had frozen on her tongue.

The torch swept over the barn from floor to rafters, dissolving the darkness from corner to corner.

There was no swinging rope.

'I'll just check the cottage,' Callie said, wringing her hands together.

Is everything okay here?

It was an hysterical question, given the circumstances.

Victoria stepped away as Callie dragged herself outside.

She sprinted across to the cottage door and fumbled under a

plant pot for the spare key. Hers was sitting in her hotel room. She'd never expected to need it tonight. Fitting it into the lock took every ounce of her concentration.

She knew she wouldn't find the boys inside, but she still went from room to room calling their names. She found the detritus of meals, dishes dumped in the sink, a towel on the floor in the bathroom. Climbing the stairs took a Herculean effort, and as she pushed open Jackdaw's door she steeled herself for something too unholy to imagine.

Moonlight flooded the room.

A damp towel lay on the floorboards, soaking up a pool of red-flecked vomit. She staggered across to the bed and pulled back the covers. They were sopping wet. Something dripped onto her hand, and her gaze drifted up to the ceiling. To the beam.

Droplets of water clung to its surface—and tiny red-capped mushrooms sprouted from the cracks.

The roof is leaking, her common sense told her. But her other sense, that instinctual one all humans have but keep buried, whispered something that was completely unhinged.

They're tears. The beam's crying.

She stood there washed in moonlight, staring out of the window, her eyes wide, her brain short-circuiting on everything that had happened since Jackdaw arrived.

He's the catalyst.

The thought derailed her to a point where she couldn't even remember her name.

Movement from outside refocussed her scattered perception. A crow hopping to the end of a spindly branch, making it bounce in the darkness.

It cawed once, twice, three times.

If Jackdaw wasn't here, that meant he was out in the night celebrating something ancient and disturbing. The gibbet that had stood for centuries was on fire… it was a sign, a forewarning of something awful. All Callie's modern reasoning withered away.

She flew down the stairs and into the yard like a woman deranged, yanking open the passenger door of the sleek, black car.

'Drive!' she yelled, her voice echoing out into the hungry dark.

The car made short work of the climb to the Gala Day site. Other vehicles rested in the dark, but there were no revellers making their way home.

It's past midnight, everyone will be in bed.

But they wouldn't have left the bonfire burning.

They wouldn't have left the gibbet still alight.

She climbed out of the car, using the sill as a footrest so she could see farther into the dark. The whole site was a ghost town. A solitary string of bunting skipped forlornly along the grass.

As her eyes became accustomed to the dark, Callie thought she saw something up ahead, towards the forest. An orange glow.

Leaving the car behind, she picked her way through the remains of a celebration. A stray red balloon bobbed on its string, snagged on a tent pole. The rich scent of burning meat drifted on the wind. She turned and saw a suckling pig speared on a spit, charred and lonely. A paper cup danced across her path.

Feathers fluttered in its wake. White feathers. She followed them, and what she discovered drove revulsion through her gut. A patch of darkness, which in the bonfire glow gleamed crimson. The carcass of a butchered chicken lay on the ground, its throat cut.

She suddenly didn't know this place at all. She didn't know its people or its customs.

Another scent reached her, and this time it was unmistakable. Smoke.

She narrowed her gaze towards the forest, saw tiny flickers of blazing light.

Oh my God.

She kicked off her shoes and ran. She ran as fast as her legs could carry her, stumbling over rabbit holes and tufts of uneven grass. She ran with her heart in her mouth.

As she neared the tree line, distant shouts came to her. They were calling two names. And as she ran into the woodland, frantic and fearful, the impact of those names settled in her marrow.

Jackdaw and Oscar were in the forest.

And the forest was burning.

CHAPTER
SIXTY-FOUR

Urgency tugged at Jackdaw's brain. But it wasn't coming from Iza or Lonan. It was coming from the boy he'd left in the present. The boy he'd left in the future.

But he couldn't return yet.

Find another point, fast forward…

Friendship.

That's what ties them together.

That's what ties him to Oscar.

History repeating itself.

Images flicked through his mind, images that brought all his senses to the fore. The boys lay on a large flat rock by the stream, their skin bathed in dappled sunlight—the same stream Oscar had taken water from. Iza teaching Lonan how to fish. Lonan soaked to the skin but triumphantly holding a wriggling brown trout. Iza doubled over with laughter as the trout slipped from Lonan's hands.

Jackdaw felt the warm sun on his own skin, could hear the stream burbling over rocks, splashes of water as a frog jumped from the bank.

Fast forward.

Iza crouched on the forest floor, his fingers pointing out

flowers and leaves, skimming over fungi co-existing on the trees.

'Can I eat that one?' Lonan's question as Iza fed him a berry or let him taste a leaf.

'This one here,' said Iza, stroking a small, white-flowered sprig near the path, 'is yarrow. Use the seeds on a wound to draw out any infection.'

Lonan declaring that these lessons were of far more use than times tables and copperplate handwriting. He plucked a stem of yarrow and placed it in a muslin pouch hanging from his belt.

Iza laughed, slinging his arm around Lonan's shoulders. 'You do not need a token. I will always be by your side. Through all seasons.' A pledge for friendship.

There was a firm bond between them. Jackdaw could feel the pulse of it like a little heartbeat across his skin.

Fast forward.

A summer evening where the boys lay on their backs watching the stars emerge from an indigo sky. The soft caress of a warm breeze. Sweat dotting their brows.

Iza's expression becoming serious as he flicked away a tiny insect.

'What do you do on a hanging day?'

Lonan's mouth twisted to one side. His throat rippled. Jackdaw felt himself moving closer, transfixed.

Lonan wet his dry lips with the tip of his tongue. 'I sing a song,' he said simply. 'When they are dead, and everyone has gone. When the moon is out, I sing a song for their souls.'

Iza rolled onto his side, studying Lonan intently.

'You do a good thing, Lonan,' he whispered, 'but I wish you did not have to.'

A silence descended and Jackdaw felt the vibration of it against his fingertips.

Iza raised himself onto one elbow.

'Too many of my folk have swung from a gibbet or a tree, accused of things they did not do. People are quick to judge us. Quick to condemn.' Iza's voice held a hint of resigned bitterness. 'But that is the way of this life.'

'I do not like it.' Lonan sighed, his eyes closing for a moment. 'I do not like it at all.'

'Do you know what your name means?' Iza asked, changing the subject. He picked a blade of grass, twirling it between his fingers. Lonan shook his head. 'It's Irish Gaelic.' An easy grin lit up Iza's whole face. 'And I should know, given my blood. It comes from the word *lon*, which means blackbird.'

'My Pa said I had jet-black hair when I was born, like my brothers. But it grew lighter each year. My mother had fair hair.' Lonan paused, a flicker of sadness passing over his eyes. 'She died a few weeks after I was born.' He pushed his hair back from his face until it was a tangled muss of blond strands. 'Is Crow really your surname?'

Iza nodded. 'My folk have a different way with our surnames. We take them from nature. My family line all have bird names. So I am the crow. And now you are the blackbird. It was meant to be.'

And I'm the jackdaw, Jackdaw thought as the pieces flowed together.

Fast forward.

Another evening, later in the year. Leaves floated down from the young oak outside the cottage. The pale disc of a full moon rested on a bough. Iza appeared, wraith-like, at the door.

Lonan slipped out, his chores done for the day.

'Where are we going?' Lonan whispered, as Iza took him by the arm. They ran through the meadow, taking a track Jackdaw didn't recognise. It brought them out on the outskirts of the forest, near where the orchard stood now. The trees enfolded them as they ran, Iza navigating the pathways effortlessly.

'You will not believe what I have found,' he whispered, and the grin on his face was part devilry, part joy. 'Look, is he not magnificent?'

Wandering in a small clearing, his head down tearing at tufts of greenery, was a horse. But not just any horse. A coal-black stallion standing at least eighteen hands high. Moonlight streamed through the treetops, highlighting the gleam of his coat. He watched them warily as they stood at the edge of the clearing, the only sound the grass as it was ripped from the ground.

The horse wore a halter with a fragment of frayed rope dangling to his chest.

Iza fell to his knees and crawled towards it. The stallion raised his head, his ears pricking.

Jackdaw could smell the scent of the masticated grass.

Iza settled cross-legged in the middle of the clearing with his back towards the horse. After a few moments the animal wandered cautiously towards him. Iza didn't move.

The stallion nudged him with its muzzle, chewed on the edge of his collar. And it was then that a soft tune fell from Iza's lips.

Lonan's eyes widened. The lilting melody washed over him. A buzz of affinity threaded through his veins.

He watched as Iza slowly stood and ran his hand along the stallion's neck. Muscles rippled under his touch. Still singing, Iza sprang onto the stallion's back, aided by a handful of mane. He beckoned Lonan over, held out a hand, hauled him up behind.

The song held Lonan in its thrall—held Jackdaw in its thrall.

Iza looked over his shoulder and grinned. 'My people sing, just like you do. But we sing for life, just as you sing the souls to sleep. Hold onto me,' he whispered. 'We will just ride him over the meadow.'

Lonan did as he was told, wrapping his arms around Iza's waist.

Jackdaw was instantly thrown back to his own ride with Oscar. It was all pre-ordained. They had replicated history. His mind stuttered, remembering Oscar tight against his back, as Lonan was against Iza's. The song still hummed in the air even though Iza had stopped singing.

The next instant the stallion launched forward. Iza bent low over its neck, Lonan clinging on.

Branches whipped past, snatching at their hair, but as the forest gave way to lush grass a smile broke across Lonan's face.

And Jackdaw was with him, inside his mind, feeling every emotion spinning through them both.

Iza urged the stallion faster with his hands, a cry of absolute delight bursting from his lips.

The moment was theirs as they raced over the pasture, the rhythmic pounding of hooves on earth, the star-drenched sky their witness.

In that wink of time Lonan knew what it felt like to be truly alive. He was no longer the boy who took down the dead, no longer the boy who sang the ghosts to rest... he was simply the boy who saw his freedom glistening like a silver-backed fish in a stream.

He could make his future with Iza, walk away from the gibbet and the burden of his family name. The idea settled and he threw back his head and whooped with joy, the sound whipped away by the wind.

Another sound rang out into the night. Lonan felt a spear of blinding pain in his side. He glanced down, saw the dark bloom of blood soaking into his shirt, spreading across his ribs.

He tilted sideways, saw Iza's eyes, wide and horrified, as he pulled the stallion up abruptly.

And then he was falling, falling, into a tunnel of spinning darkness as the ground rushed up to meet him.

CHAPTER SIXTY-FIVE

'Wake up! Wake up!' Oscar screamed the words as the crackling of burning trees amplified around them. In just a few minutes, the flames that had seemed so far away were closing in on them, drifting smoke curling into the glade.

Jackdaw's eyes remained clouded, his hand splayed across his ribs. If Oscar hadn't been holding his arm, he was sure Jackdaw would have crumpled to the ground.

This had gone from Massively Fucked Up by helping Jackdaw eat the mushrooms to We're Going To Die Now if they didn't try and get out of the woods. He couldn't hear anyone shouting now. Only lunatics would still be trying to find them.

'Need to go back…' Jackdaw said, his words thick and slurred. 'Lonan's hurt. Not Iza's fault.'

'No.' Oscar shook Jackdaw gently. 'We need to get out of here, and fast.'

Jackdaw raised his head slowly, his eyes regaining their summer blue. There was a crusting on the inner corners as though he'd been asleep for a very long time, a dappled bruising beneath.

The crackling suddenly grew more ferocious. Oscar wheeled, his gaze pinpointing a tall silver birch standing at the edge of the pathway they'd forced themselves through.

The trunk seemed to glow from within, snapping and popping filling the rapidly choking air.

Another sound came from above and he craned his head to the sky. Dozens of crows circled against the milky face of the moon, swooping and diving in a frantic murmuration.

If this was a horror movie, something would blunder out of the trees with an axe and chase them into the flames. But this wasn't a horror movie. It was something much more terrifying.

And neither of them had read the ending of the script.

They were both coughing now, their eyes streaming.

Ash floated down like filthy snowflakes.

Oscar grabbed Jackdaw's hand and dragged him in the direction of the stream. At least he hoped it was the direction of the stream. The drifting smoke was disorientating, blurring their surroundings into a single murky hue, as though an artist had dragged a finger through a black-and-white palette.

Jackdaw pulled up sharp, leaning to scrape a handful of the mushroom paste from the plate on the ground.

Even now, when they were running for their lives, his brain was still tuned into discovering what had really happened to Lonan and Iza.

It was such a noble gesture that Oscar's heart flipped over.

They ran blindly, brambles tearing at their clothes, wicked thorns puncturing their flesh—until icy water flooded over their feet. Oscar tore off his scarf and soaked it through before tying it around Jackdaw's lower face. If only one of them made it out, Jackdaw deserved it more.

Oscar had been blessed with a whole life of advantages and

rewards. How much of this was a gift from the forest he didn't know, but what he did understand to his marrow was that Jackdaw had to finish what he'd started—otherwise, all this madness would continue through more and more generations.

Jackdaw clung to him as they knelt in the freezing stream.

'The horse,' he whispered. 'They were on the horse. Like we were.'

'There's no horse now,' Oscar said, panic lacing his words. 'It left us, Jackdaw.' He wondered if Jackdaw was truly with him or still lost in the tethers of the past.

The hair on the nape of Oscar's neck prickled, and instinct made him crouch deeper into the stream.

Through the drifting smoke, he thought he saw a figure walking towards them. But his vision was filled with smarting tears, and no one could walk through that much smoke and not be affected by it.

Jackdaw had become very still beside him.

The birds above them broke into a raucous shriek, the sound melding with the ferocious snapping of burning timber.

Oscar pulled Jackdaw close, cradling his head to his chest. Stickiness coated his fingers—he looked down, saw crimson smeared across them.

Trickles of blood leaked from Jackdaw's ears and his eyes had become that awful milky white again.

'No, no, no, not now, Jackdaw!' Oscar's pulse pounded with alarm. The figure moved closer, and now Oscar could see that it wasn't walking. It was drifting with the smoke.

Is this Lonan?

The thought exploded through him like a depth charge,

shrapnel sharpening his perception.

Lonan, who he'd been warned about since childhood.

Lonan, who Jackdaw had somehow connected with in the past.

Lonan, whose home was the forest—and now that forest was burning.

Because of them.

Oscar looked away, clutching Jackdaw closer. He could feel the figure hovering on the banks of the stream. Could feel the suffocating intensity of its presence.

Find his bones.

The words punched into his mind, insistent and forceful, as though the figure had drilled them right into his brain.

'We're trying!' he shouted, even though his throat was raw with smoke. A coughing fit overtook him. A shred of courage peeled away from all the panic, and he raised his head to stare right into the figure's intangible face. 'But you have to help us.'

An aching desolation pulsed towards him. It made Oscar want to curl up into a ball and sob.

He pulled Jackdaw onto the opposite bank of the stream, where a large, flat rock sat embedded into the earth surrounded by clusters of fallen leaves—as though this small distance could save them from the wrath of something that had roamed this place for centuries.

A great rending echoed through the smoke, a tearing of wood, and then the silver birch they had left behind in the glade crashed down through the treetops, a solid, burning, angry mass.

Oscar just had enough time to drag Jackdaw to his feet, to

take three stumbling steps backwards. The heat from the flames singed the ends of his hair, his hand rising to protect them from the fireball.

Death stared him in the face as flames filled his vision and choking heat seared his lungs...

Until the ground beneath them gave way, and they tumbled with flailing limbs into the earth.

CHAPTER
SIXTY-SIX

They fell together through crumbling soil and rotted leaves. They fell into shallow, subterranean groundwater, the icy shock knifing through them.

Cocooned in silence, deep and thick and cold, tree roots pressing against their skin. They were thigh-deep in filthy water, in a large hollow under the rock that had been hidden by vegetation… a hollow that could only have been caused by the erosion of the stream at one time.

Somehow, they'd escaped the flames.

Jackdaw jolted back into the present. But the past refused to leave him. It coiled around his body like a lost shadow, the bond between Iza and Lonan throbbing in his blood.

Oscar groaned beside him. His elbow grazed against Jackdaw's ribs, where a deep ache pulsed.

A jolt of realisation rocketed through Oscar's body.

'Oh, fuck. Oh, sweet fuck.'

Jackdaw felt the breath from Oscar's startled words against his face. A flare of panic shot into him like a scythe, making what he needed to ask a pendulum blade in his chest.

'Stop,' Jackdaw said softly, his head tilting back. Root tendrils tangled in his hair. 'We're safe now.'

Or at least he hoped they were.

Still smeared across his palm was the mushroom sludge.

He drew in a shaky breath, wanting to cry at the pain throbbing through his skull. 'Oscar, I have to go back.'

He brought his hand to his mouth, lapped at the bitter paste.

'Ssh,' he whispered as he swallowed. Oscar didn't protest, just trembled against him. 'Through all seasons.'

A pledge from another age, because this was all Jackdaw had left to offer.

The present untethered like a loosed knot, and he was back spinning through the drifting mist—but this time, he had a purpose.

Jackdaw latched himself against Lonan's mind, the connection between them stronger now. This wasn't the time to wonder how the hell it was possible, it was the time to believe. Time to witness.

Lonan opened his eyes to the low throb of a drumbeat.

Thin light washed the window pane.

Something was around his head. His fingers edged upwards, found a bandage encircling his skull, another wrapped around his rib cage. He shuffled onto his side, waves of pain assaulting his nerve endings. His tongue felt dry and heavy in his mouth.

The drumbeat continued. Became louder.

A hanging. It is the sound of the death drum.

And then, what had happened sliced through him like a wire noose.

Iza.

The stallion.

The gun shot.

A desperate fear for Iza's safety overcame the blinding pain in his side.

He pulled himself up to a sitting position, walked hunched over to the window.

The outline of the gibbet stood stark and black against the pink-drenched dawn sky. A line of people, some as small as ants, meandered up the hill from the village. Outside, in the yard, he could hear Asher yoking their horse to the cart. The sound of a jingling harness and impatient hooves.

But the rest of the house was quiet, his brothers and father already absorbed in the job they had to do.

Maybe Iza had got away? Maybe he would never come back.

Lonan's thoughts skipped from hopeful positivity to abject dread. He had to get out. Ask his father, who would be checking the rope, calculating the length needed.

He remembered Iza saying how innocent traveller folk had been hanged, just so the crime could be wiped away, so those wronged would feel satisfied. Horror clutched his heart. Gritting his teeth, Lonan dragged himself to the door. On the bleached wood table was a small glass bottle, a pale liquid inside. Poppy seed tea. He could taste it on the back of his tongue.

A pain reliever.

He gulped down a mouthful, wiped the back of his hand over his mouth. Too much and it would make him drowsy. But he needed something.

The door creaked as he opened it, the chill of the morning biting against his heated skin.

'What in heaven's name is this, Lonan? You should not be on your feet.'

Farley ran across the yard, the bridle curled around his shoulder.

The drumbeat on the hill grew louder.

'I am well,' Lonan said, although he felt as far away from that statement as possible.

'You have been in your bed for five days. You were damn lucky the bullet only grazed you, half an inch more and...' Farley's voice trailed off as Lonan's gaze wheeled to the hillside.

'Who is it?' he whispered, as in the distance the crowd gathered around the gibbet.

Like they still gather, Jackdaw thought. The wickedness of it all flared behind his rib cage.

'Go inside, Lonan,' Farley said, and at that moment, Lonan knew from the look in his brother's eyes who the accused was.

A shard of ice pierced his lungs.

'No, no.' He pushed Farley aside, staggered across the yard, oblivious to the pain in his ribs and his head. The pain in his heart was greater.

'He stole Lord Parnell's horse, Lonan. You know the penalty for thievery!'

Lonan wanted to say that Iza did not steal the horse, they were just riding it back for the sheer joy of being alive—but it would not have mattered.

'Get him inside.' His father's voice as he climbed onto the cart. The creak of wood and a hoof pawing at the ground.

Asher draped his arm around Lonan's shoulder, guiding him back towards the cottage. Lonan struggled against his brother, but his strength was almost gone.

His mind began to drift from the poppy seed tea but he forced his thoughts to concentrate, even though all he wanted was to slip back into oblivion, to pretend this was all a nightmare.

'I was with him,' he murmured. 'It is my fault, too.'

'Hush your words,' Asher said gently as they stood in the doorway. 'The boy already confessed. Already said he made you go with him. That you tried to stop him.'

Lonan's throat closed up. For a moment, he could not breathe. Hot tears stung the back of his eyes.

'Let me see him,' he pleaded. He knew Iza would be trussed up in the barn, waiting.

Pain drilled through his skull as shadows moved across the yard.

Lonan turned to find Iza at the cart side with his hands tied behind his back, but his head was held high. Dark curls fell over his brow. His unwavering gaze met Lonan's.

'Thought I had lost you when that shot rang out, little blackbird.' A smile that ended in the crinkles around his eyes. 'You are tougher than you look.'

'Why did you confess?' Each word stuck in Lonan's throat like a barb. 'I was as much to blame.'

'Because they will always find a way to judge my kind, Lonan. In their eyes, I was guilty the moment I arrived here.'

'Why did you not run?' Lonan had too many questions and not enough time to ask them.

'I had to make sure you would survive. I could not leave without knowing.'

And there it was. The ultimate sacrifice.

'It is time,' Asher said, stepping between them.

'Iza.' Lonan whispered his friend's name for the last time.

It curled onto his tongue like a bittersweet berry.

Asher opened the back of the cart and pulled across the step, and Lonan thought for one moment that Iza had not heard him.

A high-pitched buzzing sounded in his ears, but he would not break eye contact with the boy he thought of as another brother.

He clutched at the cart side as if he could halt its progress. Iza smiled. His lips moved silently, but Lonan heeded the words.

Sing your song for me.

Lonan's heart lurched as the cart pulled forward.

A dark cloud passed over the rising sun. In the distance a murder of crows took flight, their plaintive cries soaring on the wind.

Lonan did not recall the remainder of that day. It passed in a blur of pain and indistinct images. Of sweat-slicked fever.

Of whispered voices and the slow ticking of time.

But all he was waiting for was the sun to set. That was when he would go out and take down Iza's body, when he would sing his song.

When he would fulfil the final task Iza had asked of him.

No one spoke as he went to the door, as he slipped out into the arms of dusk.

He crossed the meadow, skirted the church, and when he

reached the bottom of the opposite hill he finally plucked up the courage to raise his head.

He stared, open-mouthed. A small cry built in his throat.

There was no body swinging from the gibbet.

'His people took him, Lonan. It was the least we could let them do. They will honour his memory, sing their own songs.'

Lonan wheeled, found Farley waiting about ten feet away, his hands open, pleading with Lonan to understand.

A wail left his lips. It rose into the settling dusk as he half-ran, half-stumbled up to the gibbet, as he fell on his knees before it. And the song followed, a lament for a shattered friendship, for a future ripped away.

For a wrong that could never be put right.

And when the song was over, the hangman's son knelt on the earth and wept.

Hot tears welled in Jackdaw's eyes. The immorality of what he'd witnessed so intense it felt like it might rip away his skin and leave him raw and bleeding forever. This horror was what the village celebrated. They kept a haunted boy from his rest by recreating his anguish year after year.

And Lonan accepted their offerings and gifted them good fortune because he was still remembered—and that meant he could still search for Iza.

Jackdaw tumbled back into the present, the rapid change making his ears ring and his sinuses scream. He was resting against Oscar's shoulder. Jackdaw blinked away the tears—he wasn't sure if they were his or Lonan's.

'Did you see?' Oscar whispered. 'You kept saying no, no, no, and shaking your head, tearing at your hair.'

Jackdaw raised his chin. He looked up towards the narrow gap at ground level dusted by smoky moonlight. Everything was deathly quiet.

'They were devoted to each other,' he said, the edges of his words quivering. His legs and feet were frozen, his tongue coated in a bitter mixture of crushed mushrooms and poppy seed tea. Every bone in his body ached as though they'd been reassembled in the wrong place.

Despair wracked his heart for the two boys he'd connected with so briefly. He knew he'd never forget them.

Oscar took his hand and held it tight. They stayed there, shivering in the water-drenched dark, until Oscar clawed his way to ground level, pushing away the earth enough to see what was left of the forest.

CHAPTER SIXTY-SEVEN

Callie stared into the drifting smoke, saw the hungry flames leaping from treetop to treetop. Her head told her that going any farther was lunacy, but her heart didn't want to listen.

A figure emerged on the pathway to her left, one she recognised. Maggie. Her face was taut with worry, her familiar hat slightly askew.

'Callie.' Maggie coughed her name. 'This way.' She started to lead her from the forest, but Callie shook her arm away.

'Jackdaw's in there. I have to save him!'

A moment where Maggie's eyes filled with tears, then the saddest smile.

'There's only one who can save him, Callie. And it's not you.'

Rage boiled through Callie's veins. She wanted to scream at everything and everyone in this godforsaken village, but something in Maggie's expression made her stop. There were secrets there... secrets the older woman hadn't wanted to spill.

Until now.

They backtracked towards the hill, and with every step Callie's heart became a little more bruised and beaten.

Other people were drifting from the forest now, their steps sluggish, their heads bowed. In the distance, Callie heard the loud wail of a fire engine. Somehow, in all of this madness, someone had the clear-headedness to call them. She looked back over her shoulder.

All they could do was contain the flames. They couldn't stop the damage they had done.

Maggie led her over to a grassy knoll at the top of the hill. Callie's knees gave way as she slumped down.

'There's something I have to tell you.' Maggie paused.

Callie leaned towards her, desperate to know, but also stricken with terror.

'I knew your mother.' Maggie stared across the valley to the spot where Callie's cottage stood. She held up her hand as Callie opened her mouth to speak. 'But I didn't know I knew her until I received a letter a few days ago.'

'Where did you meet her?' Callie asked, and some part of her brain short-circuited because… she was sitting here calmly talking about a woman she hardly knew when… a sob throbbed in her throat.

'I met her here in Combe Hurst sixteen years ago, but then she called herself Naomi. We were younger then, although certainly not in the first flush of youth. Just wise enough to understand that beauty is fleeting, and we wanted to experience everything we could. All you need to know is that one night in that forest'—Maggie nodded towards it—'we were infatuated with each other, and something happened. That something was Jackdaw.'

Callie looked across at Maggie, the words all tumbling together in a chaotic disarray. 'I don't understand…'

Maggie glanced down and blew out a breath. 'Your mother

and I weren't alone. There was another there. A man. A man you've seen in the village.' And now, Maggie grasped her hand and took it onto her lap. 'Twig.'

Callie pulled back sharply, her brows shooting into her hairline. 'Twig? You're telling me that Twig is Jackdaw's father?' She shook her head fiercely. Judging people by how they looked wasn't something she normally did, but when someone chooses to live in the forest and eat poisonous mushrooms, that had to say they weren't quite *normal*. That last word burned a trail in her mind. Over the past week, she'd lost all sense of what was normal.

'That's not all.' Maggie released her hand and slowly tugged at her woollen hat.

As she did so, a thought took root—she'd never seen Maggie without a hat of some kind on her head.

Horror crawled over Callie's flesh. Tufts of grey hair sprouted from Maggie's scalp, but amongst them were deep, furrowed scars running from her brow to her crown.

'What happened?' she asked, her fingers rising to press against her lips.

'The crows happened. They didn't like what we had done. They didn't like what Twig was trying to do.'

'Trying to do?'

'You must have heard stories, Callie. You've lived here long enough,' Maggie said, slipping her hat back on.

Callie thought for a moment. Yes, it was true she'd caught gossip about Twig trying to use the hallucinatory powers of the mushrooms to see back into the past.

But that was ridiculous… wasn't it?

'The crows were angry because they didn't want him to see. He wasn't the one.'

The one. She thought back to standing in Jackdaw's room with the stench of vomit and the mushroom-clad beam dripping tears onto the bed.

She muffled the cry that rose in her throat with her palm. Jackdaw had been trying to eat the mushrooms, too, because he knew—somehow, he knew.

Maggie took her hand again and squeezed it. 'Think back to what's been happening. Suspend your disbelief.'

Callie stared into the darkness as the neon-blue flashing lights of a fire engine split the night apart. She thought about the barn and the stick-and-clay figure in London. The bird wings pinned to the door, the insistence that a boy shouldn't live in *that* cottage.

It was too much to thread together, and she was frazzled and worn to the bone with worry about Jackdaw.

'I think he'll be okay, Callie,' Maggie murmured. 'Because he's done what the villagers here were desperate to stop.' She slipped an arm around Callie's shoulders. 'He's forged a deep friendship with Oscar. And that fact alone terrifies the village. Because it was kinship that started this—and it will be kinship that finishes it, too.'

'Tell me everything,' Callie said, even though her mind felt like it was at maximum capacity for absorbing any more facts.

She listened, occasionally nodding as Maggie told her about what had happened here over two centuries ago. About a boy who had lived in her cottage. About another boy he had met, and the terrible injustice committed. About Martinmas and Lonan and Gala Day and what it really signified.

'How does it end, Maggie?' Callie's voice was small and quiet. She knotted her shaking fingers together.

'It ends with Jackdaw discovering how to soothe Lonan's spirit.' Maggie sighed, and the sound was bone-deep.

'But he's only a boy.' Callie's words were edged in sharp frustration. 'And he's had so much to deal with up to now. My mother basically left him to fend for himself, because she was always in her room, trying to solve some kind of crazed puzzle with notes pasted on the wall and strings and coloured markers…' Her voice trailed off at the memory.

'Your mother loved him, Callie, I'm sure of it. She was just preparing him to be self-sufficient and perceptive. All those notes and strings were her trying desperately to solve the madness of what happened here, so she could fill him with knowledge. She died before she had a chance to put all the pieces together.'

'She didn't know I lived here, though.' Callie was trying desperately to hang onto any fragment of logic.

Maggie quirked a grey eyebrow. 'But something did. Call me a crazy old woman, but something brought you here for a reason, brought Jackdaw here for a reason. We just need to believe that it was the right one.'

CHAPTER SIXTY-EIGHT

They stumbled out of the smoke-drenched forest, frozen to the bone and clinging together, trying to hold onto a tiny shred of reality when everything around them had dissolved into a melting pot of chaos and madness.

For one moment there, as he'd dragged Jackdaw back into the present, Oscar had seen a reflection of the gibbet in Jackdaw's eyes—with a boy hanging from it. Everything that he'd grown up knowing felt like his own noose around his neck.

Teach the children that this is normal. Let them grow up with Gala Day as a celebration. Feed the next generation so that history repeats and repeats… a groan sounded in his throat and Jackdaw's pale, soil-streaked face turned to his.

'Do you think they've given up on finding us?' Jackdaw asked, glancing over his shoulder. Behind them, the dark trunks of the trees stood shrouded in smoky vapour.

'Knowing my aunt, I'd say that's a no,' Oscar said, a grim smile haunting his lips. 'But for now they think we're in the forest, so that gives us an advantage, yes?' He slipped an arm around Jackdaw's shoulders. 'This whole fucked-up night has to have some bonuses.'

Oscar's teeth began to chatter as a cruel wind knifed up from the valley. A whole-body shiver ran through him. 'We have to get hold of some dry clothes or we'll freeze.'

It seemed such a mundane comment considering that Jackdaw had literally glimpsed back through history, had watched as two boys had their world ripped apart.

'There's something that still doesn't make sense.' Jackdaw clenched and unclenched his fists as though the answer might appear in the palms of his hands.

'I might be stating the obvious here, but none of this makes sense.' Something that might have been a laugh at any other time dried up in Oscar's throat.

'If Iza died, why is Lonan the one everyone fears?' Jackdaw was looking at him with slightly clouded eyes, and Oscar bit the inside of his cheek. He wasn't sure if he could handle it if Jackdaw spiralled back off again. But what he said was well-reasoned. Oscar contemplated this as they started to walk downhill, their feet slipping on the damp grass.

'Maybe because he's the hangman's son? I don't know,' Oscar said. 'And that's a scary enough fact on its own.'

A silence descended as they wrestled with their own thoughts. Oscar's feet squelched in his soaked trainers. Moving should have made him feel warmer, but all it did was remind him with each step how miserable his saturated clothes felt against his skin. He'd probably come out of this with pneumonia. If he came out of this at all.

He glanced back over his shoulder to see a few thin lights on the hill as the villagers continued to search. A flash of a hi–vis vest. *They think we're dead.* It was a sobering thought. Part of him wanted to rush back and alleviate their fears, but another, much stronger part was linked with Jackdaw and whatever the hell it was they needed to do now.

The track they were on skirted the edge of the hill, then sloped down to the valley bottom. Darkness pressed against them and every time something rustled in the grass, Oscar's heart somersaulted in his chest. The sound of running water greeted them as the meandering stream came into view, a streak of moonlight carving a pathway across it. From there, they had to climb the other hill before the meadow levelled out slightly. And then, if good fortune was on their side, they'd see Jackdaw's cottage. The hangman's cottage.

Never had that knowledge seemed so terrifying, because the past had leapt into the present.

'Is there any record in the churchyard about Lonan being buried there?' Jackdaw finally asked, as they picked their way carefully across the stream. Which, in the scheme of things, was ridiculous—as they were soaked to the bone.

'I don't think so,' Oscar said, his brow creasing. His nose had started to run and he wiped it on his sleeve. 'One time, me and some other kids dared each other to run around the graveyard to see if we could find it. It seemed like it was the middle of the night, but it was winter so it could have been any time after 4pm. We were young and stupid. My aunt came to get me after the church warden reported us. My God, she was angry.' He sighed at the memory, at the tirade of recriminations. *You don't know what you're messing with, Oscar.* And he didn't, back then. But now he knew, and the horror of it clung to his marrow.

'And?' Jackdaw nudged him for more as they began to climb

the hill.

'And no one found anything about Lonan.' Oscar shrugged and then swore softly as his foot sank into a cow pat. 'Although there is a family grave, for his sister at least. No one really bothers with it.' Which, as Oscar thought more deeply, was strange, given that the village was red-hot on preserving history. 'Maybe he grew up and moved away? Put all this behind him?'

Jackdaw's lips tightened into a thin line. 'I don't think you'd ever put your best friend being hanged for something you both did behind you.'

Oscar tucked his freezing hands into the drenched pockets of his jacket and shivered again, although if that was from the cold or Jackdaw's words, he didn't know.

Jackdaw paused halfway up the hill. He reached out and grabbed Oscar's sleeve. A crow cawed in the night.

'Oh God, Oscar.' Jackdaw's fingers tightened. 'You know I've been hearing things, and I know that at first you thought I was deranged...'

A plea ached in his voice.

Oscar took his hands out of his pockets. 'Hush,' he said, holding Jackdaw's slim wrists. 'We're standing here after fleeing from Gala Day on horseback, after watching the gibbet and the forest burn. After me feeding you seriously dangerous shit and watching you literally go back in time.' He took a breath. 'If you're deranged, then I am, too.'

'That kinda makes me feel better.' Jackdaw shook his head, then winced, his black hair falling into his eyes. He sucked his lower lip before continuing. 'I thought I was hearing Lonan. After all, he's the one who lived in the cottage. The one who wrote the journal. But then everything fell into place up on the hill, when I realised the name wasn't Isaac Row, it was Iza Crow. I thought it was Lonan telling me I had to find Iza, but what if...' His voice cracked. 'What if the voice I've been hearing isn't Lonan—it's Iza.'

CHAPTER SIXTY-NINE

Jackdaw half expected Oscar to throw his hands up in disbelief. In the list of all the crazy things that had happened, this was yet another layer on top. But Oscar didn't do that.

He just stood and stared into space for a moment.

His lips parted before uttering, 'Holy shit.'

The realisation shot through Jackdaw like a firebolt as they climbed over the fence and ran across to the cottage.

If they were sensible, they would have gone inside and changed into dry clothes... but sense had left them a few hours ago on the hill where the gibbet was now a smouldering ruin.

They passed in front of the security light. It clicked but didn't come on, and Jackdaw wondered if it was a blown bulb or some other force keeping the dark pressing around them. Moonlight crazed over the yard as it shone through the bare branches of the oak. Movement in those branches, and he turned to see a lone crow perched like a sentinel.

Iza Crow.

They stopped outside the barn, the car still embedded in the door like a piece of modern art representing how contemporary life had destroyed the past. Jackdaw laughed, a short, harsh sound, and Oscar turned to look at him.

'What now?' Oscar asked, and then he stopped and swore, his gaze tracking over Jackdaw's shoulder.

Jackdaw wheeled, and the sight that met his eyes numbed his limbs even further.

Headlights streamed down the opposite hill, splitting the dark. They could hope that everyone was going home to sleep—but they both knew that a few of those cars would end up here, just in case they'd made it back.

'In the barn,' Jackdaw hissed, pushing through the shattered gap in the door. His skin crawled at the prospect of hiding in the deep blackness.

The barn had already tried to give up its secrets, and Jackdaw still wasn't sure what everything meant—he wondered if Lonan and Iza would grow tired of these modern boys, who knew nothing of the brutality of the past.

He was so far into his own thoughts that he didn't realise Oscar had stopped in the doorway, his phone held aloft in his hand. The beam skipped across the opposite wall with its ancient farm machinery, skipped across the old, cracked harnesses and coils of rope hanging on rusted nails, cobwebs draped across them like a caul.

Jackdaw tapped his fingers against his lips as something flitted across his consciousness. He tried to grab a hold but it floated away before he could grasp it.

'Fuck.' Oscar breathed out the profanity. 'This is like stepping back in time.'

Fear unfurled in Jackdaw's gut and for a second he was back in the yard, watching the hangman's son fall apart as his best friend climbed into the cart…

He shivered, felt an ache deep in his bones.

'Come on,' he said, leading Oscar to the back of the barn. They passed the place where the cart had stood, the red-capped mushrooms still clustered there, because they loved the dark and the dark loved them in return.

Up the dusty, wooden staircase to the hayloft where bales of musty hay still rested. Jackdaw almost expected Ophelia to jump out—but inside he knew, he knew that he'd seen the little girl for the last time in the rafters.

Her gesture made sense now. A hand across her heart—telling him to trust his own.

The sound of engines echoed across from outside, tyres rolling over gravel, then the slamming of doors.

Raised voices demanding entry to the barn.

'Get off my property.' Callie's voice, filled with fierceness.

Jackdaw's eyes widened. She should be in London…

Another woman spoke, someone Jackdaw didn't recognise.

'Just to let you know, I'm recording all of this.'

He pointed to a narrow gap between two stacks of bales and Oscar squeezed himself through, crouching behind them.

Jackdaw followed, his heart a wild thing in his chest. His stomach cramped, a dull ache throbbing deep in his sinuses from his swollen nose. He could still taste the mushroom paste on his tongue.

He was tired, so very tired.

His head lolled onto Oscar's shoulder. An arm around him and he smiled, his lips trembling.

He closed his eyes and the past loomed, the drifting mist racing by until he was… here, back in the barn, drenched in sweat.

He could smell it, the ripe tang of a desperate fear. Grief held him in clawed hands, the talons sinking deeper with each step into the darkness.

Show me, he thought from somewhere deep inside his mind, even though he was so afraid to see what happened next.

Lonan standing in the barn in the dark, his breath ghosting into the frigid air. Tears streaked his face, his shoulders caved. He walked across to the wall where rakes and hoes and pitchforks hung. The coils of rope were fresh and cobweb-free. Beneath each one was a small piece of carved wood, writing etched upon them.

Lonan ran his hands over the coarse strands and the ropes swung slightly. Until he paused at the very last nail, deep in the shadows to the left of the hayloft. He was shaking now, the sobs in his throat raw and painful. He took the coil from the nail it hung on and touched his fingers to the wooden plate.

Jackdaw knew what it said before his vision tunnelled towards it.

Iza Crow.

Jacob Carter kept the ropes he had used, each with its own nameplate. Because the dead deserved to be remembered, even like this.

He never used the same rope twice, in case it had stretched and he couldn't calculate the weight and the drop properly.

Something broke inside Jackdaw's mind—because he knew exactly what Lonan was going to do. He watched as the hangman's son climbed the hayloft stairs and threw the rope over the rafter Ophelia had sat upon. He watched as Lonan settled the noose around his neck and climbed onto the rail.

He watched as the boy closed his eyes, whispered Iza's name. And jumped.

Fast forward, Jackdaw screamed internally. His mind folded in on itself, the awful knowledge of Lonan's death fused against his core.

A frozen stillness bloomed upon his skin.

He couldn't feel Lonan anymore. Only an aching gap where he had once been.

All he could hear was the creaking of a swinging rope.

CHAPTER SEVENTY

'Jackdaw!' a voice hissed.

Someone shook him, hard, and he tumbled back into the present, his head spinning as he was caught between two realities for a few seconds. He focussed his eyes on a worried face above him. Oscar's face.

Oscar held a finger to his lips. 'There's people in the yard,' he whispered. 'Please tell me there's a back way out of here if they come looking.'

Jackdaw stared into the darkness, and a desolation wrapped itself around him like an iced glove. 'I saw him die, Oscar.'

His hands started to tremble and Oscar grabbed them.

'Iza?'

Jackdaw shook his head. 'No, Lonan. Here. Here in this barn. With a rope.'

He didn't need to go into any more details. He *couldn't* go into any more details.

The boys huddled together between the dusty hay bales as this terrible knowledge seeped into their marrow.

Find his bones.

And now Jackdaw knew, with a lightning bolt of certainty, that it wasn't Iza he was looking for—it was Lonan.

Lonan wasn't buried in the churchyard unless it was an unmarked grave.

'Oscar,' he whispered as a thought settled in his mind. 'Am I right in thinking that suicides couldn't be buried in consecrated ground?'

Oscar nodded, sucking his bottom lip between his teeth.

'Yeah, it was considered immoral. My mum told me about a guy who hanged himself in prison. They tossed his body into a dug-out pit at a crossroads and drove a stake through his heart to pin him to the spot.'

Jackdaw put his head in his hands, desperately willing all the puzzle pieces to slip into place.

'Sorry,' Oscar grimaced. 'Not helping with that description.'

'I couldn't have done any of this without you,' Jackdaw said, lifting his head. Iza's voice drifted back to him. 'Through all seasons.' The words fell into the freezing darkness around them.

'What does it mean?' Oscar asked, his breath warm against Jackdaw's cheek.

'I think it meant that Iza and Lonan would always have each other's back, no matter what.'

It was a beautiful but heartrending phrase.

Oscar peered over the hay bales. 'I think the cars are going,' he said. 'But my aunt was here, and she'll be back.'

Jackdaw pulled himself up, brushing strands of hay from his damp jacket. His eyes were accustomed to the dark now. His gaze flicked up to the rafter and he swallowed. If Lonan wasn't buried in the churchyard, where would he be? He tried to juggle all of the places where he'd seen or felt something uncanny. He wondered for a brief moment if Lonan was buried under the floorboards in his room, if he'd been sleeping beneath the beam that had taken Iza's life and above Lonan's corpse.

But Callie had said his room had been renovated.

A body would have been discovered then.

He contemplated if it was under the oak which had just been a young tree when Lonan lived here. It was where the birds gathered. But there was no marker. A stinging anguish flooded his veins for the family who had lost a son and a brother so tragically.

Maybe they wanted to keep him close? Maybe they didn't trust what might happen if they buried him where others could get to him?

The thoughts exploded in his mind, and he scrambled onto the hay bales. His eyes flicked up to the rafter where Ophelia had sat, where the rope had been strung. Then his gaze dropped.

'I know where he is, Oscar. I know where he is.'

Oscar's jaw slackened as the words settled.

'Where?' he yelled, but Jackdaw was already halfway down the hayloft stairs. He sprinted across to the wall and grabbed the pitchfork.

'Get something you can dig with,' he shouted. There was an urgent thrumming in his veins and a desperate hope in his heart as he ran across to the space where the cart had stood. A shaft of moonlight through a broken roof slat illuminated the clutch of red-capped mushrooms, growing in the dusty soil.

The signs had been pointing the way all along and Jackdaw hadn't understood—until now. He began to claw at the ground with the pitchfork, but the tines were too far apart to make any impact.

He could hear Oscar scrabbling about. A whoop of triumph and then Oscar was by his side, an ancient, cobwebbed shovel in his hands. They began to dig, slowly at first, then a little more feverishly as the ground opened up to them.

At one point Jackdaw knelt and pushed the earth away with his hands as Oscar freed it. Soil impacted under his nails, sweat running down his face, dripping into the dirt. How deep had they buried him?

Oscar paused for a moment and wiped the sweat from his own face with his sleeve. Never once had he asked why Jackdaw knew, he just believed and trusted and toiled.

Jackdaw looked up and blew his hair out of his eyes, chewing on his pain, before nodding to Oscar to continue.

A few more feet of hard labour, their breaths loud and ragged—and then the shovel came into contact with something solid. Oscar stopped. The sound echoed around the barn like a gunshot.

Both of them on their knees now, hauling armfuls of soil away. A pale expanse of wood shone through the earth.

'Holy shit,' Oscar whispered, sitting back on his heels, his eyes meeting Jackdaw's. 'This is him, isn't it? This is Lonan.'

A commotion sounded from outside and they both wheeled as one. The scrabble of claws on metal, and then through the gap in the shattered doors a mass of darkness blotted out the moonlight. Feathers skimmed their faces, the sweep of wings as the air became alive with crows and ravens and jackdaws.

The birds swooped around the barn in a dizzy murmuration before settling, one by one, on the rafters.

Oscar raised an eyebrow and grinned, a smudge of soil on his nose. 'I guess we have an audience.'

Now that the coffin was partly uncovered, they were more hesitant with their digging. Oscar cleared a hole at the bottom of it, deep enough so that Jackdaw could slip in and get his hands under the rim. It was a rustic resting place for the hangman's son, the coffin made from interwoven strips of willow with a reinforced lid.

There was no nameplate and this one fact alone brought tears to Jackdaw's eyes. He stopped and dabbed at them with his sleeve. Oscar's hand came to rest on his shoulder.

They prised a crowbar under the fastened lid of the coffin, and when all the crooked nails lay in the dirt, they knelt together. They knelt together and slipped their hands under the lid.

They lifted it.

Dusty air rose to greet them and the smell of a grave.

But they didn't flinch.

Lonan lay wrapped in a dirty linen shroud that had been eaten away by insects. Bones jutted through the flimsy remains of the material. Bones cracked by time, bones that had seen so few years. The dome of the skull was visible along with one empty eye socket.

'I'm sorry,' Jackdaw whispered, tears channelling trails down his dirty face. Oscar slipped an arm around his shoulder as they knelt solemnly and silently, leaning against each other.

'What do we do now?' Oscar asked, after a few minutes.

Jackdaw glanced up at the birds, then smiled.

'We take his bones to where Iza can claim them.'

It took them more than an hour to remove the bones from the coffin and place them into sacks. They didn't rush, despite an urgency running through them both. Lonan deserved this respect. The rib cage came away whole, and Jackdaw held it in his hands and wept again.

They'd found a small pouch clutched in Lonan's fingers. Inside were the dried remains of tiny white flowers, a polished pebble, and a single black feather.

They slipped out into the darkest hours of the night, making the journey back into the forest where they'd fled from. A lone crow followed them, sometimes flying up ahead, but always silent.

The fire had been contained to the highest part of the forest, and they moved instinctively away from the smouldering trunks, their steps taking them deep into the lower woodland.

The trees pressed close, but there was no menace within them, more of a comforting shield. As they walked through the undergrowth, carrying the bones of a boy who had died more than two hundred years ago, the forest felt more like a cathedral… the bare branches above them forming great gothic arches, moonlight shredding the boughs.

Along another pathway, twisting and turning, exhaustion in their limbs but determination in their hearts, until finally they came out into a hidden glade. Smoke drifted ghostlike through the trees.

'This is the place,' Jackdaw whispered. He crouched and

opened his sack, drawing the cloth down so that the bones sat in the middle. Oscar did the same. Jackdaw pulled the pouch from his pocket and placed it inside Lonan's rib cage, where his heart had once been.

Dried yarrow, a pebble from the stream, a black feather.

The tokens had been there all along. The flowers Jackdaw had seen scattered in the bottom of his wardrobe, the pebble he'd picked from the ground the night he went around the side of the cottage, a feather for all the wounded birds.

A breeze wafted through the trees, bending the slim branches of the silver birches. Leaves rustled around them and they felt it then, an intense, charged electricity like the moments before a storm. Jackdaw's scalp tingled. Oscar's eyes widened, awe written across his face.

Iza.

A haze formed where they had placed Lonan's bones. A haze that spun upwards, little eddies carrying fragments of the forest in its wake. The crow swooped down, and as the haze spun faster it was swallowed into the rising vortex.

Two translucent figures crystallised for a heartbeat.

They merged together.

And then the sweet tang of apples burst from the darkness.

Iza Crow and Lonan. The traveller boy and the hangman's son.

A promise kept.

EPILOGUE

— One week later —

Callie and Maggie sat around the kitchen table. A weak November sun glittered against the frost covering the clematis overhanging the window. A crow cawed in the oak, and they both turned to watch it wiping its beak on the bare branches.

One week since Jackdaw and Oscar had tumbled exhausted through the door close to dawn, filthy and frozen to the bone. One week since Oscar had rung his parents in Bali and scared them half to death with a very condensed version of the night's events. The bottom line being that he refused to go back to Elspeth's house. Callie had taken the phone, and assured two people she had never met that she was more than fine taking Oscar in until they returned. It had been the easiest decision of her life.

The boys had slipped out, but she could almost hear the sound of their laughter still drifting down the stairs.

They had become inseparable.

'Are you sure this is the right decision?' Maggie asked, sipping her tea from one of Callie's rustic mugs. She nodded towards the half-packed boxes stacked up behind her on the quarry tiles.

'I can't stay here, Maggie,' Callie said. 'Not with everything being a constant reminder of that night.' Unspoken words drifted between them. The village had been no place for Jackdaw prior to the gibbet burning. Now it had closed ranks around its wounds, and Callie knew she'd never want Jackdaw to go there alone.

He had closed the door on an event that they had celebrated for over two hundred years, because it bestowed privilege and blessings, even though these were granted by a broken boy who could not rest. They had thought it was only the hangman's son who haunted the land. They still did. Iza's legacy was a secret she and Maggie would take to their graves.

They had both decided not to tell Twig about Jackdaw.

Some things were best laid to rest.

'And you're happy with Diego's offer?' Maggie asked. Her hat lay on the table. Callie had seen the very worst of her. There was no reason to hide it anymore.

'He was more than generous.' Callie picked a stray tea leaf from her drink with her thumb. 'Turning this place into a retreat for artists and crafters was his idea. He said he might even find someone better than me.' Callie laughed. 'But he doubted it.'

'Does he know everything?'

'He knows the history of this cottage and about the beam.' Her gaze flicked upwards. 'He said he'll renovate and take it out. I asked him if he'd bury it in the forest, and he agreed. It turns out that my designer-clothed benefactor has a healthy respect for things that don't have an explanation.' She paused and sipped her tea. 'I won't miss this place, but I will miss you, Maggie.'

Maggie reached across and placed her hand on Callie's arm. 'You won't miss me, because I'll visit so often you'll set a place at the table for me each night in case I turn up.' She patted Callie on the back of the hand. 'Anyway, I want to stay around here and see what the village makes of Diego if he visits. Elspeth might self-combust at all that foreign blood.'

Callie snorted. 'I'd consider coming back for that.'

But they both knew that when Callie and Jackdaw left Combe Hurst, they were never coming back.

A new life beckoned in another village.

Callie had leased a rambling old Victorian on the outskirts of Meadowford Bridge. She hoped it was just a boring, English village. It was only thirty miles away from where Oscar lived, and there was a rural train line so the boys could be together whenever school didn't get in their way.

One thing she had learned over the past couple of weeks is that the bond of special friendship has tendrils like the roots of ancient trees. That once forged, nothing can tear them apart.

Not even death.

Jackdaw and Oscar sat on a fallen log in the forest. They had tried to find the hidden glade again but to no avail. It had simply disappeared into the trees as though it had never been there at all.

A breeze filtered through the late autumn branches, bringing with it the scent of burnt wood. Even now, the gibbet was leaving its mark.

They watched as a couple of crows squabbled in the treetops. Jackdaw leaned against Oscar and closed his eyes as a shaft of sunlight coated them in a burst of warmth.

A persistent feeling ebbed through him, something it had taken him a few days to pin down.

Contentment.

He had lived his whole life fighting neglect and abandonment, although now he knew why his mother had been the way she was. She was only trying to protect him in her own misguided way. Everything had been compounded by the intimidation and hounding at school for looking like he did. But if that hadn't happened, he would never have learned about birds and nature, and the peace of a forest.

Maybe something had always been pushing him here, because that's where he began.

'Through all seasons,' he whispered, a little sleepily.

'Through all seasons,' Oscar repeated with a soft laugh, hooking an arm around Jackdaw's shoulder. 'You know I wouldn't ride bareback into a dark forest with anyone else.'

They sat in the sunlight for a few minutes without speaking, lost in their own thoughts.

And Jackdaw hoped that somewhere, in another universe, Lonan and Iza were running free, saying exactly the same words.

DID YOU ENJOY THIS BOOK?

YOU CAN MAKE A BIG DIFFERENCE.

When it comes to getting attention for my books, reviews are the most powerful tools. Much as I'd like to take out full page advertisements or put posters on buses, I don't have the financial muscle of a big publisher.

But I do have something those publishers would love to get their hands on.

A committed and loyal group of readers.

Honest reviews of my books help bring them to the attention of other readers and lets me continue to create stories for you to fall in love with. If you've enjoyed reading *The Haunting of Wounded Birds* I would be very grateful if you could leave a review (it can be as simple as a few short words).

ACKNOWLEDGEMENTS

A book starts with the writer, but there are so many other people who nurture it through its growth from seed to flower. My grateful thanks to my wonderful writing partner, Nicole Eigener, for that all important first critique. To Nicole and Sarina Langer, whose editing skills helped shape this into the tale in your hands. To Matt Coxall and Kev Harrison who received an early draft of this and waded through with comments and suggestions. To Danielle Klassen for research into the art of pottery. To my beta crew, Catherine McCarthy, Craig Wallwork and Lisa Niblock. To Kealan Patrick Burke and Elderlemon Design for my haunting cover creation. To Nicole Eigener, for beautiful interior design, hand holding, and for all those weekend hours together. Sleep is overrated, yes?

Thank you to my friends and loyal supporters on Instagram, for showing me the human side of social media. Writing is a solitary craft but I am never alone with your constant loyalty and encouragement.

And to those who discover my books through other sources—welcome, and my warmest thanks.

ABOUT THE AUTHOR

Beverley Lee is a bestselling dark fiction author who lives close to the dreaming spires of Oxford, England. Her work specialises in atmospheric horror, creeping dread, and broken boys—sometimes altogether—but are always filled with heart and the tenuous threads of relationships pushed to the brink. All the Feels all the time. Vampires are her first love and occasionally they stop whispering long enough for her to write other books. When she's not writing you'll find her rambling through the countryside, dreaming about male vampires kissing, and exploring time-worn graveyards.

Visit beverleylee.com for more information about her books.